THE BRINY BROTHERHOOD

Terry Halfhill

ISBN: 1492906581
ISBN-13:9781492906582

DEDICATION

This book is dedicated to my fabulous mother, Mikee. Her steadfastness to her moral compass forced me to write a book devoid of debauchery. It's not "Goodnight Moon", but it's as close as my mind will allow me. I truly hope she reads and enjoys it.

Introduction

This is a story of brotherhood. True brotherhood. The sort of camaraderie that you hear soldiers talk about when they are lying injured in a field hospital, trying desperately to make it back to the front line, feeling shame and guilt for abandoning their brothers.

Policemen call it the "Blue code" or the "Blue wall." The mob calls it "Omerta." Regardless of name, ethnicity, organization, or purpose, a code exists among men who take responsibility for themselves and their actions. They clean up their own messes and they certainly don't let outsiders play a role in their matters. They don't talk about the code they just live by it. In every fraternal organization on the planet, presumably since the beginning of time, man has accepted into his culture a code that guides behavior.

Describing the code is difficult, and the word *brotherhood* is the best approximation Noah Webster has to offer. If you try to define the code you quickly realize it's more like a cloud than a clock. A clock is something tangible that you can touch and understand. You can see a cloud, but you can't really touch it. You know it's there but you can't grab it. You can't move it, and you certainly can't stop it.

And so the Briny Brotherhood was formed in south Florida among a group of strangers who liked to fish. Each of the members had lived the code for a significant part of their lives prior to meeting and becoming friends. It was in their blood. It was comforting. Some had been police officers, some military. Some grew up living by the code as a matter of survival.

The brotherhood started innocently enough one day when two of the members were introduced at a Texaco gas station near the ocean. Vinny owned the gas station and Tye needed mechanical help with an engine.

Over the years a select few members were added. There was no vote, not even a discussion about who should be added. They earned their way in over time by proving their mettle and by protecting the brotherhood.

There were no overt signs of membership. No jackets or patches, no secret handshakes. In fact, if asked about the brotherhood some of the members would likely exclude members that others included, but the core was strong. Like a cloud, you knew it was there, you just couldn't touch it, or move it, and it was hard for everyone to define the same way.

But like all brotherhoods and for that matter fraternal organizations, they shared a common language which helped them identify members. Tye had a habit of calling everyone "Dumbass" and eventually had to number them. Dumbass one, dumbass two, etc..

If you earned the moniker "Dumbass", chances were good that you were considered part of the brotherhood.

This is their story.

CHAPTER 1

The sun was blazing hot on the fishing boat that particular Saturday. The middle of summer in south Florida is no place to be if you don't like the sun or its many side effects. The four fishermen were nearly three miles off-shore and the wind had picked up considerably since the morning, making for a bumpy ride as they dropped lines once again. A steady breeze kept the humidity at bay. Toward the shore they could make out the Boynton Beach water tower.

The smell of brine was in the air and the smell of fresh cut ballyhoo used for bait was on everyone's hands. The two scents mixed together to create a pungent aroma that only the seagulls appreciated. They barked their approval as they hovered above the twenty-eight foot long fishing boat, not daring to land.

Terry and Dergo were in the front of the boat and Vinny and Tyrone were in the back. All four fished from the right side of the boat as the current was strong and would drag lines underneath the boat had they casted off the left side.

Vinny and Terry hooked fish simultaneously. Terry was only about sixty feet deep so he figured he had a Trigger fish, not one he would keep unless it was unusually big and even then they would use it for bait. Vinny let everyone know that he had a yellowtail on the end of his line. The yellow-tail was what they were fishing for and Vinny was famous for bringing home big fish… and lots of them.

He was a master at the craft and the other three on the boat just shook their heads, as they had done most of the day. They all used the same bait and did roughly what Vinny did; however, he seemed to be able to reel in fish after fish as the rest of them waited patiently for a bite.

Terry's fish had almost made it to the surface when Vinny's yellowtail decided to run for deeper water. Dergo and Tyrone reeled in their lines in order to make room for Vinny. It was a big fish and his pole formed a semi-circle with the tip of his rod brushing the top of the water.

Vinny was strong, nearly six feet tall and in decent shape for a man of fifty-seven years old. He was born and raised on the island of Trinidad. He had dark features and at first glance looked like he was Puerto Rican or Venezuelan, but nobody dared tell him that. He wasn't fond of a variety of ethnicities. He was also unusually nimble for his age, undoubtedly from his fourteen years as a police officer back on the island. He was a black belt in some type of martial arts. Nobody knew exactly which discipline he studied because he never talked about it. In fact the only clue he gave about his martial arts expertise was when he was drinking. At various times he would chop a coconut in half with his bare hands or kick something several inches above his head.

His speed and nimbleness was evident as he glided from one end of the boat to the other while his fish panicked and ran. Terry was in the middle of landing an average size Trigger fish when they ran into each other

“You fucking DUMBASS, get out of the way“ Vinny said in a half-joking, half-serious, sort of mumble under his breath. His accent was thick but the other three fishermen understood him perfectly. He took his fishing seriously and mistakes weren’t welcome aboard his boat.

Tyrone and Dergo laughed and chimed in with another chorus of “Dumbass.” It was a term of endearment for them, but Vinny had a way of getting his point across by not laughing after using the expletive.

Terry, the perpetrator of the fishing crime offered a weak excuse. “Fuck all of you. You all suck.” He landed the small fish and threw it back in the water, careful not to let the sharp teeth ruin the outing. A trip to the hospital would mean an end to the fishing day.

Meanwhile, Vinny made it to his feet and continued to struggle with the monster yellowtail. Tyrone started the dual Yamaha motors and began to chase the fish, relieving some of the stress on Vinny’s fishing line. A few minutes later the fish was in the cooler, along with the others caught mostly by Vinny.

The fishermen prepared to drop their lines once more when Dergo said, “That’s about it for me… I need a beer,” in a disgusted tone, his Illinois accent bleeding through in every word. "Besides, Dumbass is the only one catching anything." Vinny smiled and lit another cigarette. The others agreed. It had been a long, hot day out on the ocean and the cooler was almost full of the day's bounty. It was time to clean the fish, clean the boat, drink some beer and have a fish fry back at the trailer.

The trailer was a small white tin box nestled on the ocean at a retirement community called Briny Breezes. Terry often referred to it as, "The Ghetto." It was a trailer park that sat between two of the highest rent districts in south Florida – Gulf Stream and Manalapan. Professional athletes, late night television hosts, and actors of all sorts inhabited the beautiful multi-million dollar homes along this part of the coast. Older, retired folks from modest incomes lived in Briny Breezes.

The juxtaposition of the trailers and the mansions – both ocean front – was a visual paradox. However, many of the Briny residents could afford the expensive homes next to their trailer park, but chose not to. Terry couldn't. He was lucky to live anywhere near the ocean and was thankful his family had the foresight to purchase the modest trailer when they did. He had the place to himself most of the year, and shared it with family on occasion, when cousins and family friends decided to stop in for a few days to dodge the cold Pennsylvania winters.

So the crew reeled in their lines and prepared to make the journey through the Boynton inlet. Passing through the inlet - going from the ocean to the Intracoastal Waterway - proved to be a bit tricky. The winds had picked up, which meant the surf had picked up, which meant navigating the long boat through the narrow passage in choppy, angry, water took some concentration on Tyrone's part. As always he did fine and the crew appreciated it, though nobody told him. Tyrone cleared the inlet and headed south toward the Briny Breeze marina. It was a short jog to their destination, maybe ten minutes at slow speed, but it turned out to be a violent, horrifying, ten minutes. The worst day of Terry's life.

CHAPTER 2

Within a few minutes the boat was approaching two of the finer waterfront restaurants in Palm Beach County. "Two Georges" was first. The fishermen could hear live music coming from the establishment and there were a gaggle of boats parked along edge of the restaurant. Most belonged to residents who lived along the intracoastal. It was easy to hop in a boat and stop at the restaurant for a cocktail and fresh fish. Vinny, Dergo and Tye sat behind the wheel near the rear of the boat admiring several scantily clad spring breakers. A few of the girls waved and they waved back. Vinny simply nodded and flicked the ash off his cigarette.

Terry didn't see the girls. He was at the front of the boat looking at the Woolbright Bridge, which was several hundred yards ahead. The bridge was down, which was no problem for their boat, but what caught his eye was the activity taking place on the bridge itself. In the far right corner he could see police lights. They had the bridge closed for some reason.

As the boat passed "Two Georges" and drew near the "Banana Boat," the men continued to look at women in bikinis and the handful of boats parked along its waterfront tables. Terry moved to the very front of the boat to get a better look. He could see policemen motioning toward him to get back… to move away. At first he didn't understand. He turned to alert the others but saw something out of the corner of his eye. For a brief second he thought better of looking back. He thought he should warn the others immediately. Perhaps he should have. Maybe it wouldn't have made a difference in the end.

On the left side of the bridge was a small enclosed room where a man sat and controlled the opening and closing of the bridge. The room had windows on all four sides and was just big enough to fit an employee and the controls necessary to lift the bridge up and down, which enabled tall boats, and sailboats with masts to pass underneath. Terry noticed the door to the small room was open, which was odd. Even more peculiar was the man who stood up and pointed a rifle in their direction. In an instant he fired and Terry dropped off the front of the boat into the water.

The three remaining fishermen heard the shot and were confused. Dergo was the first to see Terry had fallen overboard and pointed in his direction. The others looked. Tye stopped the boat and ran to the front, pushing Vinny out of the way. Without thinking he dove in and grabbed his brother by the shoulders. He shouted, "Terry…Terry." He panicked and looked to Vinny and Dergo for help. They bent over and helped hoist the lifeless body into the boat. Still confused, they were desperately trying to figure out what had happened.

Tye climbed into the boat and began to shake his brother. "Call 911" he shouted to the others. But it was too late. They all knew it. Terry's body was lifeless. He hadn't drowned and his heart hadn't stopped. CPR might revive someone with such an ailment. A bullet passed through his forehead and exited the rear of his skull, making an awful mess. His brain was dead, there was no need to keep his heart beating.

Like Vinny, Dergo was also a retired policeman. He had spent more than twenty five years on the force in a small Illinois town a little south of Chicago. He had good instincts as a result, and his instincts told him that they were still in danger. After a quick scan he told Vinny and Tye he saw a gunman on the bridge. He was taking cover behind the center console when he noticed Vinny reaching into his fishing bag. He pulled out a .45 caliber Smith and Wesson and aimed at the gunman. Before he could squeeze the trigger the S.W.A.T team located on the far left side of the bridge put a round in the gunman's head and he dropped out of sight. Dergo was dialing 911 while Tye held his brother in his arms… crying.

CHAPTER 3

Several days later a small funeral was held at the Weiss Memorial Chapel on Boynton Beach Boulevard. It was attended by a handful of family members and a few friends, including the group that could always be seen at the Texaco gas station on A1A, the road that parallels the coast in Florida south from the Florida keys north almost to Georgia. The Patriot Guard riders led the procession on their Harley-Davidsons, an acknowledgement of his military service. As the service came to an end Dergo, Vinny, Tye, and Thomas held a private conversation.

"Did you see the news this morning?" Thomas asked in deference, pointing his question toward Tye, not wanting to pour salt on his wounds, but he knew they had to talk about it. It was too important. His Swiss accent was thick, but everyone understood him perfectly.

Thomas and Tye were friends for more than ten years. They knew each other before Vinny bought the Texaco station, and before Dergo bought his apartment across the street from the Texaco station. Thomas was a Swiss national who moved to the U.S. after graduating from a prestigious university in Switzerland. A mechanical engineer by training, he now ran his own business at a private airport fixing and maintaining private aircraft. Between Tye, Thomas, and Vinny, there weren't a lot of things on the planet they couldn't fix. Thomas was a few years younger than Tye.

"No," Tye said, almost afraid of what he was about to hear.

Thomas understood his hesitation and framed his response carefully, taking his time to choose the English words he translated in his head. "There was another random shooting. That makes two now."

Dergo responded before Tye. "I have a bad feeling about this. I don't think they are random."

Vinny took another drag off of his cigarette and made eye contact with Thomas, silently coaxing him for more information. He hadn't seen the news either. He lifted his head slightly and blew out a thick blue wisp of smoke, squinting as it filled his eyes.

"Two random murders from two different gunmen, all within a week and all within a few miles of each other. It was on CNN, how the fwock did you guys miss it?" Thomas asked, accent heavy.

"I've been a little busy Thomas." Tyrone said. "I do know that the killer's tox-screen came back negative. No drugs or alcohol."

"How do you know that?" Dergo asked, his brown mustache curled a little toward the end of the question. He had lost most of his hair but kept what was left neatly trimmed. He was tanned and in shape for a man his age.

"Ocean Ridge cops called me this morning

before I left. They've been pretty good about keeping me up to date with new information. It doesn't make sense though. Why shoot Terry? I don't get it."

Vinny put his arm around Tye in a gesture of support. "Wipe that shit off your face dumbass." Tye had quit smoking a few months back and was now addicted to nicotine lozenges. For some unknown reason traces of the white lozenge escaped the side of his mouth and formed what looked like a sticky paste on his mouth and spread toward his cheek. It was a constant occurrence and on a less important day Vinny would have asked if he just finished blowing himself.

CHAPTER 4

A reception was held at the trailer after the funeral. Tye placed his brother's ashes on the kitchen table and started to hand out a few beers. People milled around outside the trailer and a few inside offered condolences as he opened a Corona beer with a cigarette lighter he found on the table. After using the base of the lighter to remove the cap from the glass bottle, he looked at it and realized that it was Terry's. Now that he didn't smoke he had no use for it, but decided to drop it in his pocket anyway. He didn't see any reason for someone else to have it.

Thomas and Dergo were outside talking with some of the friends that had gathered. Tye looked for Vinny but didn't see him. He figured he stopped at the Texaco to check in on his son who was working. The Texaco station was a few hundred yards from the trailer and Tye assumed Vinny would show up in a few minutes.

"What are you going to do with the ashes?" Thomas asked. Tye thought about it for a minute. It was tradition to paddle a surfboard out past the breaking waves and spread someone's ashes in the ocean. "Not sure yet." Terry had never really been a beach guy. He spent most of his life up north in

Pennsylvania and had only moved to Florida in the last five years. A beach burial didn't seem appropriate. He thought of riding his motorcycle up to Tennessee and dropping the ashes in the Smoky Mountains. That's where Terry would want to spend the rest of his days.

There were a lot of cars parked in the field across from the trailer that day. Two Ocean Ridge police cars stood out among the mostly blue-collar type vehicles. The cops often stopped at the Texaco to chat with the guys during their shifts and in the process, over many years, had developed close ties with most of them. Officer Payne was one of them and Tye spotted him talking to a few of the women a little further up the street. He decided to say hello.

"Any news Payne?" Tye asked as he approached him from behind. Officer Payne spun around, happy to see Tye. His smile left his face as he remembered why they were there. "Unfortunately no. The tox-screen results for the shooter are the latest news I have. Although, I did just find out that the second victim wasn't a local. Not sure if he and your brother's death are related somehow, but I'll keep you updated as best I can. We really don't know where this thing is headed Tye. Wish I had better news, but something will come up." He didn't sound very convincing but Tye knew there just wasn't much to work with.

"Thanks Payne.." As they finished up their small talk Vinny's truck turned the corner onto Briny Breezes Boulevard from A1A and pulled into an opening in the field across from the trailer. He was about to grab a beer for Vinny when he saw another vehicle turn off of A1A. A lump formed in his throat and a little bit of panic set in with the realization that it was a news van from the local channel four news.

Two of Tyrone's friends ran an intercept route to the driver side door of the news van. Bill, an old friend from Pennsylvania who now lived in Florida, and George, a friend who lived across the street, stood close enough to the van door so it could not be opened. A young man in his mid-twenties rolled the window down and asked if they knew where he could find Tyrone.

"I'm not sure this is the best time to talk to him," Bill said with a decidedly blank expression on his face. There was little room for interpretation.

George reinforced the notion. "Maybe you should come back later in the week, or better yet, don't come back." The young man sitting behind the wheel was no stranger to this type of treatment. In fact, he told Renee, the reporter, that he would run interference while she snuck out of the van's back door. Their plan worked to perfection.

While this was happening Vinny kept a watchful eye on the van as he exited his green Tahoe. He quietly observed and lit a cigarette, watching Bill and George block the van driver door while a pretty woman exited the back door of the van as though she was a teenager sneaking out of her bedroom window to meet a boyfriend.

He followed her as she made her way to the front of the trailer where Tyrone stood. She was a few feet away from him when he yelled at her.

"Hey you… what do you want?" His accent was

thick and it threw her off a little. She spun around with a smile on her face and her hand extended. Her show of goodwill and matching good looks confused Vinny a little. She thought the double punch would make him relax a little. Vinny refused to shake her hand. He took a long drag off his cigarette and spoke. “This isn’t the right time for this. If you want to talk to him do it later. He’s burying his brother.” Vinny looked deep into the young girls eyes and pleaded. His face softened as did the tone in his voice. “Please, I’m asking you to let my friend bury his brother today.”

Vinny could be very convincing when he needed to. He could be rough or he could appeal to your heartstrings. On this day he chose the latter and it worked. She turned around and headed back toward the van.

CHAPTER 5

Jules Friedman sat in his office in downtown Miami Florida on a Monday morning watching the local news. There was a report of a sniper killing a man on a fishing boat, followed by a report of the killing of a man who worked for a large real-estate investment firm out of Canada. Jules grabbed the remote from the conference table and turned up the volume on the seventy-two inch flat panel display mounted on the wall across the room. Some might have thought the screen ostentatious, but not Jules. He had more money than most people could grasp. He was worth billions. Four point two billion dollars to be more precise.

He sat the remote down on the table and listened to the attractive anchorwoman of Latin descent finish her story. "Authorities are left to wonder if the two killings are related because of their proximity and the sniper style execution involved in each murder. Both homicides occurred in the Boynton Beach area." She said with a smile on her face, getting ready to pass the spotlight over to the local weatherman.

Jules wasn't smiling. He picked up the phone and dialed a number he hadn't planned on calling this particular day.

Jules was generally a nice man who appreciated good conversation with people from all walks of life and all backgrounds. He came from nothing and built an empire over his last seventy-five years. He was addicted to the game of business and that addiction brought out a side of him that very few people saw. When it came to the game, he was a ruthless and merciless man who would stop at nothing to win. His small town appeal and down—home values disappeared. He became devoid of any pity or apathy for anyone who stood in his way. Much like the man he was calling.

"Hello!" Came a voice from the other end of the line in a thick New York accent.

"This isn't like you John. You don't make mistakes." Jules said with a disdain in his voice.

"It's not a problem." Johnny Maldone "Mal" as his friends called him – didn't like receiving phone calls from clients. He didn't know what Jules was talking about but he would be on it as soon as he hung up the phone. Mal took care of things. He was known for doing a good job and doing it right the first time, and people paid a premium for his services. "I'll take care of it immediately." He said in a convincing voice. If he had to fly to Florida himself to fix whatever was wrong he would do it.

Jules wasn't as convinced but he also knew who he was dealing with. Just because he wrote the checks didn't give him the right to walk on a made guy so he tread a little more lightly. "I've got a schedule to keep up with, I hope this doesn't set us back."

Mal was losing his patience, which didn't take

much. In the end Jules still had the power because Johnny Maldone received only half of the agreed upon price for the job. "I'll fix it!" Mal said, his voice rising slightly. "As soon as I get off this fucking phone I'll fix it! Are we done here?" Mal asked in a thick, New York sarcastic tone and hung up the phone.

CHAPTER 6

Mal pounded his fist on the table and yelled a few expletives just before he snapped the cell phone in half and hurled it against a wall. Some of the people out in the cigar shop heard the ruckus and looked at each other with confusion on their faces. A handsome young Italian man in his late twenties stood behind the counter and told the customers that everything was OK.

"The walls are thin around here, I'll see what the problem is." He smiled at a group of tourists from South America who were smoking Black Dragon – Gurkhas. The cigars fetched twelve hundred dollars each, and between the five men smoking them at an oak table, they had laid down six thousand dollars upon entering the cigar shop for an hour of cigar heaven.

Tony, the cigar shop attendant moved quickly toward the back door and knocked twice before opening the door. "Everything OK boss?" He asked Mal.

"No it's not Tony. Get me a prepaid with Gutsy's number on it. Now!" He said to Tony as his mind wandered off to another place. Tony left the back room and returned to the counter, assuring everyone that all was well. When he was finished smiling and making eye contact with everyone he pulled out his cell phone and made a call.

In the back room Mal remembered the good days with his pal Guts, from when they were kids trying to make a name for themselves. Guts was a standup guy and Mal loved him like a brother. But if he fucked this job up he would simply become a casualty.

This worried Mal a little, not because he was his friend, that sort of thing happened in his line of business. What really worried him was that Guts was in the Witness Protection Program. If he had to take him out it would be risky for several reasons. Reason number one involved the Feds. He was pretty sure he could pull that off without drawing attention to himself. He wasn't sure that he would live much longer if his "family and friends" ever found out that he was associating with the snitch. But Guts had skills and Mal knew first-hand how he operated. In this particular situation, with this particular client, he couldn't pull off the job without him.

He looked at the clock on the wall, it was close to ten o'clock in the morning. Mal ran a daily poker game out of the back room of the cigar shop every day at noon. It was a high dollar game and his cut was ten percent when the chips were cashed out. He opened the cigar shop as a front for the game. He didn't expect to do so well selling cigars. In fact, he had done so well with the cigar shop he thought about opening a second store. He didn't think about it very long because he knew where his real money was made. He was a cigar fan and a poker enthusiast. Cards and smoke were two of his favorite hobbies so he decided they would occupy much of his time between jobs. It was his way of staying out of trouble… when he wasn't consciously looking for trouble.

CHAPTER 7

A few weeks had passed since Terry's death and they hadn't heard much from the Ocean Ridge or Boynton Beach police. Officer Payne stopped a few times at the Texaco station to deliver updates. Nothing much to speak of. The only new bit of information he delivered was that the second victim was a representative from a large land development corporation out of Canada. Officer Payne wasn't even sure if he was in south Florida for business or pleasure.

"Well Dergo, that shoots a hole in your theory." Thomas said with a thick Swiss accent as he sipped on a Corona beer.

"For now anyway." Dergo shrugged a little. His instincts told him that the two homicides were related, but he agreed with Thomas that there was not a clear link between them. Dergo was fifty-five years old and almost always had a smile on his face. He was a jovial sort of guy who always had a bad joke to share. He liked to drink Beck's beer when he wasn't fishing or buying or selling rare coins or guns. Collecting coins and guns was a hobby he had pursued since childhood.

Nobody had went fishing since Terry's death. It was a taboo subject around the gas station until

Tyrone broke the ice. As Dergo and Thomas continued to chat Vinny was replacing brake lines and an air conditioner in a white Honda Accord inside the garage. At three thirty in the afternoon the unmistakable sound of Tyrone's Subaru WRX came roaring down A1A and turned into the gas station. He parked in front of the garage, blocking Vinny from moving anything out of both bays of the garage.

Vinny met Tye as he was exiting the blue car. "Move that piece of shit out of the way you fucking dumbass."

"Whaaats up dumbass!" Tye replied with a smile on his face. The elongated expletive signaled to Vinny that Tye was in good spirits. He decided to turn the knife a little.

"I told you to buy a good car. Get rid of that piece of shit. It's nothing but a money pit." Vinny had a serious tone to his comment. Tye ignored him as usual.

"Let's go fishing tomorrow." Tye said.

"What time?" Vinny asked.

"Does it matter? You never get here until nine o'clock in the morning. So let's make it nine." Tye said as he popped another nicotine lozenge in his mouth. Two were under his tongue from the drive home and the newest one he attached to the roof of his mouth. A long white strip of crud was already stuck to the right side of his lip and was slowly migrating toward his cheek.

Thomas and Dergo made their way from the front of the gas station over to the garage and joined the conversation. The four of them agreed to meet at nine o'clock in the morning – Saturday – to go on their first fishing expedition since Terry's death

Once the details were worked out Dergo asked Tye who the lucky guy was.

CHAPTER 8

All four were at the Texaco before nine o'clock the next morning. At eight thirty the boat was loaded with bait and fishing poles. Dergo brought a twelve pack of Beck's and the other's brought water and snacks. Word at the bait shop was that the Wahoo were running along a weed line just past the reef. Vinny had every intention of filling the cooler before noon. After cleaning the fish and equipment he could finish a brake job on one of the four cars waiting to be serviced in his shop. They were parked on the other side of the garage. Normally he would attend to the paying customers before fishing, but this was an important day for all of them and because of that he didn't mind putting off the work for another day.

The retired police officer form Illinois popped the top on his first beer of the day at five minutes before nine as they all boarded the boat. The air was warm already, close to ninety-degrees, and the sun was brutal. Tye rubbed sunblock over his bald head and popped another nicotine lozenge, white shit already seeping out of the corner of his mouth. Thomas settled in behind the wheel and fired up the motors, constantly playing with the depth finder.

Vinny lit another cigarette and took his place at the very rear of the boat – just as they always did when they went fishing.

Fishing involves a lot of ritual. Each of the fishermen had a routine and Vinny was glad to see that everyone was settling back into their routines. He hoped for a good day on the ocean but understood that just getting out there was a big step for them. A step toward normality.

Thomas handed over the controls to Tye just before entering the inlet. The water was calm and there was no apparent danger this particular day, but once again it was habit. The trip through the inlet was uneventful and after a few minutes of heading directly east Tye and Thomas switched places again. Thomas steered the boat while Tye grabbed a bag of ballyhoo and began to chop them into small pieces to be used as bait. Vinny smoked and Dergo opened another beer. All was well aboard the "WHAT"S HER NAME" the official fishing vessel of the A1A Texaco gang.

They headed to deeper water and everyone settled in for a few hours of fun. Thomas hooked a sailfish and Tyrone cut his line. The group had made a pact years before that everyone gets one sailfish. After that they agreed to simply cut the line as it took hours to land the mammoth beast and nobody else was able to fish until it was landed. After sitting around for a few hours waiting on a buddy to land a fish that may or may not be of legal size wasn't everyone's idea of a great fishing day.

Just before noon the group had pushed south to Delray Beach and had caught half a cooler of fish.

Vinny was singing to himself in the back of the boat, a terrible rendition of "No Woman No Cry" by Bob Marley. His accent made the chorus sound a bit staccato which had the effect of butchering the song even more. Thomas had pleaded with him on several occasions to quit and was promptly met with a "Fuck You" each time, and each time Vinny spoke the words a thick plume of blue smoke passed through his mouth and nose. The third time Thomas begged him to quit singing Vinny ignored him and simply sang louder.

Tye asked Dergo for an old war story from the police force and Dergo was quick to respond. They were all sick of hearing Vinny sing.

"Well I tell ya," Dergo started off with a smile on his face and paused briefly to make sure he could recall the entire story. The fishermen on the boat knew him well enough to know that this was probably a good story if it made him smile. Even Vinny quit his noxious Bob Marley impression. Dergo opened a new can of Beck's and started his story. All eyes and ears on the boat were locked onto him.

"There is a little bar on the edge of town called the Willow Inn… big Willow tree out behind the parking lot. It's famous for some pretty bad fights so I would pass by occasionally on a Friday and Saturday night just in case I saw someone laying in the parking lot or such."

He took a swig of his beer and started to reel his line in. "So out walks this guy drunker than a skunk with his keys in his hand, ignition key jutting out from between his fingers. He walks right up to the police car and motions for me to roll down my window. I roll it down and the dumb fuck asks me where his car is."

At this point Dergo's line was out of the water and he was looking for the box of bait. Tye kicked it toward him and he bent down and grabbed a strip of cut up Bonita and began attaching it to his hook.

Dergo took another swig of Beck's and remembered where left off. "So I ask the guy where his car was the last time he saw it. He looks at the keys in his hand and says – *'Well shit, it was attached to this key the last time I saw it.'* So then I notice his pants are down and his dick is sticking out of his pants. I point this out to the guy… he looks down at his dick and says, *'Fuck... they stole my girlfriend too!'*"

Everyone laughed and the mood was light, until Tye's phone rang.

CHAPTER 9

Shortly after ten o'clock in the morning Gutsy heard a strange noise. He had woken at dawn to go for a walk along the beach, then spent an hour fishing off the shore. By the time he cleaned his Spanish mackerel and soaked it in marinade he decided to take a short nap. That was at nine thirty.

He had a prepaid cell he kept locked in a desk drawer. When he realized it was his friend Mal calling from New York he jumped up and fumbled for the key to the top drawer. After a few rings he had freed the phone from captivity and flipped open the receiver.

"Yeah!" He said loudly, cautious not to say his name or even assume he knew who was on the other end of the line.

"It's me." Mal said in a low voice, his unmistakable New York accent crisp as ever.

"What the fuck are you doing down there? Why am I having to make this call? You know this is bad for me.. and anything bad for me gets worse for you. You understand friend?" Mal tried not to sound sinister. He wanted Gutsy to hear him loud and clear, hoping the clarity would have more of an effect than any type of threat.

Guts wasn't buying it. He understood perfectly what was happening. He had been in the business long enough to understand that a phone call was coming today and the contents of the phone call could almost have been scripted by Guts himself.

"Yeah I got it." Guts said in a monotone voice. He had meant to sound more interested. Having been in Florida for so many years his New York accent seemed to carry a sort of dramatic tone all by itself for the locals. Mal would have been able to sense the apathy even with the thick accent.

"You better hope you got it, and you better hope whatever needs fixed gets fixed – today!"

They both understood how much was riding on this job. They were both professionals. Neither of them even needed to have this conversation. It served more as a warning of what would happen if things weren't fixed right away.

"So this is the last phone call I'm gonna have to make … right?"

Guts opened a new pack of cigarettes and lit one. "That's right." He heard a click from the other end and hung up his phone. He placed his cigarette in the ashtray that sat on his desk and then replaced the prepaid in the top drawer and locked it with the key. He spun around in his chair and took a look at his one room loft. It was small and in desperate need of updating. If fit his needs well however. It didn't require much maintenance. The tile floors were easy enough to keep clean, even with all of the sand that was tracked in and the cheap blinds were easy enough to dust. The salt from the proximity of the ocean had a tendency rust anything metal, so he made sure all of the metal windows and railings outside were treated. A modest expense considering he would have had to replace them every few years if he didn't pay for the treatments. His little place was nice enough for him. It was a far cry from the grandiose living arrangements he was accustomed to in New York. But this was Florida, and small and tidy suited him just fine in his new life. Besides, his only job now was staying alive, and in order to do that he needed to fly under the radar. Regular chats with old friends from his old life weren't conducive to flying under the radar.

His mind shifted toward the day's events. He had to make a few phone calls and get this job back on track, not that it was derailed, just going a little slower than anticipated. He pulled on a pair of board shorts and a tank top. On his way out the door he slid his tanned feet into a pair of flip-flops and locked the door behind him.

CHAPTER 10

The others were laughing at Dergo's story when Tye felt his pocket vibrate. He knew better than to keep his phone in his pocket in case he went overboard or it stormed enough to soak him. He was feeling a bit lucky that the phone rang… until he answered it.

On the other end of the line was Bill, Tye's old friend from PA. Sometimes Bill went fishing with the gang but had recently hurt his back in an auto accident that sidelined him from such activities. He still hung out at the gas station when he could and usually had a few beers every Saturday after work. He was on his way to the Texaco this particular Saturday afternoon. He had just crossed over the Woolbright Bridge where Terry had been murdered when he saw heavy traffic congestion on A1A. He was at the intersection of Woolbright and A1A intending on turning right and driving the quarter mile south to the Texaco when he saw flashing lights. Traffic wasn't going anywhere and he thought about going straight through the intersection to Old Ocean Ave but saw that route was congested as well. It took a few moments to register in his head but when it did he simply turned his car off and left the keys inside. He tried to run but his back wouldn't allow it. He just had surgery a few weeks earlier to replace one of his vertebrae. He walked briskly toward the station, hoping that everyone was OK.

He saw fire trucks and ambulances. There were five or six police cars from various locations including Boynton Beach, Ocean Ridge, Delray Beach, and Gulf Stream. It was bad, he could feel it. He made it as far as the outer ring of police cars. The yellow tape was already stretched across the street and there was no way of making it to the gas station – the obvious center of whatever happened.

Bill had a horrible feeling inside his chest. A few short months ago he and his two good friends – Terry and Tye - seemed bulletproof. They were young and healthy and on top of the world. Today, Bill couldn't run and had a fake vertebrae in his back, lucky to even be alive. Terry was dead, and Tye seemed a little older than his years. Maybe it was his brother's death bringing him back to reality, maybe he was just getting older.. maybe they were all getting older. Either way life had changed for him and his friends and it would never be the same.

These thoughts flashed in front of him as he tried to find a way inside the yellow tape. He was good friends with these people and he could help. He believed he could help somehow… if he could just get past the damned yellow tape.

The police were adamant about keeping everyone out so Bill circled the tape to the other side looking for a way in. He ran into a lot of people he knew as most of the folks that lived close to the

Texaco were regulars and hung out on occasion. Bill saw an older guy, Frank, and thought he might be able to help. If not help, perhaps he knew something.

"Paisan! What happened?" Bill asked Frank in a slightly panicked voice.

Frank was a retired caterer from New Jersey who still did some light catering for extra cash. He was a jolly fellow that everyone liked, in his early seventies. "Jeez Billy… I don't know how to tell you this." Frank had true hurt in his heart and his eyes were welling up with tears. "It's Darryl. He's dead. Someone walked into the gas station and just shot him. I was one of the first one's there. I heard the gunshot."

"Does Vinny know?" Bill asked, fairly certain that Vinny would be fishing on such a beautiful day.

"Naaaw. I think he's fishing with Dergo and Tye.. maybe the Switz." Frank always referred to Thomas as the Switz.

"I'll call Tye and tell him what happened." Bill said to Frank, half hoping for some advice. It seemed the best thing to do for some reason. Part of the reason was that Bill didn't want to have to tell Vinny that his son was dead. He also figured that Tye would know what to do. He always did in the past. Frank offered no advice.

Bill dialed Tye's number and waited for him to pick up. When he did, Bill went straight to the point before Tye could say anything.

"Tye… it's Bill. There's been another shooting. This time at the Texaco. Darryl is dead. I figured better to let you know than call Vinny."

CHAPTER 11

"Thanks for the info." Tye said and hung up his phone. "Pull up the sea anchor, we have to go… now!" Tye fired up the engines as he spoke. The others stopped laughing and fell silent.

"What's up dumbass?" Vinny asked as he lit a cigarette. His eyes were larger than normal and his head moved from low to high, as if asking a question.

Dergo's instincts told him something was terribly wrong. It wasn't like Tyrone to act so quickly without any sort of justification. He immediately understood Tye was hiding something for a reason and he didn't want to complicate matters by asking questions. He was sure they'd all find out soon enough.

Unfortunately Vinny had cop instincts too, and he also knew something was wrong. "What the fuck is going on?" Vinny asked in a more serious tone.

Tye hesitated, searching not for the right words, those didn't exist. He racked his brain trying to think of anything that might work.

Finally he just blurted out what was on his tongue. "It was Bill. Some sort of trouble at the Texaco. He says we need to get there now. Didn't say exactly what happened."

Vinny sat down on his chair on the back of the boat. He knew his son was working by himself. He knew that if anything happened to his son he would blame himself for not being there to protect him.

The sea anchor was retrieved and most of the lines were reeled in when Tye throttled the boat and cut the wheel, turning due north toward the Boynton inlet. Everyone grabbed hold of something solid and braced themselves as the ride became dangerous. Instead of riding with the waves to minimize the chop Tye made a beeline directly to the inlet. The boat planed off the top of waves and the nose dug into the base of waves all along the way. It was hard on the boat and harder on the men, but it cut travel time. Tye also knew that with the throttle pegged the sound of the motors was too loud for any of them to talk. He didn't want to talk so it was a good trade-off. He didn't make eye contact with anyone, just kept his face pointed toward the inlet and the throttle down.

He didn't slow down as they approached the mouth of the inlet. Everyone held on tighter in anticipation of something bad happening. The mouth of the inlet is only so big, and if another boat is exiting the inlet there isn't much room to maneuver. At the speed they were travelling there wouldn't be much time to maneuver anyway. Thomas thought about telling Tye to slow down but at that moment the nose of the vessel dug into the bottom of a wave and cold, salty spray covered all of them. Heads were toward the floor in an instant and stayed there until Tye cleared the inlet. Once inside the intracoastal they all assumed he would slow down, but he didn't. Within thirty seconds he was passing underneath the Woolbright bridge at a speed of fifty miles per hour. Past the big "*slow speed – no wake zone*" signs, past the Banana Boat and Two George's restaurants. Past the place where his brother was murdered by a random sniper

Another thirty seconds and they were closing in on the Briny Breezes Marina. Vinny moved toward the front in order to be the first off the boat. Thomas made way for him.

As Tye pulled into the dock, Thomas and Dergo readied themselves to grab ropes and secure the boat. Vinny jumped out and immediately started toward his gas station. The Texaco was out of view even though it was a mere two hundred yards away.

Suddenly everyone noticed the helicopters flying in the air. Once Tye shut the boat motors down all anyone could hear were the helicopters. One was a police helicopter moving swiftly up and down A1A, seemingly searching for someone. The other was a channel four news helicopter hovering just over the ocean, which was only a few hundred yards east of the Texaco.

After a few minutes Vinny was gone and the boat was tied to the dock. Dergo opened a beer and sat on the dock, facing the boat. Tye and Thomas were still on deck collecting fishing poles and supplies.

"So what happened Tyrone?" Dergo asked in his cop voice. He knew Tye knew more than he told Vinny. He also called him Tyrone instead of Tye, further reinforcing his "Don't bullshit me" stance on the subject.

Tye lowered his head and spoke, “Darryl is dead. Gunshot to the head.”

“Oh shit.” Thomas said under his breath.

Dergo handed each of them a beer. “Let’s get up to the station.” He said as he got to his feet. Leave all this stuff here. I have a feeling we’ll need a reason to come back to the boat.

CHAPTER 12

It took less than two minutes for Vinny to make it from the boat to the Texaco. Officer Payne met him at the yellow tape on the southern end of the property. Bill was standing next to him.

"I'm not sure you should go in there yet Vinny. The crime scene guys aren't finished yet." Payne wasn't very convincing, but like Bill he didn't know what to say. Until recently being on the Ocean Ridge Police force had been a cake walk. It was a retirement community with almost no crime, and Payne wasn't prepared for what was happening.

Vinny on the other hand had seen it all in his days as a police officer in Trinidad. Because of that experience he knew exactly what was going on, nothing was left to the imagination except for the *who* part. Who was lying dead in the gas station and who did it. Most people would have wanted to know the *why* part – but in all the years of being a cop knowing why never seemed to help any of the victims' families. Knowing why didn't bring anyone back from the dead. Knowing who helped you get justice.

Vinny steadied himself as he grabbed hold of the door to the candy shop. He reflected for a moment on the words “candy shop.” His son had always referred to the small convenience store as the candy shop and everyone else seemed to go along with it. He’d never really thought about it until now. Darryl had often said that beer and candy sales paid the electric bill and that brake jobs and new air conditioners paid the mortgage. Darryl was well liked by everyone in the community. He always tended the full serve pumps with a smile and treated everyone with respect regardless of the car they were driving. He was just as nice to the people driving Buicks as he was to the folks that pulled in with a Ferrari or a Bentley. In fact there were more Maserati’s and Lamborghini’s at the full serve pump than Ford’s or Chevy’s. It just came with the territory on this strip of land. This was where most of the big money in south Florida lived.

Vinny opened the door and all of his fears were realized in an instant. He saw his son lying on the floor in a pool of blood, single gunshot wound to the head. His body was lifeless. There was nothing he could do. He turned around and left the candy shop and immediately took a seat on one of the chairs outside the door. Without thinking he took a pack of cigarettes out of his shirt pocket an lit one. People were talking to him… Bill and Frank included, but he didn’t hear anyone. His mind went blank and he started to cry. His gaze never wavered. He stared straight ahead, directly east toward the ocean. In the top of his view was a helicopter pointed directly at him. He figured it must be hovering directly over the coastline. The beach at Briny Breezes.

Tye, Dergo, and Thomas all stood about twenty feet south of Vinny. For a while they just sipped what remained of their beer and tried to think of a way to console their friend, but nothing came to mind. Vinny never saw them.

After a few more awkward minutes of silence Dergo finally broke the ice. "I don't know about you guys but I think it's time we figured out what's going on here."

"What makes you think something is going on?" Thomas asked, not necessarily doubting Dergo but hoping there was more information to be shared.

"Just a gut feeling at this point. Two people from our circle of friends are murdered within weeks of each other. There's a motive somewhere… we just have to find it. Once we know the motive, we'll know who is doing this."

Thomas nodded in agreement. Tye popped another nicotine lozenge in his mouth. After traveling at high speeds with his face in the wind his white crud line had migrated almost to his ear. He wiped his cheek on his shoulder knowing that he must have had white crap on his cheek. Thomas just shook his head and laughed. Tye understood it must have been bad and spit out all of the lozenges.

"Fuck it, I'm quitting the lozenges." Tye said in disgust.

"Go buy a pack of cigarettes for goodness sakes." Dergo said. "You'll probably ingest a lot less nicotine."

They all went their separate ways that evening. Nobody heard from Vinny for a few days. The gas station remained closed for a few days until the funeral took place.

CHAPTER 13

Jules had invited a small group of people to join him aboard his boat for the weekend.. His “boat” as he called it, was a three hundred foot long – five story floating palace. He purchased it from a Hollywood movie producer for a mere one-hundred and seventy million dollars, and immediately gutted the inside and had it tailored to his liking. After renovation the yacht contained ten separate suites with accompanying bathrooms and hot tubs. It was capable of holding a crew of twenty-seven. On the main deck he had an infinity pool installed, complete with a forty foot movie screen that disappeared with the press of a button. The top deck boasted a helipad and tennis court.

A few days earlier he had confirmed that everyone was able to make the excursion so he told his assistant to make the necessary plans. It took several days’ preparation to stock the vessel with the necessary accoutrements, fuel, and staff.

Jules showered and got dressed for the day. He could afford any attire he desired, but coming from humble beginnings his preferences were solidified at a much younger age. He had seen the pictures of the Hollywood elite on their yachts with Ralph Lauren linen pants and lightweight sweaters wrapped around the neck. It was a perfect look for him and being in his seventies he felt he looked the part. A nice pink colored polo with a mint green sweater complimented the tan linen pants and deck shoes he wore. He instructed his assistant to make sure there were plenty of clothing options aboard the boat in case the weather changed. What Jules had forgot was that the boat was fully stocked with a month's worth of clothing at all times. His assistant just nodded his head in agreement fully aware that Jules's memory had recently lapsed. It wasn't bad at this point, but he knew it would get progressively worse in a few years, maybe less.

After dressing he walked across the master suite of his ocean front home in Miami to the glass windows that faced the ocean. The view was beautiful, uninterrupted by nothing except for his yacht approaching the front of his landscaped yard. His property was more than four hundred feet of ocean front and stretched west from the ocean to the intracoastal waterway. The seawall on the ocean side was constructed specifically to be able to dock his mammoth yacht for occasions like today.

When the yacht finally stopped moving Jules noticed, as he always had, that the boat nearly blocked out the entire view of the ocean, even from where he stood upstairs. He saw the very large boarding door open and a set of custom constructed stairs slid slowly down a mechanical guide rail, coming to a halt as they touched the patio in his yard.

It truly was a sight to behold for those who had never witnessed such a thing. The boarding door was nearly two stories tall and opened from bottom to top like the doors on a Lamborghini. From where he stood, almost even with the second deck, he could see a handsomely dressed woman standing behind the second floor bar on the boat. She noticed Jules and gave a short waive. As Jules returned the gesture he felt like a child again, a little giddy inside. His stomach fluttered and he wanted to play with his toy. He noticed that the bartender, a woman who was always at that station when he took the boat out, raised a glass to him, inviting him to come have a drink. His favorite, Jack Daniels and root beer. The home-made root beer was flown in from West Virginia just for this occasion.

With a smile on his face he made his way downstairs and out to the courtyard past the giant water fixture and infinity pool. As he approached the steps to his boat he could hear his helicopter returning from the Miami airport.

"Perfect timing." He thought to himself, and his smile grew a little bigger.

CHAPTER 14

Gutsy loaded up his beach chair, towel, sheet and cooler on his golf cart. It was only a hundred yards from his front door but he didn't feel like carrying everything. He decided at the last minute to grab the prepaid cell phone from his locked desk drawer. He put on his flip flops and locked the front door behind him. As the electric golf cart took off he remembered his last conversation with Johnny Maldone. Mal, as he referred to him since childhood, would likely be calling soon given the events that had taken place a few days ago.

It was a perfect Florida day. The sun was bright and the temperature was in the mid-eighties. A constant, cool breeze was coming off the ocean blowing right into his face. It was salty. The waves were small, maybe two or three feet. Perfect for a short swim. Guts wore nothing but a pair of board shorts he bought at a discount at Nomad's surf shop down the street from his house. His chest was bare, hairy, and tanned. He wore a bright orange University of Tennessee ball cap and a pair of aviator sunglasses. He looked the part, and aside from his thick New York accent it was impossible to tell that he wasn't a local.

He parked his golf cart on the sidewalk and started to unload his effects for the day. After a short stroll of maybe twenty feet he started to place his supplies underneath the tiki hut. The tiki hut was nothing more than a small palm tree that a few folks had built a makeshift roof cover to protect them from the sun. Thick palm leaves were laid on the small roof and nailed down. They were stacked six inches thick and provided protection from rain as well.

So Guts laid out his sheet and put a scoop of sand on each corner to keep the wind from blowing it away. His beach chair sat on one corner of the sheet and underneath the shade of the tiki hut. His cooler full of Budweiser's and ice was placed beside the chair He kicked his flip flops off and grabbed a cold beer. It tasted good in his mouth. The first swallow always did. He relaxed and soaked up some sun for a few minutes until he finished the first can. He pulled out the latest James Patterson novel from his beach bag and opened another beer.

He had finished a few chapters and his second beer when the prepaid cell rang from inside his beach bag. He took a deep breath and prepared himself for the call, grabbed the phone, flipped it open.

"Yeah." He said with his unmistakable accent. He knew who was on the other end but didn't say his name.

"I told you I didn't want to have to talk with you again. Now I gotta come down there myself.

Why you gotta make shit hard for me Guts?" Mal said in a pissed off tone.

Guts knew full well he wasn't going to fly down from New York. Not yet anyway, but his grace period was just about over.

"Listen." Guts said. "I went myself to take care of it and he wasn't there. I sent a message though."

"A fucking message?" Mal was yelling now. "I'm not paying you to send a message. I'm paying you to take care of a simple job and you're making fucking national headlines."

Guts listened intently. He waited for Mal to calm down, or at least stop talking so he could update him. When Mal finally did quit talking he saw his opportunity.

"I got a plan. I'm too close now but I got this guy… he's from another family. He knows what to do. Gimme a few days. Things are a little shady down here right now."

There was a short silence followed by another round of yelling. "I don't wanna hear about a plan you cocksucker. I wanna hear that the job is done. Last chance friend. I swear to you this is the last call I'm gonna make." Mal hung up the phone as his last words came through Gutsy's earhole.

Guts opened another beer and closed his eyes, soaking in more sun. He was unaffected by the conversation. However, he was happy that Mal didn't ask about his friend from "another family." Had Mal known about the next step in his plan he would certainly have flown down to take care of things himself. Nobody from his old life would have approved of what he was about to do. Bring in someone from the outside.

Guts opened his eyes and scanned the ocean. Among the fishing boats was an unusually large boat that appeared to be a cruise ship from where he was sitting. He thought it rather odd that one of the Carnival Cruise lines or a Disney Cruise line was heading north out of Ft. Lauderdale or Miami. They typically headed south to the Bahamas.

CHAPTER 15

Jules boarded his yacht as his helicopter was landing on the top deck. He instructed his assistant to meet his guests upstairs and bring them to the second story bar.

Upon entering the oceanic palace his assistant turned left toward the elevator that would take him to the helipad and Jules turned right toward the rear of the vessel. He gazed out upon the open area surrounded by darkly tinted windows. He was able to remove his sunglasses and placed them on top of his brow. The boat was beautiful. The grand scale of everything reminded him of his humble upbringing. No matter how well off he would ever become he never forgot where he came from. The breathtaking beauty of this ship reminded him that he had work to do, and he headed up the spiral staircase to the second floor.

Eva, the bartender who waived at him earlier greeted him with a loud "Hola senior Jules!" She was a beauty in her late twenties with a perfect figure and a matching personality. Jules had always been too smart to allow himself to fall for a young beauty like Eva, but he told himself each time he saw her that if he ever did lose his edge she would be the one who made it happen.

She was educated and spoke perfect English, but she knew Jules liked it when she spoke Spanish.

"Hola yourself Eva!" He replied with a childish grin as he reached for her outstretched hand. He grabbed the frosty mug full of his favorite elixir held it up to what little sunlight was peeking through the windows.

"Nice color." He said. Then he closed his eyes and held the mug up to his nose. He sniffed once or twice before one long inhale. He exhaled and opened his eyes with another smile on his face. "Mmmm …smells perfect." He took a sip, sloshed it around in his mouth then swallowed. He followed the swallow up with an entire mouthful of the concoction and swallowed that.

"Perfect temperature. Not too cold. I can taste all the elements of the root beer… one note above the Jack Daniels. Perfect Eva. As always you are perfect."

Eva blushed a little and curtly smiled. Fifty-five degrees Mr. Jules. The only temperature to serve such a drink.

Jules was about to say something else when the elevator door opened at the other end of the bar.

"Hey! How are you? You old coon-dog you?" A very tall man wearing a cowboy hat and cowboy boots walked out of the elevator with his arms raised in a welcoming hug. Jules met him half-way and they embraced.

"Michael, it's been too long. How is Texas?" Jules asked, knowing full well that the oil business in Texas was second only to the natural gas business in Texas, much of which Michael was involved in to some extent.

"Well…I gotta say things are pretty good right now." Michael said with a Texas slang, his words almost syrup-like. He took a dramatic look around at his surroundings with his arms raised. "And I see you're almost broke, did you gamble your fortune away?"

They both laughed, however, Jules and Michael had known each other for years and at one point Jules did have quite a gambling addiction, but hadn't engaged in such behavior in years. Because he was on the wagon Michael thought it was OK to joke about it.

"Things are going well here as well. I spent a fortune buying property when the Florida housing market fell out, but it's coming back and I've already made my money back with the potential to make a killing."

Michael looked at him in disbelief. "I know you better than that my friend. You never break even. You've probably doubled up already." He didn't wait for a response. He indeed knew Jules well enough to know that if he wasn't raking in money he never would have mentioned it in the first place.

Jules tried to look behind Michael to see if anyone else was getting off the elevator. Michael was such an imposing figure that Jules had to take a step to his left and curl his neck to see around him.

"Just me amigo. Were you expecting someone else?"

"I was expecting two others. Was anyone else on the helicopter?" Jules asked with a twinge of disappointment poking through in his voice.

"Just me partner." Michael said with a touch of sarcasm. "If I'm not good enough to dance with maybe you shouldn't have invited me."

"Nonsense." Jules said with a smile. "We'll just have to make all this money ourselves… that's all."

Michael smiled a little out of curiosity. He didn't know exactly what Jules had in store for him but he did know their last few ventures had made him money, and lots of it. He was a busy man but he knew Jules was a straight shooter. If he had went to all this trouble to wine and dine him there was the potential for a big pay day on the other end.

Eva muttered from behind Jules. "Mr. Jules.. your drinks. Jules turned and found Eva had prepared two more perfect Jack and root beers. He thanked Eva and handed one to Michael.

"Are you still drinking root beer in your whiskey?" Michael said with disdain. "Why don't you sit at the big boy's table and order up a shot of tequila. Hell.. I'm buying!" He said with a smile on his face.

Michael looked at Eva. "Honey… two shots of your best tequila."

CHAPTER 16

It had been a week since Darryl was murdered at his father's gas station. Tye was trying to sort through all of the events that had taken place in his life in the last few weeks. He decided to go kite-surfing and called Thomas. The two of them had grown up on the beach and had graduated from surfing to sail-boarding, to jet skis to catamarans and now their salt-life passion involved kite surfing.

Five years prior, Thomas worked at a fledgling kite-board company as an engineer who designed boards and sails. The company downsized once the sport took off and competition drove down prices on everything. In the meantime however, Tye and Thomas had become quite good at the sport and were entrusted to test all of the new equipment that was produced by the company. It was a form of relaxation for the two of them, as well as a tremendous workout.

The winds were right, about fifteen knots blowing directly from the east. Thomas met Tye at the trailer and they grabbed their equipment and headed for the beach. They had a system. They had done the same thing for years and didn't need to speak about who would bring what. Thomas picked up a case of Corona Beer on his way. Tye provided the five gallon bucket full of ice and attached it to the back of his golf cart. Barely a word was spoken as they loaded up the small air compressor that was attached to a piece of plywood. They bungee corded it to the roof of the golf cart. They needed the compressor to inflate their kites. Manually pumping them up would have been a workout by itself. They were old enough to make things easy on themselves.

Thomas was strapping into his harness and Tye was stretching out the lines that attach him to the kite along the sand when the wind changed.

"Fwock" Thomas said as he looked at the storm cloud brewing directly above him.

Tye laughed. "Say Fuck."

"Fwock." Thomas said and looked at Tye like he was retarded.

Tye laughed again. "How long have you lived in this country you dumbass?"

"Fwock, Fwock, what the Fwock?" Thomas said angrily, just about tired of their current conversation.

"Fwock you, you dumbass." Thomas started peeling off his harness while Tye continued to laugh.

"Fwock you too!" Tye said in his best Swiss accent.

They settled down in the sand and drank a few beers, hoping the wind would change back. They started to discuss the Texaco when Frank came walking down the beach.

"Hey it's Tyrone and the Switz." Frank said

with a smile on his face. They were happy to see him. Frank was a little older but he always had something kind to say.

"Say fuck - Frank." Tye said to Frank trying to hold back a laugh.

"Fucka you." Frank said with his thick New York Italian accent.

Thomas edged in. "See, I'm not the only one who can't say it right."

"What the fucka you talking about?" Frank asked. "I say it just like you two assholes do."

"No… no you both sound like you are from different countries trying to speak English." Tye said seriously. If you would learn to speak the language then people wouldn't give you a hard time.

Frank looked confused. "What the fucka you talking about you cake-eater? I was a-fucking born and a-raised in New York.

"Get the fwock out of here." Thomas said, laughing at Frank's accent.

"Fwack? What da fuck is Fwack? You fucking Switz? Frank asked Thomas.

They were all laughing almost uncontrollably when they noticed the storm cloud disappeared and the wind shifted back out of the east.

"Thank goodness for that." Thomas said. "I don't feel like going to the Bahamas." He was referring to the shifting wind that would have pushed them east off the coast and toward the islands.

"We have enough beer to wait it out for a while if you want." Tye said to Thomas. But it was too late. Thomas, tired of engaging in an entire conversation centered on the pronunciation of the word "Fuck" had already slipped his harness back on and prepared to launch. In the old days someone would have needed to lift the kite off the ground into the wind but with the advent of some of the things Thomas had designed that was no long necessary. He simply yanked on the control bar attached to his harness and the kite strings pulled taught, launching the kite upward into the gust. He walked slowly toward the water with his board in one hand, dropped it into the water, slid his feet in and wrestled the kite to a position where it would accept the east wind.

The kite caught the wind and jerked him out to sea. Tye and Frank sat on the beach and talked for a while.

CHAPTER 17

Jules and his buddy from Texas sat toward the front of the boat as they cruised north. They had left Miami early in the morning and had already passed Fort Lauderdale and the Hillsborough inlet, still heading due north up the coast. They were only about a mile off the coast, just as Jules had directed the Captain.

They were sitting inside with the air conditioning on as they passed Del Ray beach and continued north. Jules had instructed Eva to back off the Jack Daniels in his drinks. Michael didn't know the difference and didn't care. He was drinking tequila and chasing it with Lone Star beer. It was impossible to find Lone Star beer in this part of the country but Jules made sure there was plenty on board for this trip.

"Let's take a walk outside." Jules said as he stood from where he was sitting. "There's something I want to show you." Michael played along. He was buzzed at this point from the alcohol and truly enjoying his time with his old friend.

He took another look around at the sheer opulence of the vessel they were on. "What did this set you back Jules? A couple hundred million?"

"Pretty close… give or take. Once the renovations were completed it was pretty close to two hundred million." Jules didn't like talking about spending money. He preferred to talk about making money, which is exactly why he brought Michael along.

He motioned for Michael to follow him and stood up from where he sat. He turned and made his way toward the elevator. "Follow me. I'm going to present you with an offer you can't refuse."

"I had an ex-wife tell me that once. Cost me more than this boat cost you." Michael said as a smile ran away from his face.

Once in the elevator Jules hit the number five and they ascended to the top of the boat, nearly fifty-five feet above sea level. The elevator doors opened and Michael was surprised at how cool the breeze was from this high up. As they neared the front of the boat, just past the tennis courts, the boat turned left and pointed due west toward the beach. They were a little more than a half mile off the coast.

"There it is amigo, what do you think?" Jules asked, feeling a little giddy again.

"What exactly am I looking at Jules?"

"Excellent question my friend. You are looking at close to a billion dollars in your pocket, directly in front of you."

Michael started to sober up a little. "Billion dollars huh? I'm interested."

"What you see directly in front of you is the very last piece of real estate left to develop on Florida's east coast. From the Keys to Miami all the way to St. Augustine. This is the very last piece of land available.

"I'm not tracking Jules. It looks developed already. I see houses. I see… I think I see a trailer park for Christ sakes."

"You do see a trailer park. You see a forty-two acre plot of land that was developed before any of the houses up and down the coast. They have their own water and their own sewerage."

"OK, so why is this particular piece of land so valuable. You can only put so many houses on forty two acres. None of the houses I see are above two or three stories."

"That's just it Michael. They don't have to answer to Palm Beach County. There are no height restrictions on building. There are no zoning restrictions. They don't have to pay Palm Beach taxes."

"I'm just an old oil and gas guy Jules. I don't know what you know about this sort of thing. I'm just not seeing it yet."

Jules could see Michael wasn't getting it the way he needed to. He had planned for this to happen. He looked at one of the staff attendants standing next to the elevator and motioned to him. When he arrived Jules told him to have the model sent up immediately.

A few minutes later the elevator door opened and a man dressed in black like the other staff pushed out a cart that had something on top of it, all of which was covered with a black silk blanket.

When the cart arrived Jules moved it in front of them, so it was between the two men and the shoreline. He positioned it correctly and pulled off the silk blanket.

Michael's eyes lit up and a broad Texas smile illuminated his face. "Holy Shit Jules." The words extra syrupy and drawn out. Michael threw back his last shot of tequila and chugged what was left of his Lone Star.

"This is what that forty two acres will look like when we are finished." He wanted to explain everything but decided to let Michael take it all in for a moment.

What he saw was a small city for adults. An "R" rated Disneyland if you will. There were two skyscraping condominium towers. In-between the residential towers was a state of the art casino that Las Vegas would be proud of. All of this was ocean front. On the other side of A1A were two high end hotels fully equipped with a grand marina for boats and yachts, as well as a concert venue for entertainment of the Cirque de Soleil and Elton John Variety.

"And what is this place called? What is this trailer park that we are looking at." Michael wanted to know.

"Briny Breezes."

"Briny Breezes?" Good enough I suppose.

"It will cost us five hundred million each to purchase the trailer park. After that, the two of us will be the primary investors in all of the real estate and casino. We will double our investment in four years.

Michael thought for a minute. "I'm interested Jules. You sold me on it. I'll just need to see some numbers before I start writing checks, but I like it." Michael said, not smiling this time. His brain had clearly clicked into business mode. He had passed once on an opportunity to invest in a casino and had always regretted it based on the numbers he saw come out of the establishment. He wasn't going to let this opportunity slip away.

CHAPTER 18

Guts had a small problem. He walked in to the Texaco intending on finishing the job himself. Drastic measures for a man in his position, but it needed to be done. The only problem was that he wasn't counting on Darryl being alone in the candy shop. His real target wasn't there that day. Not wanting to waste an opportunity he did what he could. He killed Darryl.

However, now he had a true dilemma on his hands. He had cycled through the hired guns he knew personally and was out of people to call. He couldn't risk finishing the job himself, he was too close to the shenanigans as it was.

He told Mal he had a plan, and he did. It just wasn't a good plan. The only professional left that he could trust to do the job was a man he barely knew. He came highly recommended by some folks in the business, but Guts didn't know him very well. He had met him once before and they seemed to get along well enough, but in this business that doesn't mean much.

He had arranged for the two of them to meet at

a local bar called "Sweetwater's." It was within walking distance from Gutsy's bungalow and this guy owned a business in the same shopping center that Sweetwater's was located in.

At five o'clock P.M sharp Guts walked through the door. It was new and it was beautiful. Large open spaces were punctuated with tables that had beer taps at each table. Novel concept. Guts wondered why nobody had thought of that before. Put the tap right at the table and you'll likely sell more beer, and the customer does most of the work. The floor was decorated with huge white marble tiles and the décor was decidedly German. As were the little outfits the servers wore. They looked like Bavarian teenagers dressed up for Oktoberfest. All of this eye-candy came at a price however. The first thing Frank noticed was the large board on the North wall with prices for the half-liter and liter. He could just about buy a twelve pack of Budweiser for the cost of one liter of imported German brew.

The second thing he noticed was the man he came to meet. He was already seated at the bar, which was a huge square set directly in the center of the open space. The ceiling above the bar arched into a dome and had to have been close to twenty five feet high.

"It's good to see you again." Frank's hand was extended to shake but he forgot the man's name.

"Deepak." He said in a friendly tone, understanding that many people forgot his name. "It's good to see you again." His accent was East Indian, and he looked Indian. Frank's Italian family back in New York wouldn't understand this meeting, but then again there were resources in New York that Frank didn't have access to while in Florida, while in the Witness Protection Program. He had to scramble to get this job done and he needed help.

Deepak stood and motioned for Frank to follow him to one of the open tables in the corner. When they sat down Deepak poured a beer for Frank and handed it to him. "On me." He said. He poured one for himself, took a long drink, sat his mug on the table and looked Frank in the eye.

"How may I help you on this fine Florida day?" His accent was terribly thick and Frank had a little trouble deciphering what he said, but he got enough of it to get the point.

Frank looked intently back at Deepak and took a long drink of beer from his mug. "I hope you don't take this personally, but I'm not sure you're even qualified to do what I want you to do. I'm not sure what experience you have with this kind of work."

Deepak smiled. "You think the Italians and Mexican's have the copyright on organized crime? We have been dealing in the opium markets for centuries. Where there are drugs there are gangsters. I was part of the Mumbai underworld most of my life. If you are uncomfortable with this I understand. I do not wish to push the issue."

Frank took a long look at him. He was put together well as far as dress was concerned. Khaki pants and a black polo shirt with his business name embroidered on the chest. His hair was cut neat and combed. His mustache was well-groomed, though it looked like your stereotypical nineteen-seventies porn mustache. He was methodical in his actions and both agreeable and conscientious in his choice of words and dialogue. It was hard not to like this guy, not to trust him. But Frank knew better than that. He was however, currently out of options.

CHAPTER 19

Vinny had shut down the Texaco for a solid week in order to take care of personal business. Dergo, who lived directly across the street from the gas station thought it was best. Looking out his second story window across the street into the Texaco parking lot he had seen all sorts of news crews and busy-bodies trying to see what they could see.

Dergo hadn't spoken to Vinny since the funeral, nobody had. Vinny fell into a sort of silence that everyone understood. They gave him his space and patiently waited for his mental return.

In the meantime Dergo had contacted some old friends in the Chicago Police Department. He didn't find much but it was a start. He called in some favors and had the second murder victim investigated using FBI and CIA resources. He wouldn't have the ability to call in many more favors of this sort so he was hoping for at least a sliver of something that made sense or tied the three murders together. Anything that could get him on some sort of investigative trail. A UPS overnight envelope arrived at ten o'clock that morning containing all the information his buddy in Chicago could squeeze out of his Federal contacts.

He poured a fresh cup of coffee and sat at the

small table in his small apartment. He opened the UPS envelope and sorted through the information. The second murder victim was Canadian. His name was Mark Henry Jean-Louis. He was a young man with a Ph.D. in finance from McGill University – Canada's equivalent of Harvard. Single, no children. He lived modestly and was accumulating a nice bankroll. At thirty-one years old his bank account topped six hundred thousand (U.S.) dollars. Bank history showed no out of the ordinary deposits. He saved his money and invested wisely. There were no big expenses, no large checks. His house and car were paid for, nothing extraordinary or anything that would raise a flag.

"It seems Mark Henry was a good kid with a good head on his shoulders." Dergo thought to himself. He poured through the rest of the file and found much of the same. Nothing out of the ordinary. He worked for the Wellington Group since graduating from McGill at the age of twenty-five. The Wellington Group was a multi-billion dollar investment group with a finger in just about everything. They bought and sold commodities, invested in technology, real estate, biotechnology, privatized prison companies, railroads, etc. There was almost nothing they didn't dump money into.

Dergo picked up the phone and dialed the number listed for Mark Henry's boss at the Wellington Group. The conversation was short and sweet. After identifying himself as a private investigator, Mark Henry's boss gave him a very canned response. "I'm sorry but we do not provide personal information for any of our employees. If you have questions you may contact our legal department or the local authorities. Please hold for more information."

Before Dergo could say a word he was transferred to a secretary who provided the number for the local authorities and offered to transfer him to the legal department.

Once transferred he got more of the same. It was a dead-end as far as he was concerned. He sat at the small table inside his small apartment and looked out the window, feeling a little defeated. He noticed a young couple heading toward the beach with towels wrapped around them and sunglasses on their heads, not much else. She was young and beautiful and mostly naked. He loved Florida.

Suddenly he sat up straight and thought to himself. "Our Canadian goody-two shoes must have had a love interest. He was young, handsome, well-off, smart, educated. He might have had a stable of women."

Dergo searched through the stack of papers he had been through several times before until he came across the phone records again. He cleared the small round table of everything else and spread out the phone records in chronological order.

He sifted through the numbers and wrote down the one's he would forward to Illinois for investigation. Some were made late at night to his home. These he figured to be a love interest. A group of calls to the Boston area. As he was finishing up he noticed a few calls to the Boynton Beach area code.

He picked up the piece of paper with the local

numbers on it and moved to his couch. His laptop was sitting on the small coffee table. He did a Google search for the local numbers and what he found surprised him. He had actually placed a call to the Texaco station the day of his death.

"Now we're getting somewhere." Dergo said with a sigh of relief. He picked up the phone and called Thomas.

CHAPTER 20

"What the fwock do you want?" Thomas said in a jovial tone.

"Can you get me a ride to Canada?" Dergo asked with hope in his voice.

"What? Why do you need to go to Canada?"

"Just answer the question. Can you put me on a plane to Canada."

"Not today. I have one going back to Toronto tomorrow. Just finished upgrading the engines on it. I don't know how you would get back though."

Dergo thought for a second. "Just get me on the plane. And can you go with me?"

"Are you fwocking crazy Dergo? I can't just walk away from my business. How long are you talking about."

"A day, two at the most." He said.

"Why don't you come over here. You can buy me lunch since I'm putting you on a plane. You can fill me in."

"Sounds good you Swiss prick!" I'll be there in a half hour."

Dergo hopped in the shower and drank his first Beck's beer of the day. It was just after eleven A.M. He put on a clean pair of cargo shorts and a Harley-Davidson shirt he picked up while in the Florida

Keys. Once outside the door he looked over into the Texaco parking lot. He saw someone trying to open the bathroom door, not realizing the station was closed. Dergo could tell he was visiting because he was Indian looking. Maybe from one of the islands.

He yelled from the second floor landing he was about to descend. “They’re closed!” The tourist turned around and got back in his car, not looking at Dergo. He didn’t think much of it until he was already inside his red Dodge Durango heading north on A1A. He brushed it aside for the moment. He needed to hop on interstate ninety-five and head north a few miles to the Lantana airport. A private airport used by people like Donald Trump and Presidential candidates when they flew in for fund-raisers and such. Donald Trump had recently finished building his Florida dream home – Mira Largo – just a few miles north of the Texaco. His helicopters could be seen shuttling back and forth between the Lantana airport and the helipad on the east side of his ocean front mansion. Dergo remembered seeing Air Force One and the Trump Jet parked side by side at Lantana during the weekend of a big Presidential debate in Boca Raton. That hangar was exactly where he was headed to.

He pulled into the entrance of the airport and was stopped by security at a small guard shack. The guard made a phone call to Thomas, who verified that he was expecting him. Once inside the airport he made the short drive to the north end of the airport hangars where Thomas had set up shop. He parked the Durango and walked inside.

CHAPTER 21

"Good to see you old friend." Thomas said with a smile. They shook hands and made their way to his office.

Dergo took a backpack off his shoulder and sat it on the conference table at the end of the office. They both took a seat and Dergo revealed the contents. He cooked several pieces of fresh fish, mostly Pompano and Mahi-Mahi for them to eat for lunch. There was some homemade beef jerky and a bowl of cut up fruit to round out the meal.

Thomas approved of the lunch menu and went to the refrigerator to retrieve a couple of sodas. As he sat down and opened two cans of Coke, Dergo reached into his backpack and pulled out the file his friend from Chicago sent to him

"Working lunch." He said, and opened the file. He took several papers off the top and handed them to Thomas. He allowed Thomas ample time to review the paperwork while he helped himself to some lunch. They had caught the fish two days earlier.

Thomas ate as he read. Dergo could see that he

was struggling a little. "Am I reading this correctly?" Thomas asked Dergo with a mouthful of fruit.

"Depends. What are you reading?"

"This guy worked for the Wellington Group. I've seen their corporate jet here many times. They park it a few hangars down. Hell… I've probably seen this guy before."

Dergo dropped his fork on his plate and told Thomas to focus on the phone records. He switched a few pages around until he came to the right page. Thomas scanned for a while, not sure what he was looking for, and then his jaw dropped.

"Is that the Texaco number?" He asked in disbelief. "What was he doing calling the Texaco?"

"Exactly!" Dergo said.

"No, seriously. " Thomas asked, "What does it mean?"

"I don't know, but I think we can find out if we go to Canada and ask some questions. Surely someone will have to know.

"Can't you just call? Do we really have to go to Canada? Isn't it cold up there this time of year?"

"I tried to talk to his employer but got stonewalled."

"And you think showing up in person will change their minds? Thomas asked.

"Won't know till we try." Dergo answered.

"I don't know man. Seems like a long way to go for possibly nothing."

Dergo became a little upset. "It's not a long way to go if we can figure some of this out. Vinny and Tye are missing family members, and this guy holds the key to us figuring out why. I think we have to take the chance at striking out… for our friends."

Thomas nodded his head in agreement. "You really think this guy will help us figure it all out?"

"I do. His phone call to the Texaco wasn't random, it's part of the story. An important part of the story. I've been a cop for more than twenty years. If I know anything… it's that I have to go to Canada."

Thomas thought about it while he tasted Dergo's latest jerky concoction. It was spicy and tender. As good as any he'd made before.

"What kind of meat is this?"

"Rat." Dergo said with a straight face.

"Fwock you." Thomas laughed a little as he choked on a piece of jerky. "I'll go with you. We leave tomorrow at seven A.M. I have to pick up a Gulfstream IV in upstate New York. I was going to do that next week but we can fly back on it.

"What's a Gulfstream IV?" Dergo asked tentatively, hoping it had jet engines instead of propellers.

"A Gulfstream IV is the nicest plane you will likely ever fly in. A guy in Boca Raton just paid seven million dollars for it. I have to pick it up and service it for him before the end of the month."

Dergo gave a sigh of relief. "Thank god, I was afraid we were going to be in a sardine can with propellers. I'm afraid of flying."

"Good. There's something I want you to see." Thomas smiled and it made Dergo's stomach turn a little. They got up from the conference table and made their way to the hangar, Thomas's workshop. There were three planes inside the hangar, though it could have fit five or six as big as it was. In the very center of the hangar was a beautiful private jet, a Cessna Citation CJ1. Not as luxurious as a Gulfstream IV, it was still in the neighborhood of two million dollars. A comparable jet was on the right side of the hangar.

On the left side was Dergo's worst fear. A Beechcraft Kingair F-90-1, twin turbo propeller – flying sardine can. Thomas pointed to it and smiled. "That my friend, is what we will be taking to Canada in the morning."

CHAPTER 22

Vinny opened the gas station for the first time in ten days since his son had been murdered, and four days since they put him in the ground. It was eight o'clock in the morning and the warm Florida air was already approaching eighty five degrees. There was a breeze coming off the ocean, and even though he was only one block from the water there was still humidity in the air. Beads of sweat collected on his forehead. Everything was open and accounted for. The garage bay doors were open. The candy shop was open. The pumps were on. Everything was ready.

Vinny walked outside and sat in one of the chairs along the front wall where he and his friends had always congregated. He was alone for a few minutes and was enjoying it. Soon the day would begin and all of the well-meaning customers would want to stop and offer their condolences. He knew their intentions were in the right place but he wasn't looking forward to talking to everyone about his son's death.

As he sat, he pulled a cigarette out and lit it without thinking. Blue wisps of smoke curled up into his eyes, making him squint. He was deep in thought when Tyrone pulled in on his motorcycle. In true Tyrone fashion it was a Kawasaki ZX-14. The fastest production motorcycle ever manufactured. The roar of the fourteen hundred cubic centimeter engine could be heard half a mile away. It wasn't thunderous like a Harley-Davidson, but had a low growl that bellowed. It was a unique sound that could be identified easily.

Vinny was accustomed to the growl but he was so deep in thought that he didn't notice Tyrone until he had pulled up beside him in front of the gas station and shut the motor down. Tye pulled his helmet off and put the kickstand down. He sat in a chair next to Vinny.

"How come you're not working today dumbass?" Vinny asked, truly concerned.

"I don't know. Thought I'd come over and see how you're doing. Haven't heard from you in a while."

Vinny suddenly felt better. Other than Dergo, Tye was probably one of his best friends in the world. He appreciated the fact that Tye took the time to check in on him. He was friendly with most of the customers that patronized his business, but he realized that he felt better for the first time in ten days. And by better, he didn't feel like he was going to vomit at any second because his stomach was in knots. For that… he truly appreciated seeing his old friend.

What Vinny didn't know was that Thomas called Tyrone the night before to tell him that Vinny was opening the gas station in the morning and that he and Dergo were going to Canada to investigate the second murder. Tye had decided he would go to the gas station to have a chat with Vinny. He missed his friend. Both of them were missing family members now and he thought misery might like some company.

"Have you talked to Thomas lately?" Tye asked, knowing the answer.

"No." Vinny said. "Why?"

"He and Dergo made a trip to Canada today. Coming back in the morning."

Vinny gave Tye a confused look. Under normal circumstances he would have followed up with some questions. He simply didn't feel like it today.

Tye sat quietly waiting for Vinny to speak. He didn't. After a while he pulled out a nicotine lozenge and added it to the two that were already in his mouth. The two of them sat there and watched the cars roll past on A1A for a while until a Bentley pulled in to the full serve lane at the gas station. For a brief moment Vinny expected Darryl to come out of the candy shop, air pressure gauge in hand, restroom key in the other, and greet the customer with a smile. That didn't happen either.

CHAPTER 23

"Oh God… I don't know about this Thomas." Dergo said. "Seriously, maybe we should rethink this."

Thomas laughed, he was truly enjoying the look on his friend's face. "Don't you fwocking throw up in my plane dumbass." He handed him a bag just in case. The small twin propeller plane was just about at take-off speed. After a quick visual check of the instruments he pulled back on the control bar and the wheels left the ground, briefly. He touched back down again and screamed, "Oh shit – oh shit." Dergo's face turned completely white and he threw up in the bag for the first of many times that day.

Other than a constant stream of vomit followed by whatever juices Dergo's stomach produced – the flight was uneventful. They landed close to noon and Thomas thought he might have to take Dergo to a hospital. He was in pretty bad shape. Once on the ground he drank some Gatorade and made a phone call to Illinois. He had an address forwarded to his cell phone. He and Thomas rented a car and he punched the address into the navigation system.

"According to the GPS we have about an hour's drive to get to her house." Thomas said, checking his friend's face to see if any of the color had returned. It hadn't. "Why don't you let me drive, maybe you can relax a little."

"I'm fine." Dergo said in a raspy tone. His throat hurt from all of the vomiting. The acid had torn it up pretty bad. Along the way he stopped at a convenience store to get some gum and lifesavers. He grabbed a Beck's while he was there as well. After twenty minutes of driving and a beer to settle his stomach he felt much better.

They left Toronto and headed east toward the town of Quinte West, a small town forty miles north of Lake Ontario and seventy miles east of Toronto. This was where Rachel lived.

Rachel was owner of the phone number that called Mark Henry every day. The group from Illinois had emailed a picture and quick background check, along with a few other tidbits they found.

She was a twenty-four year old graduate student at the University of Toronto, working on a Master's degree in accounting. The semester had just ended and everything indicated she was back at her parents' house for the summer, in Quinte West.

There was little conversation on the way to her house. Dergo didn't feel much like talking. He had investigated thousands of cases in the past, so he had little to do to prepare. He understood how it was going to play out.

For the most part Thomas was in agreement, as far as trusting Dergo to call upon his past life to get what they needed. He may not be able to hold down his lunch in a plane, but he was sure to be able to get some answers from this woman.

As they pulled in the driveway they could see

multiple cars, indicating at least someone was home. "Let me do the talking." Dergo said, and Thomas nodded his head.

"Just try not to throw up on anybody."

Dergo didn't see the humor in that comment and chose to ignore it. They walked to the front door and knocked. A few seconds later a pretty young woman answered the door. It was Rachel. Dergo introduced himself as a private detective investigating the murder of Mark Henry Jean-Louis.

They made some small talk and introduced themselves. Rachel's parents prepared some coffee and they all sat in the comfortable sized living room.

"I'm sorry for your loss Rachel." Dergo said with humility in his voice.

"Thank you." She said quietly. "I had been expecting the police to reach out to me but I haven't heard from them. I suppose I won't after this much time has passed?" She looked to Dergo for an answer.

"Likely not at this point I'm afraid." He wanted to be honest with her. "Our main concern is with the nature of his trip to south Florida. Do you know why he was there and what he was doing?"

"I'm not exactly sure, but I do know it was a business trip. He mentioned something about his boss wanting to buy a trailer park in Florida. He wanted me to join him but I couldn't. I was in the middle of taking final exams."

Dergo jotted some notes down. "According to your phone records I see that he called you the morning of his death. Can you tell me about that conversation?"

"Sure." She said. "He was going to meet with a group from the trailer park at ten A.M. He called me as he was leaving the hotel. He said he would be home the following day. The last thing he ever told me was that he missed me and loved me."

She began to cry and her mother, who was sitting beside her, held her in her arms. "Is there anything else we can help you with?" The mother asked. Her tone was telling Dergo that the interview was over.

"No, that's all. Thank you for your time."

Thomas rose to his feet and shook hands with Rachel's father. Dergo did the same and then they left.

In the car they had a brief discussion. Thomas asked if anything was gained from the conversation. Dergo was confident that they had but couldn't pinpoint the relevance yet.

"So what now?" Thomas asked.

"Now we talk to the people he met with."

"And who is that?"

"It has to be the management group at Briny Breezes." Dergo said.

"There are a million trailer parks in Florida dumbass. Besides, Briny isn't for sale." Thomas said.

Dergo looked at him and raised his eyebrows. "You sure about that you Swiss prick?"

Thomas wasn't sure. Just because there was no realtor sign in front of the office didn't mean it wasn't for sale.

Thomas changed the subject. "Are you going to

survive the flight tomorrow or should we hire a nurse to take care of you?"

"I'm thinking about driving this car down to Florida. I'll just drop you off along the way."

Thomas laughed. "You should be O.K. tomorrow. You'll be able to lay down and sleep. This jet has a bedroom in it."

Thomas punched in the address to the plane in the GPS while Dergo made a stop at the convenience store. He returned with a case of Beck's.

CHAPTER 24

Gutsy woke up in his little bungalow and took a shower. It was early, six o'clock in the morning. As he dried off in the little bathroom, mostly the color of nineteen-seventies avocado and the accompanying yellow of the era, he wondered if he had time to do some fishing before his meeting in Delray.

He decided against fishing. Today's meeting with the U.S. Marshall was too important. He had to check in each month. Typically someone would just show up at his house dressed like a local and chat with him for a few minutes at his house. However, he received a phone call the night before with instructions to meet in Delray. This only happened twice each year and it made him a little nervous.

He thought about it for a while before deciding to let it go. "It is what it is." He thought to himself. "If they know, I'm going to jail. If they don't know I'll be back by nine o'clock."

At five minutes before eight Guts got in his car and headed three miles south on A1A to Atlantic Boulevard. The local probation office was only a few blocks off Atlantic. This is where he met the U.S. Marshall twice per year. He remembered each time he went inside the small building. It was an odd color, some variation on salmon. It was one-story and terribly old and in need of maintenance. It smelled like insulation and floor polish, though the floors never appeared to be polished.

The air conditioning never seemed to work, or maybe State employees had to leave the thermostat on seventy-seven degrees. Either way it was uncomfortably warm. There was usually a pest-service truck parked outside as well. Guts wasn't sure if they somehow shared the building but his instinct told him they simply had a bad pest problem.

What confused Guts most about the place was why they asked him to meet there. A hotel room or restaurant would have been better cover. Hell, even the beach would have been a more incognito place to meet. A probation office? He wasn't on probation like the rest of the small time offenders sitting in the waiting room for their turn to check in with a probation officer. He was in the Witness Protection Program for fuck's sake. He felt he deserved better.

"Mr. Canale?" A voice called from the door that had just opened. Guts stood up and walked toward the large African American woman that called his name. He followed her through the door and down a narrow hallway. She stopped at the last door and motioned for him to step inside. He did. It was a small room, maybe ten feet by ten feet. It contained one desk, one chair, one table, one painting, and one U.S. Marshall. It smelled like dust.

"Anthony… how have you been?" Asked a very tall, lean man. As he stood to shake Gutsy's hand, the U.S. Marshall badge, attached to his belt, peeked into view.

"I been good Marshall. You?" Gutsy asked in a slow, raspy New York tone that revealed he could give a shit less about the answer .

"Call me Austin, please." The Marshall said, but as long as they had known each other Guts called him Marshall, as though it was his first name and not his job title. And even though Anthony wasn't Gutsy's real name, it was the identity the Federal Government had issued to him. Austin, the ever-so-rule-conscious agent that he was, would never think of going off-script. Anthony it was, and always would be.

"So why we meeting here… something wrong?" Guts asked, wanting to get it over with if there was a problem.

Austin looked at him and cocked his head a little. "Well you tell me Anthony. Is something wrong here?" His accent had a little southern twang to it, but not much. It wasn't Texas or Alabama, probably Arkansas, or southern Missouri.

"I'm good Marshall. Everything is fine. I had plans to go fishing today that's all. Maybe you guys don't want me to fish no more… afraid I'll take off for the Bahamas or something." Guts laughed. Austin laughed a little as well.

"No Anthony, just a routine – random drug test." Austin pulled open the top drawer of the desk he was sitting behind and retrieved a clear cup with a screw on lid. He tossed it to Guts. "Piss in this."

"In all the years I been in this program I never been drug tested. What's this shit about?"

Austin's smile decreased to a smirk. "Just piss.

And do it now."

"Right here?" Guts asked.

"Yes. I have to watch you. It's the rules. And don't make any jokes about..."

Before Austin could finish his sentence Guts had unzipped and started peeing in the cup right in front of him.

"I ain't never touched drugs in my life. You guys know that." He was upset and Austin found it a little refreshing. Here was this tough guy who had done God knows what in his lifetime, was offended that he had to prove he didn't do drugs.

When he finished he handed the cup to Austin, but Austin put his hands in the air as if surrendering and backed his chair up a good two feet. "Not me muchacho, give it to her." He said, and pointed to the lady who had escorted him to the room.

She took the cup from Guts and placed it on the small table, picked up a small strip of paper and swirled it around for a few seconds. She removed the paper swatch and held it up to the light. "He's clean." She said.

"Good job Anthony, you passed the test." Austin said with a smile, still two feet behind the desk. He nodded toward Gutsy's crotch. "You can zip up now."

"Are we done here?" Guts asked.

"We're done."

"Been a pleasure Marshall." Guts said and left the room.

Austin sat back in his chair and thought for a moment. When he had finished he turned to his partner. "We need to keep an eye on him. How fast can we get a team authorized?"

"I'll put the request in today. Should have someone here by the end of the week."

Austin pulled his chair up to the desk again. This time he put his elbows on the table and his chin rested in his palms. He was thinking.

"He's nervous. I've never seen him nervous before. He's up to something.."

CHAPTER 25

A couple of days had passed since Dergo and Thomas returned from their trip to Canada. Tye had been in Key West on assignment for his job and Thomas was shuttling a plane to Colorado. Once everyone was back at the Texaco he would debrief them on what he knew up to that point. Vinny was busy with a backlog of repair jobs in the shop and hadn't emerged from inside the bay for several days, other than to go home at night.

Dergo kept his eye on the Texaco from his second floor landing across the street. He had a bird's eye view of the property. He sat at a small round metal table with a cup of coffee and his notebook, jotting down things that popped into his head. He knew he wanted to schedule some time with the Briny Breezes management team. He had thought about walking across the street to the office himself but wanted Tye to go with him. Tye knew everyone at Briny and he thought things might go more smoothly if he was there.

He watched a few folks stroll past. Eager beach goers wanting to soak in the sun. Many of whom were young and scantily clad. In stark contrast to young and naked, he saw Frank make his way over to the candy shop to buy a pack of Marlboro lights and a Mt. Dew, as he did most every day. Dergo waived to him and Frank waived back, turning to face him and then deciding to ascend the small group of stairs to chat with him face-to-face. As Frank topped the last stair Dergo stood and met him with a smile.

"How's it going Frank?" He asked, and offered him some coffee.

"No thanks, I got the Dew this morning." He said as he opened his new bottle of green liquid and took a swig. "Damn shame what happened over there, the boy and all." Frank motioned toward the Texaco with his head.

Dergo agreed. "Something's going on. Not quite sure what it is exactly…" His voice trailed off as he noticed someone pumping gas across the street. It was the Indian guy he saw looking for the restroom the other day before he left for the Lantana airport. He took another sip of his coffee and made some notes.

"What are you writing there?" Frank asked calmly.

"Not sure. I saw that Indian guy at the Texaco the other day. He wanted to use the bathroom but it was closed. When I yelled over he ducked his head, got back in his car, and took off. I didn't think much of it at the time, but here he is again. Just writing down the time and date. Probably nothing."

"Well I gotta go Dergo. Got a small catering job I got to take care of." Frank said as he stood up and stretched a little.

"I'll see you later." Dergo said. Suddenly he felt dizzy and his stomach hurt. Frank was walking down the steps and back to his little bungalow when

Dergo decided he needed to head straight to the bathroom. In fact, he wasn't sure if he was going to make it in time.

He stood up from the small metal table and hurried the ten or fifteen feet to his front door. He made it another fifteen feet to the bathroom and barely lifted the toilet seat before emptying his guts into the bowl. He suddenly felt better. For a moment he thought it might have had something to do with his airsickness he experienced a few days back, but only because the pain in his stomach felt similar.

Once he stood up he realized his error in judgment. This was worse, much worse. He was so dizzy he fell back to his knees for fear of falling down. While he was there he threw up again, violently. His guts hurt and the vertigo was horrible. He slumped back against the bath tub and passed out. In his unconscious state he continued to vomit involuntary. Luckily he was smart enough to turn his head toward the bathtub before everything went black.

CHAPTER 26

When Dergo woke up everything was black and his body hurt. His arms were tied behind his back and his feet were bound together. Based on the smells and the sound of his environment he concluded he was in the trunk of a car that was travelling at a fast pace. He tried to get his hands free but it was useless. Whoever tied him had done a good job. Same with his feet.

He tried desperately to get his thoughts together but he was still experiencing nausea and his stomach hurt. He felt the need to vomit again and tried to move his head to the side so he wouldn't choke. He blacked out before he could turn.

When he regained consciousness again he realized that he had indeed thrown up. Much of it was on the side of his face, the rest of it in front of him. His mind was more clear this time and he remembered getting dressed that morning. He wore cargo shorts as he usually did. He put a knife in one of the pockets as he always did, along with a small twenty-two caliber pistol. He always put the gun in one pocket and a small clip that held five rounds in the other pocket. He lifted his hips up and rolled a little, trying to feel if there was anything in his pocket. Nothing. He rolled onto his other side and did the same. Again, nothing.

He decided to lay on his back and relieve some

of the pressure on his wrists. The knot was so tight it cut off circulation to his hands. He could no longer feel them, and that would be a problem if he was going to make an escape.

He started to black out again when he saw a glint of daylight. He was on his back now and he was looking out a window. He realized he had a blindfold on. All of his movement had loosened the blindfold enough for a sliver of daylight to sneak in. As he blacked out again he realized he was in the back of his Durango, in his own vehicle. This made him happy. He started to crack a smile but drifted out again.

As a twenty-five year veteran of law enforcement, not a day went by that Dergo wasn't carrying at least one gun on his person, whether he was on duty or off duty. As a result, he had become quite the gun collector and kept one in his vehicle as well. He had a Glock nine millimeter in a plastic case under the rear seat of his Durango. He was hoping that whomever emptied his cargo pockets didn't search under the back seat.

When he regained consciousness again he was able to put his back against the back seat and force his bound hands underneath. He could barely feel his fingertips, but he had no choice at this point.

His stomach felt better and the vertigo seemed to be fading. He was confident that he could hold on to consciousness long enough to retrieve the weapon…if it was there. As his fingers moved back and forth he realized he didn't have much longer until his hands would become useless altogether. Then he heard the Durango pull off the road and onto the unmistakable sound of a Florida dirt road. He assumed his captor had shuttled him out into the swamp somewhere. Undoubtedly a place where the alligators would consume his body before anyone even noticed he was missing. Panic set in.

His hands moved faster but still found nothing under the seat. The Durango came to a stop. More panic set in. He had to take a deep breath to keep from hyperventilating. Adrenaline was rushing through his body at an alarming rate. He knew this feeling. He'd experienced it many times while in uniform. He'd been shot twice and run over in a patrol car by a train, but that was mostly his fault.

The adrenaline was helping. Blood coursed through his hands and he was able to bend them at the wrists a little more. He heard the column shifter move from drive to park with a thud. Next the driver door opened, then slammed shut. He tried to stay calm. He remembered his training. Try to remember the sights, sounds, and smells of this environment. Any little detail may prove useful in the future. If there was a future.

He felt his hand brush up against the plastic carrying case of the Glock. It was a simple case with no lock, just two tabs, one on each end. His fingers were on top of the case and he carefully scooted it out from under the seat toward his back. He couldn't grab it, his fingers wouldn't cooperate. The case was now underneath his hip and he put downward pressure on it to keep it from moving. One finger pulled at a tab and it clicked open!

At the same time he heard the rear cargo door open. He continued to work on the case, sliding his wrist as far down toward his feet as he could in order to find the other tab. He needed time.

"Who are you?" He shouted at the top of his lungs. "What do you want with me? Why am I here?" One thing Dergo understood from hostage situations was to try to talk to your captor. If he spoke at all – you could get him to tell you whatever you wanted before he killed you. Something of a psychological cleansing or need to be honest or some other bullshit he had learned in a training class years ago. Either way it was all he had to go with at the moment. On the other hand. If he didn't talk to you it meant that he was there for business only. His conscious and your peace of mind meant nothing to him. It wasn't something he thought about.

CHAPTER 27

Thomas had just landed at the Lantana airport and turned his phone on when it rang. It was Tyrone.

"Are you back in town yet?" He asked. Thomas explained that he had just landed

"Why don't you meet me at Vinny's when you finish there?"

Thomas had pulled the plane into the hangar and shut down the engines. He was in the middle of a post-flight inspection as he was talking to Tye. He heard another plane approach the hangar and instantly became interested. No planes were scheduled to park in his hangar for the next three days.

"Tye I have to go. I'll see you at the Texaco when I'm done here." And he hung up his phone. From his other pocket he pulled out the two-way radio and started to communicate with the pilot on Lantana's designated channel – seven.

He read the call sign of the plane. "November Six-One-Six this is hangar three operator. You do not have permission to park here." There was a squawk and a brief moment of silence before he heard anything.

"Roger that Hotel-Three-Operator. I'm looking for hangar five. Sorry about the confusion." The plane kept moving north to hangar five and pulled in. As it passed in front of him Thomas noticed the markings, as he always did. The plane was based in

New York.

Lantana airport was small and Thomas basically ran the place. No flights from New York had filed a manifest or flight plan with the control tower. This was an unscheduled stop and it was a little out of the ordinary.

Even more peculiar were the unsavory fellows who disembarked and walked out of hangar five. Two of them lit cigars and the third fired up a cigarette. They were dressed in thousand dollar suits that looked like a wool or cashmere blend. Much too hot for south Florida this time of year.

He kept an eye on them from a window, not wanting to be seen. One of the bigger fellows took off his suit jacket and loosened his tie. His shirt was soaked with sweat. He also noticed the shoulder harness. That in itself wasn't a big deal. What caught his eye however was the long cylindrical silencer attached to the end of the gun, jutting out of the bottom of its holster. Further, the holster hadn't been cut to accommodate the silencer. The entire piece was handmade.

"These guys are for real." Thomas said to himself under his breath. He was about to walk away when a vehicle pulled up to the front of hangar five and the men climbed in. It was a solid black Suburban with black wheels and tinted windows.

He finished what he was doing and filed the paperwork necessary to complete his trip. Instead of putting it in his flight manifest box he decided to hand carry it to the tower.

When he opened the control tower door and

entered he handed his paperwork to the controller in charge and asked about the plane that had attempted to park in his hangar.

"Not sure." Henry said. "Their original flight plan was for Miami International but they said they were unexpectedly low on fuel. Said they would only be on the tarmac for an hour and then they were moving on."

"They didn't tell you they were leaving the airport for any reason?" Thomas asked.

Henry frowned a little. "I didn't ask them, and I really don't care. Maybe they are hungry Thomas."

Thomas thanked Henry and said his goodbyes. He wasn't sure what to make of the whole thing but he didn't like it. He decided it was time to meet Tye at the Texaco.

CHAPTER 28

"My name is not important. And you are here to die." His accent was east Indian, thick but he could tell the man had spoken English for years, perhaps even studied it formally. His inflection points were in the right place, even if they sounded a little odd. That wasn't typical of your average immigrant.

Dergo was still trying to buy time. His hands were now on the other tab of the case that held the gun. The Indian reached down and took off his blindfold. Temporarily blinded by the Florida sunlight he couldn't see his captor. He pulled open the second tab of the case and pushed the top open, just enough to get a finger inside and feel the cold steel.

"Why are you doing this?" Dergo asked, desperate to stall for just another minute until he could think of something...anything.

"You know too much. You are making some people very uncomfortable and they have paid me a lot of money to make you go away. It's nothing personal. Just a job."

"I have no idea what you are talking about." Dergo said as he fumbled for the weapon. His hands were almost completely numb but he could feel enough of the cold steel to know that he had secured the weapon. The good thing about a Glock nine millimeter is that there is no safety mechanism. You aim and squeeze. As numb as his digits were he would never be able to feel a safety switch. That was the good news. The bad news was that he never kept a round in the chamber. He would have to cock the gun by pulling the top slide rearward, which would load a bullet from the magazine into the chamber. He was trying to figure out how he might accomplish this nearly impossible task when Deepak stepped between him and the sun, allowing him to see his killers face.

Dergo tried to say something else but Deepak was very task oriented and was finished with the chit-chat. He grabbed him by his arm and rolled him toward the bumper. Since the rear hatch opened upward Deepak didn't need to lift Dergo, simply roll him out onto the ground and finish the day's business.

Dergo was confident that he had one hand on the gun's trigger assembly and the other hand was on top of the slide that needed to be pulled back a mere three inches. If he was wrong this was his last day on earth. If he was right he still had some work to do. Suddenly he had a plan. Not a moment too soon.

As Deepak rolled him toward the bumper Dergo spotted the eight inch trailer hitch extension jutting out from underneath the back of the truck. Instead of landing on his back, as Deepak intended, he would use the short metal rod and two inch ball as a platform to rotate another half turn on the way down. It was going to hurt, but if it worked he might save himself. A fair trade.

As Deepak pulled him over the bumper he did indeed hit the tow bar and then forced himself to spin violently in another half circle. He used his momentum on the way down to cock the weapon. He landed hard on his face with a thud.

Deepak was an observant man. He paid attention to things. He was always watching and listening when others seemed to be doing things blindly. He had survived the mean streets of Mumbai by being alert. To him, alert was synonymous with alive. And Dergo's overdramatic roll confused him. He stepped back from the Durango's rear cargo area quickly. He understood something was out of place. By the time he recognized the metal clicking sound was a gun and not Dergo bouncing off the trailer hitch, it was too late.

Dergo's face hurt. His stomach hurt and his knees…especially his knees hurt. They had taken the brunt of the contact with the steel ball at the end of the trailer hitch extension. But he knew two things at this moment. He knew his gun was now loaded and pointed in the general direction of the asshole that was going to kill him. He also knew that he had to be quick or he was going to die. Years of practice at the police shooting range took over and Dergo unloaded sixteen rounds in less than five seconds. He was face down with his hands tied behind his back. His assailant was somewhere behind him. Not knowing exactly where, and not being able to see him, Dergo rocked his numb body to the left and right as he squeezed, covering a six foot wide area with lead.

He was out of rounds now. The next few seconds were the longest of his life. If he missed, or simply wounded the Indian, he was in trouble. After a few moments of silence he tried to turn over. On his first attempt he felt nothing but a hot pain in his leg. In an instant he knew he had been shot. He couldn't be positive until he saw it, but he'd been shot several times before and he knew that feeling of heat, like someone was holding a lighter to your bare skin kind of heat. It was unmistakable

The sun was hot. Dergo realized he was soaking wet. Not sure if it was humidity, sweat, or maybe he pissed himself out of fear, he decided it might be all three. Ten seconds had passed and he was still alive. He was confident his plan had worked.

He steadied himself for the big reveal. He rocked to one side to gain momentum. As his body dropped back toward the ground he twisted hard and fast the other way, rolling himself onto his back. He peeked his head up off the ground and could see the Indian lying in a pool of blood. He hit him with three of the sixteen rounds. Two grazed him and one hit the carotid artery in his neck.

Dergo saw the Indian's gun on the ground and could tell he had not fired it. He realized one of his sixteen rounds ended up in his own leg. "Fuck it, I'll take it." He thought to himself.

After a solid five minutes of trying to get himself to his feet he gave up and simply rolled over to the Indian. His hands still tied behind him he backed up to the dead man and found his gun in the Indian's pocket. Not what he was looking for.

He rocked back and forth again till he conjured enough momentum to roll over the Indian. It was the only way he could search the other pockets. Once there he did indeed find what he was looking for. His trusty old Swiss Army knife, given to him by none other than Thomas after his last trip back to Switzerland. "Thanks you Swiss prick." He thought to himself as he worked his way free of the ropes.

Eventually he freed himself and then found his cell phone in the glove compartment of the truck. He searched the Indian. Nothing unexpected until he got to his wallet. Had he not been thorough in his search he might have missed it. Tucked under a credit card in one of the leather slots was a name and a number. It was a name and a number that he knew.

Dergo sat in disbelief for a few seconds before he was able to think clearly. "You motherfucker!" He said to himself. Then he picked up the cell phone and called Tyrone.

His fingers weren't working but he was regaining some feeling in his wrists. He knew it might take a while before his digits were functional. Tye was on speed dial – number seven. He pressed the number with a finger that he couldn't feel and waited for it to connect.

Tye answered his phone. "What's up dumbass?"

"Tye listen to me. Get over to the Texaco and keep an eye on Frank."

There was a brief moment of silence before Tye responded. “Too late Dergo.”

“What do you mean?”

“It’s better if I tell you when you get here. Where are you by the way? Nobody has seen you all morning.”

“You wouldn’t believe me if I told you. I’ll explain later. It’s going to be another few hours before I can get to the Texaco. In the meantime can you schedule a sit down with the Briny Breezes management board?”

“Is everything O.K.?” Tye asked, genuinely concerned.

“Yeah…I shot myself though. Gonna have to make a trip to the hospital.”

“Dumbass.” Tye said.

Dergo hung up the phone and dialed nine-one-one.

CHAPTER 29

Tye and Vinny sat in front of the gas station and talked like old times. It was good for both of them. Vinny chain smoked and Tye had a mouthful of nicotine lozenges, and a trail of white crud sneaking its way out his mouth and migrating toward his cheek.

"Wipe your face dumbass!" Vinny yelled at Tye. "Looks like you been sucking something you shouldn't be sucking on."

Tye wiped his face. Even he didn't know why the nicotine lozenges leaked out of his mouth, but they did. It was enough to make him want to start smoking again.

Tye had recently married and had a son. It was a life changing event and he decided to quit smoking. That was six months ago and now he was addicted to the lozenges.

They were both enjoying the warm sunny day when Thomas pulled into the gas station in his beat up Chevy pickup. It was old but ran great and he saw no reason to get rid of it. The briny Florida air would rust through the American steel eventually, but until then he would continue to use it as a work truck.

Thomas said hello to the two of them and entered the candy shop to grab a beer. Vinny's wife was working behind the counter. She was a nice woman, beautiful inside and out, and she loved all of the guys that hung out with Vinny. Most of them anyway. Thomas shared a brief conversation with her and purchased a six pack of Corona's. He put them inside the walk in cooler and grabbed two of them.

Once outside he handed one to Tye and opened his own beer with a cigarette lighter. The top made an uncorking sound as it flew through the air. Thomas picked it up off the ground and deposited it into the garbage can next to the gas pumps.

It was too windy to fish and not windy enough to go kite boarding so they decided to drink. It was a beautiful Saturday in sunny south Florida and everyone sitting at the gas station was trying to forget something painful. Vinny didn't drink much and when he did it was Johnny Walker Black. He was working so there would be no drinking for him today. Truth be told, he only imbibed a few times each year, and even that was becoming a thing of the past.

Tye had purchased a new fish finder for the boat that he and Thomas shared. They had purchased one earlier that didn't work and were finally getting around to replacing it. The three of them decided to head to the marina and install it on the boat. All of the cables were run for the old unit, they simply had to mount the new unit somewhere near the steering wheel and plug in the old cables.

So Thomas grabbed his six pack from the

cooler and they loaded up on Tye's golf cart and made the short ride down to the marina.

They parked next to the dock and Thomas and Vinny grabbed the new unit and boarded the boat. Tye decided to stay on the golf cart where he was shaded. He popped open another beer and enjoyed the cool breeze coming off the intracoastal. Things were good again. Until he heard gunshots.

He wasn't positive what he had heard, but he was pretty sure. He looked at Vinny and Thomas who were arguing about the best way to mount the fish finder.

"Fuck you then. You never listen to me anyway. Do what you want." Vinny said to Thomas as he lit another cigarette. Tye could see the blue wisps from twenty feet away. They hadn't heard the gunshots.

"I'll be back, I left my phone at the station." Tye yelled as he put the golf cart into reverse. The shots came from the gas station, if they were shots. They were muffled. If Vinny's wife was involved he didn't want Vinny to see it. He wasn't sure what he was going to do if something else happened, he just knew he didn't want Vinny to be the first on the scene. Somewhere in the back of his mind he knew it would be too much for him to handle.

He pointed the golf cart toward the Texaco and took off. Thomas and Vinny ignored him. When he got to the station he was relieved to see Vinny's wife standing outside looking across the street. He parked the golf cart in front of the chairs outside the candy shop and greeted Gemma.

"Did you hear gunshots?" Tye asked.

"I heard something, but I don't know what it was. Sounds like it came from Dergo's building across the street.

Tye knew that Dergo wasn't home. Nobody had seen him all morning. He decided to investigate. He got back in the golf cart and crossed A1A to Dergo's complex. Nothing out of the ordinary. He pointed the cart north and crept slowly, still nothing. He passed the Coastal Star newspaper headquarters, the Triathlon shop, and Colby's barber shop, all nestled in a little building that had apartments over the top. He noticed that one of the apartment doors was open. It was Frank's apartment.

CHAPTER 30

Tye turned the key off in the golf cart and pulled his phone out of his pocket. He hadn't left it at the station, he just used it as an excuse to leave Thomas and Vinny at the boat. He dialed nine-one-one and put his thumb on the send button. Tye was the only one in the group that didn't carry a firearm on his person. At this particular moment he was wishing he had one.

He climbed the stairs on the right side of the building and made his way to the middle apartment, the one directly above Colby's barber shop. As he approached the open door he stopped and listened. Nothing. Not a sound came from inside. He knocked on the side of the window. "Everything O.K. in there?" He asked loudly, wanting to alert anyone of his presence so as not to be shot. Still he heard nothing.

Finally Tye entered the room, slowly and fearful that someone was still there. The place was small. It was a studio apartment. Tye was able to see the entire place except for the bathroom with one look inside. He stepped inside the door and repeated himself loudly. "Is anyone here? Is everything O.K.?" Still nothing.

Tye wasn't a detective, but it didn't take police training to realize a struggle had taken place in this small apartment. Things were knocked over and broken. There was a small table lying on its side. Everything seemed out of place. There was only one place left to look. Tye was nervous. He took out another nicotine lozenge and put it in his mouth, careful not to take his thumb off the send button on his phone. If something happened he wanted the nine-one-one operator to hear everything.

He took the final three steps to the bathroom and knocked. Once more he asked loudly if anyone was in there and if everything was O.K. Still nothing. He opened the door but it caught on something. He wasn't able to open it fully. He looked down and saw two bare feet.

At this point Tye knew something was terribly wrong. He let his thumb press the send button on the phone and then stuck his head back in the door to see what was blocking the door. When he finally pushed hard on the door and was able to poke his head through he saw Frank's body lying lifeless with his head in the toilet. It looked as though Frank had kneeled in front of the toilet to vomit, but once Tye saw the blood around the surface of the toilet he knew that somebody had drowned Frank.

Tye almost choked on a lozenge when he took a deep breath. He coughed in order to keep the lozenge from getting wedged in his throat. He backed up into the living room area, just a few steps and looked for something to sit on. His knees were weak and he thought he might fall down.

As he sat, something brought his thoughts back into the real world, because for a moment he had checked out. He heard a faint sound. "Nine-one-one

–what is your emergency?" Tye looked at his phone and put it to his mouth. Once again he heard, "Nine-one-one, please state your emergency."

"Uh… I need an ambulance… and the police." Tye said in utter disbelief. She asked a few more questions about location and if anyone was currently in danger. Tye answered as best he could and said he would wait until the police arrived.

Within minutes the police were on scene. Shortly after an ambulance was parked outside Colby's barber shop. A small crowd had gathered across the street at the Texaco, including Vinny and Thomas.

Officer Payne was on duty and was the first of the Ocean Ridge policemen to show up. Tye met him at the bottom of the steps and told him what he saw. He explained that he had heard what he thought to be muffled gun shots from the marina, which is only two hundred yards from Frank's apartment. After five minutes of questions Officer Payne told Tye he was free to go and that he knew where to find him if he had any more questions.

As Tye was getting back into his golf cart to go across the street to the gas station his phone rang. It was Dergo.

Officer Payne interviewed a few more people who lived in the building. One of the employees at the Triathlon shop stated that she saw a black Suburban with black wheels and tinted windows parked in the lot earlier. She wasn't able to give a plate number or description of anyone driving the vehicle.

CHAPTER 31

Later that afternoon a cab pulled into the Texaco station. Dergo was sitting in the backseat. He smiled at the men sitting on the chairs outside the candy shop.

Tye suddenly remembered his conversation from earlier that day. “Oh yeah I forgot to tell you guys. Dumbass shot himself.”

“What the fwock?” Thomas asked in disbelief. Had he not just seen Dergo smile he would have been concerned. Vinny’s eyes lifted a little and he started to laugh, not believing Tye.

The cab door opened and a pair of crutches found the pavement. Dergo shifted his weight in the cab and turned to face everyone as he exited the cab. His leg was wrapped in a cast from just below his left knee to the bottom of his foot.

Dergo paid the cab driver and turned to look at his friends. As the cab left the Texaco and headed north on A1A he spoke to them with a concerned tone of voice. They were alert and waiting to hear what happened.

“Apparently there is more to Frank than meets the eye.” He said, unaware of what took place across the street a few hours earlier.

Vinny interrupted him. "Frank is dead. He was found dead in his bathroom a few hours ago. Somebody drowned him in his own toilet."

Dergo stopped for a moment. Tye had grabbed one of the chairs and sat it on the pavement for Dergo to sit on so he wouldn't have to climb the twelve inch ledge that the rest of the chairs sat on in front of the candy shop. His chair faced the others, his back was now to A1A. As he processed the news of Frank's death he shook his head in disbelief. "I don't know what's going on here guys, but for some reason we seem to be stuck in the middle of it."

"All of these killings you mean?" Thomas asked as though he wanted proof. "Why would anyone target us? What the hell do we have to offer, or what have we done to piss someone off so bad that they would kill all of us?"

"I'm starting to think Dergo is right." Vinny said as he took a hit off his cigarette.

"Me too." Tye added.

Dergo told them the story of what happened to him earlier that day. He started at the beginning, going all the way back to the first time he saw the Indian at the gas station. He told them how Frank stopped by to chat with him earlier and how he must have poisoned him or sedated him by putting something in his coffee. How he woke up in the back of his Durango and narrowly escaped with his life, shooting himself in the process.

"Holy fwock." Thomas said. The mood was solemn. None of them realized how close to death Dergo had actually come, and now that they did they felt a bit of remorse for making light of his misfortune.

Now that he had their attention he finished his story. “So, after I get myself untied and back on my feet I decided to search the Indian to see if I can figure out who sent him. I search everywhere and find nothing. I had already gone through his wallet once but decided to take everything out, just in case. And that’s when I found it.” He hesitated a second to make sure everyone was following him.

“Found what?” Vinny asked, not happy about the drama Dergo was inserting into the story. He took another drag from his cigarette. “What did you find dumbass?” He was losing patience.

Dergo reached into his front pocket and pulled out a slip of paper. He showed it to the others. It had Frank’s name and phone number on it.

Not everyone understood immediately the significance of the find so Dergo spelled it out for them. “Frank hired the Indian to kill me!”

On any other day, given any other circumstances nobody would have believed Dergo. Frank was a regular at the gas station. He bought cigarettes every day and talked to all of the guys, they all knew him for years. He seemed harmless. A nice guy from New York who ran a small catering business in the twilight of his life.

“I don’t understand why Frank would be involved in all of this.” Tye said. Everyone else was thinking the same thing, including Dergo.

At that moment an Ocean Ridge police car pulled into the station, as they often did. Payne was driving. Normally he didn’t exit his vehicle when he talked to the guys, but today he wanted to see what was going on with Dergo and the new cast on his leg.

"What the hell Dergo. Are you O.K.?" Payne asked. Dergo went through the entire story and at the end Payne had a shocked look on his face.

"You know I'm not supposed to divulge any details of an on-going investigation." He said to Dergo. But you're an ex-cop and now I can see that it involves you directly." Payne was hesitating.

"Fucking spit it out Payne." Vinny said. His patience was wearing thin today. He also had a dog in this fight. Whatever Payne knew could help him figure out what happened to his son.

"Well, I just had a long conversation with a U.S. Marshall who knew Frank."

Dergo's face lit up. So did Vinny's. They understood having been in this line of work before what it means when a U.S. Marshall inserts himself into a murder investigation.

"Frank?" Vinny asked Payne loudly. "Are you kidding me? Frank?"

"What are you guys talking about?" Tye asked, genuinely confused.

Vinny filled him in. "U.S. Marshall's handle the Witness Protection Program. Frank must have been in it."

Payne nodded without saying anything. One more thing you might want to know. I interviewed everyone in the building after we found Frank. Nobody saw or heard anything except for the gunshots, and they weren't even sure it was a gun. Frank had two slugs in the back of the head. He was dead before he drowned. That must have been for show… to send a message I guess."

Dergo paused for a minute. "Anything you can tell us about the Indian?"

Payne frowned. "Sorry, not my jurisdiction, but I'll make some calls and get back to you when I get a chance. Sorry I don't have more." Payne started to leave, then stopped just as he opened the squad car door. "There was one more thing, trivial as it may sound. One of the Triathlon shop employees reported seeing a large black Suburban with black wheels and dark tint."

Thomas perked up a little. "Did they see anyone get in or out of the vehicle?"

Once again Payne frowned. "No, no description. Nothing."

Officer Payne got back in his squad car and pulled out of the station. Thomas looked confused and Tye called him out on it.

"What do you know?" Tye asked Thomas.

"Nothing." He paused. "I don't think so anyway. It's just…at the airport today, I saw a black Suburban with black wheels and dark tint. Had a few unsavory looking fellows in it. At least one was packing. I saw the shoulder holster when he took his jacket off. But what are the odds?"

CHAPTER 32

Johnny Maldone closed the door behind him as he left Jules' plush Miami office. Jules was happy to see him go.

Johnny made it clear that their working relationship was now over and that he would not be finishing the job he set out to accomplish as outlined in their first conversation. Jules was disappointed but felt relieved at the same time. It was too difficult to work with men of that ilk. They played by their own rules. Johnny was certain that the Feds would be investigating and he decided it was time to pull out for good.

"Just getting too damn complicated." He had said. And he was right. Things were becoming too damn complicated, even for Jules. After a few minutes he picked up the phone and called his partner in Texas to inform him the deal wasn't going to happen.

"Well why the hell not?" He asked. Jules wasn't able to tell him the truth. He wasn't able to say that his mafia connection couldn't handle the job he had paid him to do. He was left with a simple, "It just didn't work out buddy."

The Texan hung up on him. Jules didn't feel bad. It was business. Sometimes business deals went bad. Besides, nobody had invested anything up to this point. The Texan made it clear that he made some strategic decisions with respect to some of his companies and holdings in order to prepare for the eventual purchase, but he hadn't lost a dime at this point in the game.

Jules was feeling bad however. He felt like he had lost, felt defeated. This was a huge financial opportunity that only a handful of people in the world could pull off, and he was one of them. He had the vision to make it happen and the capital to fund the purchase himself. Having the Texan go half with him was his safety net. If for some reason he lost everything in the deal he would still be financially solvent. It would hurt less if the Texan shared in the financial loss, but it wasn't completely necessary. Jules had been doing this sort of thing his entire life and if ever he saw a no-brainer in front of him, it was Briny Breezes.

He sat for a few more minutes, and in those few minutes he decided to pursue the purchase on his own. However, it would take time. More time than he anticipated, but he could still pull it off. He'd have to wait for things to quiet down before he could make a move. He wasn't sure what that move would be, but it would have to wait whatever it was.

He needed a new strategy. Jules never did anything without a backup plan and never did anything without stacking the deck in his favor in whatever fashion he was able to. He had an insider at the trailer park. He had put her there six months ago. Michelle was the new property manager at Briny Breezes. She had supplanted the existing manager who unexpectedly decided to quit after six years on the job. Jules talked to a few people in the industry and mentioned Michelle's name. Three weeks later she was hired. She didn't realize how important her role would become in this process, and up until a few minutes ago neither did Jules.

Michelle was a go-getter. She appeared on his radar a few years back when she turned around a property in the West Palm beach area. Jules owned the development. It was a great investment initially, but after a while the housing market crashed and everyone sold their condominiums. The owners would rent to whomever would put money down in an attempt to stall foreclosure. As a result the environment went from upper class to lower class within a year. Jules was about to write it off as a loss and sell it when he started to notice a turnaround.

Within six months of taking the job Michelle increased the occupancy rate to over ninety-seven percent, brought down operating costs, and actually had two-hundred thousand dollars in the coffers for future maintenance and repairs. Jules had never seen a property turn around that quickly before so he decided to travel north to West Palm to see for himself who this magician was.

When he first entered the office she didn't know who he was. He had introduced himself as Ira, which was his birth name. Jules was his middle name, though most people were not aware of that.

He liked what he saw. A little unexpected, but a treat to his eyes. "She was a tall cool drink of water," he'd described her once to a friend. Five feet ten inches tall, over six feet with her heels on.

She had long flowing blonde hair and blue eyes with a firm body and perky breasts for a woman of fifty years old. On this particular day she was wearing a blue and white sundress that accented her baby blue eyes and showed off her long, tanned legs. Though the dress came below her knees, her legs were long enough to be sexy even from the tops of her calves to her perfectly manicured toes.

She was a no-nonsense sort of girl. Ohio born and raised, she came from a small town close to the Michigan border. She ate pork and sauerkraut, preferred beer to wine, cheered for the University of Michigan instead of Ohio State, and didn't accept bullshit from anyone. Nobody. Including Jules. And that was exactly why he adored her.

Michelle thought highly of Jules as well. And when he asked her to take the Briny Breezes job she never questioned him. She had come to know Jules very well over the years and she understood how shrewd he was when it came to business. She assumed this had something to do with business, and since Jules bought and sold property, her natural inclination was to assume that Jules would somehow buy Briny Breezes. However, she was beginning to question her own logic.

It had been months since she started working at the trailer park. It was nice enough, she enjoyed it very much. Everyone paid their bills on time and there was very little drama to deal with. Everyone owned their own trailer and simply paid taxes and maintenance dues twice per year.

Occupancy was high from December through March, but it was almost a ghost town the rest of the year. There were always children and grandchildren visiting for a weekend or sometimes a week, but other than that only a handful of people were full-time residents. And all of this made life easy for Michelle. She was enjoying the slow pace that Briny offered, until Jules called her late one afternoon.

CHAPTER 33

Tye had scheduled a brief meeting with the Briny Breezes management board at Dergo's request and now they were headed that way. The main administrative office for Briny was only one hundred feet from where the chairs sat in front of the candy shop, elevated by a twelve inch curb. Thomas wasn't able to attend the meeting. He had work to do at the airport.

They moved slowly, giving Dergo time to get accustomed to his new crutches. He wouldn't take any of the pain killers offered to him at the hospital so each movement brought with it a new jolt of pain. Vinny didn't mind. It gave him time to finish a cigarette in case the meeting ran long. As if on cue, Tye popped a nicotine lozenge in his mouth. And within a few minutes they found themselves at the front door of the administrative building at Briny Breezes.

Vinny held the door open for his two friends and followed them inside. It was cool. Air conditioned to a nice seventy-two degrees. It was small and hadn't been updated in a few decades. Wood paneling covered the walls and linoleum covered the floors. There were a few fake plants on either side of the entry way. Once inside the door a counter with a bell on it greeted residents of the trailer park. Along the right side wall were mailboxes.

The threesome approached the counter and were greeted by Jamie, a middle-aged secretary who always had a smile on her face. “Well hello there Tyrone.” Her Georgia accent was unmistakable. “And how are you today Vinny?” She asked, just as happy to see him as she was Tye. Vinny smiled back at her. He felt horrible today, and every day since his son died. He didn’t let on.

“I’m good Jamie, how have you been.” Vinny continued to smile.

“I’m so sorry about your son Vinny.” She said, as the smile ran away from her face. Vinny didn’t know what to say and started to stumble a little bit. His patience was thin already and Jamie’s well-intended comment just seemed to bounce off him the wrong way.

“We’re here to see Ms. Michelle.” Tyrone said before Vinny could reply. Jamie was astute. She recognized that Vinny was struggling and welcomed the save from Tye.

“She’s expecting you. Won’t you three just come around the corner and I’ll let you in the door.” Dergo went first, hobbling a little more as the pain was becoming much worse. At that very moment he was second guessing his decision not to take some pain killers.

The three of them sat down in the conference room. In accordance with old Florida construction, the room was small and a bit stuffy. There was only seating for eight people in total. Tye wondered how the management board actually met in this room. Then he remembered that most of them weren't living in the state of Florida nine months out of the year.

After a minute Jamie brought in a pitcher of ice water and four glasses on a tray. "Ms. Michelle will be with y'all in a minute. She's on the phone."

A few doors down Michelle had just hung up the phone with Jules. She took a minute to process everything that was happening and to determine what her next move would be. She stood and looked at herself in the mirror before moving to the conference room. Fixed her hair and made sure her dress was smoothed. There was no purpose behind it. She always checked herself in the mirror before she left the office. When she was satisfied that she looked good she opened the door and went to the conference room.

She knew of these three but had never been formally introduced. She saw Vinny over at the station most days she came to work, but had never been there herself. It was the same with Dergo. She had seen him on numerous occasions but had never met him.

Tye on the other hand, she had met several times. Twice in the office, and once on the beach. She was hoping he might not remember that day on the beach several months ago. She had just started the new job at Briny when she met Terry, Tye's brother. She had spent time with him even though she made it a point not date anyone in the park. Tye had not mentioned their chance meeting on the two occasions they had seen each other since. Both of which occurred after Terry's death.

CHAPTER 34

"Hello gentlemen! How is everyone doing today?" Ms. Michelle said with a big smile. She made her way to the other side of the table and took her place. She had a small notebook in her hand and a Mont Blanc pen that she placed on the table. She opened the notebook, wrote down a few quick things and asked once more.

"We're doing fine, thanks. And how are you today?" Dergo asked with a small grimace. His foot was hurting.

"Good… good." She looked at Tye. "You called this meeting, what is it that I can do for you?"

Dergo interrupted. "Just a few questions if you don't mind." Michelle shifted her focus back to Dergo, who was sitting directly across from her. He had grabbed the first seat he could when he entered the room in order to get off his feet. Vinny was to his left and Tye was to his right.

"Not at all. Shoot." She said. Her tone was upbeat.

"I've looked into the murder of Mark Henry Jean-Louis."

Michelle kept eye-contact with him. "I'm sorry, are you a policeman?" She asked in a slightly condescending tone, though not enough to be rude.

"I'm a retired policeman." He said, looking a little confused. "Anyway... it turns out he made a phone call to this office a few days before he died." Dergo stopped talking. He didn't want to divulge everything he knew about the Mark Henry case. He wanted to see how cooperative Michelle was going to be. After a long pause she spoke.

"Well, that's true, but I'm not at liberty to discuss the park's business. Some things are private."

Dergo hesitated another moment. Nothing else came from Michelle. "Is it true that he made an offer to buy the trailer park?"

Michelle hesitated for a second while she sized up Dergo. When she did answer she decided to be careful. "I can tell you that the investment group that Mr. Jean-Louis represented put an offer on the table to buy the trailer park, yes."

"Can you tell us anything else?" Dergo asked.

Michelle was taken a little by surprise. "For example… the price? Of course not." Michelle said, trying to side-step the original question

Dergo countered. "For example, why one of the last calls he made before he died was to the Texaco across the street. Was there something mentioned in the sale of Briny that had to do with the Texaco?"

Vinny, basically uninterested up to this point perked up a little in his chair. He stared at Dergo with a confused look.

Michelle smiled. She knew she had the upper hand. She had knowledge that the others didn't, including Vinny. "I have no idea why Mr. Jean-Louis would contact the Texaco. Perhaps you are giving too much weight to the notion that it had something…anything, to do with his death. Maybe he was just calling to see if they were open?"

Dergo wasn't buying it for a second, but there

was nothing he could do about it and he knew it. Better a friend than an enemy he thought to himself, so he backed off a little.

Michelle on the other hand had already decided that Dergo might be difficult to deal with, and she made a note of it. What she hadn't told them, and for good reason, was that the Texaco had everything to do with the sale of Briny Breezes. And it all went back to Jules.

Jules was connected. Jules was a land developer. He knew every pertinent official up and down the coast that could help or hurt him in any way. Nobody built anything on the ocean in Palm Beach county without going through the Mayor's office. The mayor controlled the zoning board, and a moratorium on any type of commercial zoning was in place county-wide along the coast. There was just too much money involved. Billionaires who put millions into their homes don't want a Wal-Mart or a Subway popping up across the street from them, or God forbid, blocking their view of the intracoastal or ocean. It was impossible to obtain a variance to change the rules. No matter how much money you threw at the problem there was an equal amount of money on the other side blocking any commercial activity.

But… as the mayor pointed out to Jules early on in the process, if he was able to acquire the Texaco along with the trailer park he wouldn't need a variance to build a casino or high rise condominiums. The plot of land that the Texaco sat on was originally part of the Briny Breezes trailer park. Since the land was grandfathered in prior to the moratorium, it was essentially zoned commercial already and didn't need approval from a zoning board.

Jules had been conducting business along the coast long enough to know that the Texaco was a deal breaker. Without it, the trailer park was worthless to him, or to any other developer.

Michelle knew that Mark Henry Jean-Louis was going to approach Vinny with an offer. Mark Henry had made it clear that he was going to meet with Vinny and that was the true purpose of the phone call to the Texaco. When he walked out of the very conference room that they were sitting in now, she stepped outside and made a phone call to Jules.

Until today she had only suspected that Jules was somehow involved in the killing of Vinny's son. Now she was sure of it. It all made sense, wrapped up with a nice little bow on top. Now she knew what she was going to do. She sat for a moment in her office, thinking. When she was finished she picked up the phone and called Jules.

CHAPTER 35

Jules agreed to meet Michelle for lunch at a small restaurant in Deerfield Beach along A1A. It was a bit north of Ft. Lauderdale where he was wrapping up a meeting, and a bit south of Briny Breezes where Michelle had just finished her own meeting. Forty-five minutes later she walked into the Whale's Tail and found Jules sitting at a booth near the back of the restaurant.

The restaurant had a beach theme with various types of shells and starfish littering the brightly colored walls. Soft reggae music played in the background and the wait staff was skimpily clad, young, and attractive. A large sign sat just inside the open front doors with pink neon colored chalk that read, "Fish Taco's – 4 for $5."

She walked past the sign along the terra-cotta colored floor tiles toward the back where Jules sat. She dropped her bag on the bench next to where she would sit and flattened out her sundress underneath the back of her legs and slid into the booth.

"Well hello there sir!" She said with her trademark smile. She was a lovely woman and Jules, like most men, showed their appreciation with an uncomfortable stare into her eyes. Michelle was used to it.

When Jules spoke it became clear that he wanted to know everything that was discussed at the meeting she had with the Texaco gang. As she recounted the conversation to Jules a waitress took their order. He settled for the fish tacos and Michelle decided on a mahi-mahi salad.

When he was satisfied that she had told him everything he took a drink of his water with lemon and then another long drink. She waited for him to start another conversation thread. He didn't. She decided to go on the offensive.

"Jules…we've known each other a long time." She said in a slow – here it comes – tone of voice. She was choosing her words carefully and he could see that she was struggling a little. Very unlike her he thought to himself. His attention piqued a little and he leaned in.

She looked him directly in the eyes and asked, "What the hell is going on with Briny Breezes?"

He thought for a second and smiled a little. "Well dear, it's business. I handle the business end of things and your job is to be my eyes and ears from within Briny." In the back of his mind he understood that Michelle was too smart to settle for what he had just said. He braced himself.

"Don't bullshit me Jules. I've been loyal to you for years and obviously you trust me or I wouldn't be working at Briny Breezes." She paused, waiting for him to acknowledge her value. He nodded and she proceeded.

"People are dying for God's sake. I didn't buy in to this sort of thing. You tell me what's going on or I'm going to have to walk away. Jules…understand that I need to know what I'm becoming part of." She over sold it a little. Even though she wasn't used to playing the drama queen she pulled it off perfectly, throwing in a tear at the end for good measure. Jules bought it completely.

"It's complicated Michelle. There are things I can't tell you, but understand that I would never put you in harm's way."

"Not on purpose." She said, still playing the victim role. "But I'm getting tangled up in this mess…your mess. And if I'm going to subject myself to any more of this, well, well, there should be some payoff for me."

"Ahh… there it is." Jules said. It was clear to him now what was happening. He smiled. When he was done smiling he started to talk but then broke out in a contained laughter in which he closed his eyes and lowered his head. His teeth were visible and after a moment he had to force himself to stop in order not to bring attention to their table.

He looked at Michelle. Only this time he looked at her differently. Perhaps she had the intestinal fortitude to become a shark, to play with the big boys. The idea of her being able to call some of the shots he'd called in the last several weeks almost made him start laughing again. This time he knew she would take offense to it so he held back.

"What an enjoyable lunch this turned out to be." He said to her as the waitress delivered their entrees. Jules nodded his head at Michelle and then nodded at their food. He would explain as much as he could after they finished eating.

She was content with that. Besides, it would give her a few minutes to think. She was hungry and the mahi was fresh.

CHAPTER 36

Once outside the Briny Breezes office Vinny looked at Dergo and demanded an answer. Dergo knew this was going to happen and he thought he was ready for it. He wasn't.

"What the fuck is wrong with you?" He asked, lighting up a cigarette. "You are one of my best friends in the world and you don't tell me that you knew there was a connection between the Canadian and my boy?" Vinny was at a full yell at this point. Some of the Briny residents enroute to check their mail at the office were staring at them. Vinny didn't see them.

"Tell me!" Vinny yelled

"Let's sit and I'll tell you." They were only a few yards from the chairs outside the candy shop. Dergo went inside and grabbed a beer. When he came out Tye and Vinny were sitting, waiting patiently.

"There's not much to tell." Dergo said as he popped the top on his beer, which he slid neatly into a brown paper bag. He was careful not to speak too loud as he didn't want Vinny's wife to hear. He would let Vinny tell her on his own terms, when she was ready for it.

"When Thomas and I went to Canada we interviewed a girl that he was dating. She told us that on the morning of his death he talked to her, from his hotel. Said he had to meet with some folks at a trailer park."

Vinny interrupted. "And he made an offer to buy the trailer park?"

Dergo didn't make eye contact with him. Tye popped a nicotine lozenge and listened intently.

"Yeah, It seems that way. So after talking to her I had a buddy in Chicago pull his phone records. I noticed that the Canadian made a phone call to the Texaco just before he was murdered."

Vinny took a long drag off his cigarette and thought for a minute. "Darryl was working that day. He would have answered the phone."

Tye chimed in. "I guess he never told you anything about that phone call?"

"No, I never knew anything about it." Vinny said without looking at anybody, just staring off into space a little. Tye knew that look. Vinny was trying to figure out the connection but was coming up blank. He tried to console him.

"Look Vin…you couldn't have known. There was nothing you could have done." Tye said.

Vinny remained lifeless, deep in thought. Tye looked at Dergo, who had a pale expression on his face. Tye could see that Dergo hadn't told Vinny about the phone call because he knew Vinny would somehow feel that he should have been able to foresee trouble, and ultimately save his son. Tye knew from experience that we all try to do that. We try to rationalize and second guess our decisions and logic until you drive yourself crazy. He guessed Dergo understood it too.

Being an ex-cop helped Vinny understand that second guessing was a losing game. He'd seen it done many times before and it never helped. Never.

It hurt him as well. His mind was in overdrive trying to put together a puzzle that didn't have all of the pieces. Tye and Dergo let him sit in silence for a while, not saying much of anything.

Vinny's wife opened the door to the candy shop and handed him the phone. She noticed his head was somewhere else and asked if he was O.K.

"I'm fine." He said, and smiled at her. Tye and Dergo were thankful she broke the ice. Vinny answered the phone. "Texaco, this is Vinny."

"Vinny, my name is Austin Seebeck. I'm a U.S. Marshall and we need to talk."

CHAPTER 37

Toward the end of lunch Jules ordered a bottle of wine. A run of the mill chardonnay to dress up the fish a little bit. Michelle already had a glass and was pouring her second when Jules decided to talk.

"So what is it that you would like to know sweetie?" He said in a fatherly voice. During dinner he had done some thinking of his own.

"Did you have anything to do with the murders that took place at the Texaco. The Canadian or the station owners' son or any of the others?"

Jules poured his second glass of wine and gave her a look of consternation. "You know dear," he said as he swirled the wine in his glass and put it to his lips taking a small drink, "once you open this door you can't always control what comes through it." He placed the glass back on the table. "Sometimes it's best to leave the door closed."

"Honestly Jules," she said, "My foot is stuck in this door. I don't think I could close it if I wanted to."

He could see that she was not phased at all. "O.K. then." He said. "I have personally never killed anyone in my life. But sometimes business dictates that one does some ruthless things. You simply don't get to be in my position without rustling a few feathers here and there."

"A few feathers? I think you've done more than rustle a few feathers." She finished her glass of wine, suddenly wishing there was another bottle on the table.

"Be careful what you say dear. I don't want you to get the wrong impression. I have not admitted to anything… nor should you ever get an urge to repeat any of this conversation." His tone was stern now and Michelle got the message. She understood that she could be next if she decided to talk about any of this. She backed off.

"I don't get it." She said, genuinely confused. She knew more than she let on but she still didn't have all of the answers. "Why don't you just buy the damn Texaco? Offer him a few million dollars and be done with it. Buy everything and do with it what you want."

"I wish it were that simple." He said and leaned back in the booth.

"Seems pretty straight forward to me."

"Well let me spell it out for you then. About ten years ago an investment group approached Briny Breezes with an offer. After a year-long campaign the board finally voted to sell. The sale was contingent upon the Texaco being bundled in with the trailer park. Vinny wouldn't sell then and the deal fell through."

She thought about it for a minute. "And you think he won't sell now."

Jules nodded his head. "That's right. I'm sure of it. The bank loan is paid off and he owns it outright. He's worked his entire life to build a successful business and he's proud of it. Money isn't important to him anymore. His business is his way of life."

Michelle paused for a second. “I didn’t see that coming. You would think anybody would sell in a heartbeat for that kind of money.”

“I understand Vinny. Better than most people. I understand him because we’re cut from the same cloth. We both came from nothing and built what we have with our own sweat and blood. He wakes up every day of his life happy to go to work. Proud to go to work.”

“I’d still sell it and build another one.” She said matter-of-factly.

Jules suddenly wanted another glass of wine as well. He thought better of it. He sat back in his booth and shrugged his shoulders a little bit. He looked a little unnerved. He stared out the window as he explained it to her.

“This country wasn’t built by people who created businesses just to sell them. The Rockefellers, the Carnegies, the Mellon’s, Ford – Bill Gates. They built their businesses to change the way the world works. They changed the way American’s live their lives. Their legacy…their gift to the world was their reason for starting a business…not to sell it and then sit around and do nothing.”

Jules looked at Michelle to see if she was paying attention. She was engrossed in the explanation as it made perfect sense to her once it came from his mouth.

“You see…I’d rather die penniless fighting to keep my business alive than sell it to someone who doesn’t understand the sacrifices I made to build it.”

“And you think Vinny feels the same?” She

asked.

Jules laughed a little and smiled. "I know he feels the same. He has a great life. All he has ever wanted he now has." They both thought about mentioning that the absence of his son changed things for him. Instead Michelle asked her final question.

"So how do you get around this problem Jules? I've known you long enough to know that nothing can stand in your way when you decide to do something."

"Well that's just it my dear. Vinny's wife isn't as attached to the brick and mortar as he is. I'm sure she agrees more with you when it comes to selling the place. If Vinny were to say…unexpectedly pass… dealing with his widow would be much easier."

"I see." She said, slightly more confused now than when she sat down an hour ago. "So your next step is pretty clear."

"Careful my dear. Watch what you say…and be even more careful with what you insinuate." He waived to the waitress asking for the check.

"So what now?" She asked. She was afraid. He was right about opening the door. She should have listened.

He could see the confusion… and a bit of panic.. in her eyes. "What now my dear…is that you go back to work. You continue to be my eyes and ears from within the park as though nothing has changed, as though we never had this conversation." He stood and made his way to the front of the restaurant.

Michelle gathered her things and followed him out the front door. She was getting good at this. She needed answers to several important questions and he had provided them. She needed him to believe that she was afraid and he did.

Most importantly, and unexpected, was the insight she had into his psyche with respect to his business. He wanted to leave a legacy, and it was more important to him than his money.

"Interesting." She thought to herself as she gave him a hug and turned to leave.

CHAPTER 38

Vinny agreed to meet with Austin Seebeck two days after he had requested the meeting. Austin showed up to the Texaco at exactly eleven A.M., as agreed. Vinny identified him as the Marshall before he introduced himself. He watched as Seebeck exited his truck, an older Chevrolet that was in desperate need of a new paint job. He was a tall, thin man who looked to be in his mid-forties. He wore cowboy boots and a Stetson hat, both a khaki tan color that nearly matched. He wore jeans and a black silk shirt that seemed appropriate for the Florida weather. He was by all accounts a very attractive man. Vinny had not given his movie star looks much thought but when he saw two young women in bathing suits saying hello to the Marshall it registered. They were still giggling and watching Austin as he opened the door to the candy shop and took his hat off. He wiped the sweat off his brow and looked up at Vinny.

"You must be the owner of this establishment?" He asked with a big smile. It was hard not to like him, Vinny thought to himself. He had no reason not to like him. If anything, the Marshall might be able to help him figure out who killed his son.

Vinny's grieving period was just about over. He was filling up with anger now and he was looking for a way to relieve the pressure. Finding out who killed his son was becoming his main purpose in life. He was quickly coming to the realization that there was a void in his heart that couldn't be filled until he identified the person who took his son from him and dealt with him – Trinidad style.

The Marshall didn't need to know any of this of course, so Vinny smiled right back at him and welcomed him inside.

"Can I get you a cup of coffee?

"That would be wonderful. Cream if you have any."

Vinny poured two cups of coffee, added skim milk to both of them and invited Austin to sit with him in the back room. The small space that connected the candy shop with the garage had a sink and a small shelf with the coffee pot and a microwave sitting on it. On the other wall was a small table with two computer screens. The one on the right Vinny used as a television to check the weather and catch up on news when the garage was slow. The one on the left contained the software he used to diagnose vehicle problems. It contained engine specifications and schematics for brake lines, air conditioning information and everything else he needed to work on any make and model that pulled into his garage. It was expensive software and critical to his livelihood, so he kept the two machines separate. Nobody was allowed to touch the computer on the left. The remainder of the space contained fishing equipment, mostly poles and reels, nearly one hundred different setups. Some were used for yellow-tails, some were larger, heavier duty with much stronger line used to troll for big game fish. Each fishing rod served a different purpose, whether it was the type of fish sought, type of water fishing in, technique used to catch a fish, even the weight of each particular lure came into play.

Austin sized up the collection in one word. "Wow." He said. "You are obviously pretty serious about your fishing."

Vinny smiled even though he didn't feel like it. "Yeah… it's what I do. You know." He said rather flippantly. "Do you fish?" He asked the Marshall.

"I do. But I don't take it seriously. Often times it's more about the beer and a day off then about catching anything."

"Well, we all have our passions." Vinny said.

Austin took a sip of coffee and put the cup down on the table. "That's true Vinny. May I call you Vinny?" He asked, not necessarily waiting for an answer. Vinny nodded his approval.

"My passion is catching bad guys. That's something that I do take seriously." He looked at Vinny. "It's as important to me as fishing is to you. And right now I believe I have a bad guy on the loose. I was hoping you might be able to help me… reel him in, so to speak."

Vinny appreciated the play on words, even though he thought it just a bit cheesy. "I'd be happy to help. Who is this bad guy that you are looking for?"

Austin was speaking slower now than he was before. His accent sounded a little bit Alabama or Mississippi. Vinny wasn't sure. "Well, honestly Vinny, I don't know who the hell he is. All that I know is there are a handful of dead people that lived within walking distance of this gas station, one of whom, I'm sure you've heard already, was a member of the Witness Protection Program. A man who I was responsible for."

Vinny lit a cigarette and took several long drags off it before responding to the Marshall. "You're talking about Frank, right?"

"I believe that's the name he went by, yes. Lived across the street, above the Coastal Star."

Vinny smiled a little thinking about Frank. "Yeah that's him. Used to come in every morning and buy a pack of cigarettes and a Mt. Dew." Then the smile trailed off and he looked Austin in the eye. "Why was he in the program by the way? What the hell did he do?"

Austin sat back in his chair and sighed a little. Vinny noticed that his legs were so long they almost stretched across the room to the microwave. He figured Austin to be every bit of six feet five inches tall. He carried it well. For some reason he didn't appear that tall when he was talking to you. Then he spoke.

"Well, normally I'm not at liberty to talk about anyone in the program, past or present, but I think you can help me."

Vinny interrupted him before he divulged anything he couldn't take back. "I can't help you Marshall. I knew Frank, but just to say hello and shoot the shit once in a while. We never really hung out. Never went fishing together."

Austin smiled and took another drink of coffee. He wanted one of Vinny's cigarettes but didn't ask.

He had quit two years ago and still had strong urges when he drank coffee and drank whiskey.

"Well, be that as it may, you've got skin in the game. Whoever killed Frank likely had something to do with your son's murder. On top of that you are an ex-cop. And on top of that your business seems to be the epicenter of whatever is going on here."

"What *is* going on here Marshall?" Vinny asked, wondering if he knew something about his son's death.

Austin set his cup down, leaned forward toward Vinny and looked him in the eye. "I intend to find out. And I will. It's what I do."

Vinny believed him. This guy didn't play around and he was happy that they were on the same side. He could tell from talking to him that he would be a formidable opponent.

"So tell me about Frank. What the hell did he do?" Vinny asked, hoping to lighten the mood a bit.

Austin obliged. "Nothing really. Frank, as you call him, ran a small catering business in New Jersey. It turns out he catered to some of the most famous mob bosses in the world. Mostly parties for their children, the occasional meeting between the families, holiday parties, etc. One day Frank was catering a party for the Genovese family in New York when the party was raided. Everyone was arrested, including Frank. We knew right away that he could be an asset to us since he had unparalleled access into the syndicate."

Vinny laughed and took a long drag off his cigarette. Austin watched the blue smoke trail off up into the rafters of the old building.

"You want a cigarette?" Vinny asked, extending his hand toward Austin, a pack of American Spirits in it.

"That obvious huh?" Austin asked. "No thank you. I quit two years ago." The Marshall continued his story.

"So anyway, Frank tells us to go fuck ourselves, that he wouldn't rat on anyone, friend or no friend."

Vinny laughed, "Yeah that was Frank."

"But somehow, word gets around that Frank is working for us and there were two attempts on his life."

"No shit!" Vinny gasped. "He never told me any of that."

"It gets better." Austin said. "And he couldn't tell you any of it or he would have lost his protection status. The second attempt on his life happened during a catering job. It was a setup. He was packing up everything after a party, his van was parked in an alley. He was loading it when an assassin walked up behind him. Frank saw his shadow and turned around and put a bullet in him before he got one himself. Then he got in his van and ran him over… twice. He actually backed up so he could run him over the second time. When we asked him why he did it he said that he wanted to make sure the guy never had the opportunity to try and kill him again."

Vinny just shook his head. "Man, you think you know somebody."

The Marshall continued. "Anyway, it was our

fault Frank was in this mess so we had to put him in the program in order to save his life. He agreed to testify against the Genovese family when the time came. They were responsible for putting the hit on him."

"And I take it the time never came?" Vinny asked.

Austin shook his head. "No, but it was coming. We think that might have had something to do with Frank's death, but we're not sure."

"That's all good Marshall, but I don't seem to be connecting the dots. Why do you think I can help you?"

Austin looked him in the eye again. "Vinny, I've been doing this a long time and I can tell you what I know. I know that you're about to start looking for the man who killed your son. I know that you possess a certain skill set that comes in handy when you go looking for someone, when you are passionate about finding someone, and I know that men like you tend to get things done. So in the end, what I know is that eventually you will find out who killed your son, and that person is going to be someone that I'm interested in meeting."

Austin stood up and moved to the sink. He poured out what remained in his cup and rinsed it, carefully placing it back on the towel where it had come from when Vinny picked it up. When he was finished he turned around to face Vinny, who looked disinterested in the whole conversation thus far.

"Listen Vinny. I don't expect you to understand what I'm trying to convey here, not yet at least. But the time is going to come when you need a friend on this side of the law, and I'm telling you that I'm going to be here for you. I'm your ace in the hole."

Vinny wasn't moved by the speech, but he was impressed that Austin was reaching out to him in general. And it couldn't hurt to have a lawman in your corner, of that Vinny was sure.

They said their goodbyes, shook hands and parted ways. As Austin made his way back through the candy store he heard one of the female customers say hello to him. The Marshall tipped his hat at her and gave her a smile.

CHAPTER 39

Michelle sat silently behind her desk as she thought about her next move. For the last few days she couldn't control the uneasiness that filled the bottom of her stomach. There were two options left on the table and she didn't particularly care for either of them, but it was time for change. One was too weak and the other too strong. Water and whiskey. She needed something in the middle, a diet coke with a splash of rum maybe. But this was a microcosm of her life up to this point and she forced herself to finish her train of thought. Option one was simple. She would quit her job, quit Jules, and move on to another job that would at least be devoid of all of the bad things that were presently in her life.

But she wanted change in her life. She was fifty years old now and she had a nagging voice in the back of her head that kept asking, "If not now…when?" She had always chosen the safe route. Her entire life was made up of conservative choices and it had got her nowhere. Conservative was easy. She knew how to take that path. Being risk-free was simple. Taking the risky path wasn't as clear to her. She simply didn't know how to proceed because she'd never gone down that path before.

Nevertheless her mind was now made up. She smiled a little at the idea and promptly stood up, deciding she needed to walk the property and get some air.

It was a beautiful Florida day, a little on the hot side but the breeze kept the humidity in check. She strolled around the marina looking at the boats and eventually ended up by the intracoastal waterway. The intracoastal was the western boundary of the property and on the north side of the marina was a small station for cleaning fish. The fish and boat club had it installed back in the fifties and it hadn't been updated much since then.

It was a simple structure consisting of a roof to keep the sun and rain out, a chest high table with a hard plastic surface and a bench for sitting. Across the top of the table was a small plastic pipe with holes in it. Water ran through the pipe and exited the holes, running down the table keeping the filet surface clean. There was also a garden hose on the left side of the table for larger messes.

As she walked by the filet station she noticed two anglers cleaning fish and decided to investigate. It was Thomas and Tyrone. She wanted to chat with them.

"Any luck today?"

Thomas turned around to investigate. "Oh, hi Michelle, yeah, we caught a few."

She decided to join them at the filet station, taking a seat at the end of the bench, as far as she could get from the bloody fish. "I was just taking a walk, checking things out, making sure no boats were sinking, you know."

Tye laughed a little but kept his head down. The filet knife was razor sharp and he didn't want to cut himself.

"Ewww...Tye? What is that on your face?" She

asked, genuinely concerned, laughing at the same time.

Thomas answered for him. "He was blowing me out on the boat."

Tye thought twice about stabbing Thomas with the filet knife and waived it at him. They had both had a few beers while fishing and Thomas was feeling pretty good. He laughed and danced his way to the other side of the filet station, next to Michelle, and out of harm's way.

"It's my cigarette." He said and went back to fileting the Kingfish on the table. Michelle was confused and looked to Thomas for help.

"It's those nicotine lozenges he sucks on. For some reason it leaves white drool all over his face."

Michelle countered. "Maybe you should go back to smoking Tye? It seems like it would be less messy."

Tye just rolled his eyes and motioned to the intracoastal in front of him. He picked up the Kingfish carcass and threw it in the water. Thomas stood up and waited for it to be sucked up by a large fish, as had the rest of the carcasses they had thrown into the water. As they waited a giant fish surfaced and pulled the Kingfish remains under water. Tye and Thomas smiled at each other. For some reason that counted as entertainment on a day when the beer was flowing. It reminded Michelle why she stopped in the first place.

"So Tye?" She started in her most innocent voice. "Have you heard any news about your brother?"

He stopped in mid-slice of a blackfin tuna he

was cutting into sashimi. He didn't look at her, he just stopped. Thomas took a drink of beer and listened intently.

"What would I have heard? He's dead. Not much more to say about it." He took a deep breath and continued slicing. Like Vinny, Tye was beginning to feel more and more anger. He had waited patiently for the police to do their job and figure out what was happening, but they had done absolutely nothing.

"Vinny mentioned that a U.S. Marshall was investigating, guess it's a federal case at this point. I don't expect they'll be of much help." Tye flung the tuna carcass out into the water and waited for the monstrous beast to grab it. After a minute or two he gave up and picked up a large bonita which he intended to cut up for use as future bait.

Tye had become angry thinking about his brother. He was hacking at the bonita and making a mess of it. Thomas stood up and took the knife out of his hands. Tye sat down on the bench next to Michelle and pulled a beer out of the cooler. He took a long swig, squinting as the sun was almost directly in his face. Beads of sweat formed on his forehead. He popped another lozenge in his mouth and wiped his face on his sleeve, which was already white with nicotine lozenge drool.

"Have *you* heard anything Michelle?" he asked, not expecting much.

She looked him in the eye. "I have actually."

Tye nodded his head for her to continue. Thomas stopped cutting the bonita and turned to face them.

"Apparently the feds or somebody…I don't know who…interviewed some guy down in Miami. I guess he's rich."

"What's his name?" Thomas asked before Tye could spit out the same question.

"Jules... something or another. I'm not sure."

Tye, ever the skeptic, wasn't amused by her new information. "And how did you hear about this Michelle?"

She lied. "I used to manage a property down there. I still know a few of the police officers in the Fisher Island area. I had lunch with some colleagues the other day and they were talking about it."

"So this guy lives on Fisher Island?" Tye asked in a tone that let her know it was hard for him to believe what she had just said..

"Where is Fisher Island?" Thomas asked.

"It's one of the islands off the coast of Miami. Star Island, Hibiscus Island, they are all restricted access areas. You have to own a home on the island to set foot on them. Very high end stuff. If he lives there it means he's more than rich. He has sinful amounts of money."

Thomas went back to working on the bonita. Tye stared off into the sunset, deep in thought. Michelle got up and excused herself.

"Maybe this isn't as hard as I thought it would be." She thought to herself. In the back of her mind she could hear Jules' advice from a few days earlier. "Once you open that door you can't control what comes through it."

"Bullshit." She thought to herself. "I'll open and close doors as I please."

CHAPTER 40

Dergo said his goodbyes to everyone in front of the candy shop before he left for Illinois. He was a retired police officer who routinely went back to work for ten days at a time. None of the guys understood it, and truth be told neither did his wife, but they didn't question it. He didn't like leaving the beach, but once he was surrounded by friends and family in Illinois he didn't mind so much.

However, Illinois would be a brief stop on his journey this time but he didn't tell anyone. He normally drove home but a bullet wound in his leg kept him from driving for long periods. The shuttle picked him up at the Texaco and headed south on interstate ninety-five towards the Fort Lauderdale airport.

When he exited the cab he left the crutches inside and stood outside the vehicle. The brace that was now on his leg had replaced the cast. The wound had scabbed over and the few stitches that were left he would take out himself when he felt the time was right. He could have done all of this earlier but he didn't want the guys at the Texaco to give him a hard time. He took the cast off and put it in the backseat. He tipped the driver and gave him another twenty dollars to discard the medical supplies in the backseat and walked inside the airport.

It was a little strange walking without the

crutches at first. He had become accustomed to them in the weeks that passed after his self-inflicted gunshot. After the first few steps his confidence increased and by the time he checked in at the counter and passed through security he no longer limped or even thought about the wound. Dergo was a tough guy. He had been shot before and even hit by a train once. Vinny, Tye, and Thomas knew about the train, but not many other people. He had told them about it one day while fishing. One of his knees had swollen to the size of a large melon and they had to end a day on the ocean in order to get him to a hospital. After grilling him about it he finally caved in and told them. As he sauntered down the hallway in search of his departure gate the idea that his knee might buckle ran through his head. He quickly dismissed the idea as he approached his gate, number twenty-eight, and saw Thomas standing in front of him.

Dergo smiled and said, "What the fwock Switz?" They shook hands and exchanged smiles. Dergo asked where he was heading to.

"Thought I'd go to Illinois and check on a friend of mine, make sure he stays out of trouble."

The smile on Dergo's face disappeared. He looked at Thomas and his brow bent to the left a little. "Are you talking about me?" The inflection in his voice increased a little, resonating his disbelief.

"I am talking about you."

Dergo was speechless. "I don't understand. I'm just going home for a few weeks to put in some time on the beat. My old supervisor needs some help covering a few vacations." He sounded convincing.

"Don't try to bullshit me Dergo. I got a call a few days ago from your contact in Chicago. He's worried you might be getting yourself into something that's above your pay grade. And by pay grade he meant skill level."

Dergo's jaw dropped and then his head dropped. He was still speechless. "What did he tell you?"

"He said that you won't leave this thing alone. That he dug up a name in New York, Johnny Maldone or something like that. Says he has mob ties and that you made it sound like you were heading up there to investigate on your own. He knew that I went with you to Canada and he reached out to me, hoping I could talk some sense into you."

He thought about it for a second. His cover was blown, no sense denying it at this point. "O.K, then, start talking."

Thomas laughed. "I know you well enough to know that talking to you won't do anything. I'm going with you...to babysit your dumbass."

Thomas pulled his boarding pass and ticket out of his back pocket then pointed to his carry-on bag that was sitting on the chair behind him. "See, I'm ready to go." Thomas smiled and waited for a response.

"God dammit you Swiss prick." His tone was fatherly at this point. He was a few years older than Thomas. "You can't go with me. My contact was right when he said we were dealing with some bad people here. You're out of your league on this one."

"Apparently you are too, according to your contact. Why do you think he called me? I promised him I would personally escort you back to Chicago and call him when we got there."

Dergo thought about it for a second, cracked half a smile and said, "O.K. then, let's go."

Suddenly Thomas wasn't smiling anymore. He knew damn well Dergo had something up his sleeve. He never conceded anything this easily.

He was about to ask him what he had planned when a pleasant woman's voice came over the intercom, "Now boarding flight fifty-five seventy, Ft. Lauderdale to Chicago through gate twenty eight."

"What seat are you in?" Dergo laughed and slapped Thomas on the shoulder. He turned toward the gate and made his way toward the plane. Thomas noticed for the first time that Dergo was without crutches.

CHAPTER 11

Tyrone worked in Deerfield Beach, which was approximately half way between his house in Boynton and Fisher Island in Miami. On a few occasions since his chat with Michelle he'd thought of driving down to Fisher Island and doing a reconnaissance of this *Jules* character. He had no idea what his last name was and no plan about how to get onto the island. There is no road to drive out to the island which is three miles due east of Miami Beach

He decided to dig a little deeper and find out who Jules was and what – if any - connection he had with the murders that took place in Boynton Beach. He was troubled by a few things that he hadn't unraveled in his head just yet. First, he knew that Vinny could help him find out about Jules, who he was, what he did, etc. The problem with bringing Vinny into the fold in this situation was that…Vinny would be involved. He couldn't risk that as of yet. Tye was upset and looking for answers, but Vinny was ready to exact revenge. He wasn't thinking clearly right now and Tye didn't want to expose him to this sort of thing. Not until he had proof of a link between the man Michelle mentioned and their dead family members.

Every day that Tye went to work the thought of driving down to Fisher Island consumed him. Finally, he decided to make the trip. He hadn't planned on it when he left his house at four-thirty A.M. on his motorcycle that morning, but when his boss sent everyone home at ten A.M. due to a major electrical outage he decided to go.

He was new to the art of investigation but something told him he needed to be secretive about what he was doing. He took a shower at work, got dressed, popped a few nicotine lozenges in his mouth and put his helmet on. He decided to take interstate ninety-five since it was the middle of the day and traffic would be light. Thirty minutes later he was in downtown Miami. He followed the signs to A1A and then took the MacArthur Causeway over to Miami Beach, which is an island itself. Miami Beach is just north of Fisher Island.

When he got onto the island he made a right and headed toward South Beach. Once he found a safe place to park his motorcycle he took off his helmet and stood up. He needed to stretch. The trip had taken less than forty five minutes but his back hurt. There was a trade-off when it came to motorcycles. Typically you exchange comfort for speed. He owned the fastest motorcycle ever built, and his back felt it. After he stretched he looked in the small mirror attached to his handlebars. He wasn't checking his hair, he was bald. He wanted to make sure his goatee was devoid of nicotine slurry. No such luck. He wiped the corner of his mouth and checked again. Still a white line remained. He scrubbed at the corner of his mouth until he was sure he had broken the skin and looked again. Content that his face was clean he turned to face the south and saw Fisher Island. The eastern side of the island was less than six hundred yards from where he stood. To his right he could see the dock where the ferry that shuttled people and cars across parked. There were several boats racing up and down the waters in between the two dots of land. This gave Tye an idea.

He turned around and headed back toward South Beach proper. There were several jet-ski rental shops and he decided to take his own tour of the island, even if he wasn't allowed onshore.

He entered the first shop he came to advertising jet ski rentals, and in true Tyrone fashion had to go with the fastest machine they had, even if he would only be putting around the outside of the island. He justified the added expense just in case he had to run from somebody, which seemed ridiculous even to him. It was the middle of the day and people were everywhere. He wouldn't be able to hide from anybody even if he could outrun them.

Tye paid cash up-front, left his credit card for the necessary deposit. He paid the owner an extra hundred dollars cash, not to run his credit unless it was absolutely necessary. When the owner objected he handed him the keys to his motorcycle and assured him that it was worth twice what the jet ski was. The owner looked at him reluctantly and then slid the extra hundred dollars into his pocket. Tye showed him the bike and the owner agreed.

Fifteen minutes later he was on the water. Tye had several jet skis in the past and was no stranger to them and how they worked. He throttled up to half speed and headed south toward Fisher Island. He cruised slowly around the island. For the most part there was very little to see when it came to private residences. There were a handful of high rise condominiums dotting the small island and those were easy enough to see, but many of the homes were shielded from onlookers by large shrubbery and trees. He drove the jet ski around the entire island several times and nothing, nothing at all seemed to jump out at him.

Tye headed back to South Beach a little deflated. He'd waited a long time to make this trip and he had come up empty. He hadn't expected much, but he felt he owed his brother a little better than what he was able to come up with on this day.

He was about to pull in to the dock where he would return the jet ski when a large boat, maybe forty feet long passed in front of him. He was forced to wait until the slow moving vessel passed. Not wanting to make a total loss of the day he decided to move around to the rear of the boat and maybe jump a wake or two, see what his mini-boat was capable of.

He throttled up and cut it hard to the right sending off his own wake. The boat was large and its wake was big enough to surf on. Tye hit one at an angle doing about twenty five miles per hour and it launched him a few feet into the air. It felt good. It also reminded him he had been working too hard. Ever since his brother's death he had thrown himself into work more. He hadn't thought about it until he realized he was having fun.

The boat had passed the dock. He played in the wake a few more times and decided to call it a day. He wanted to head back to Briny Breezes and go kiteboarding. He made his last turn behind the boat and was ready to head to the dock when he noticed the name of the boat, “WASTED SEAMEN.” It made him laugh. Then it made him think. He hadn’t checked the marina. He rode past it on his jet ski but didn’t pay attention to any of the boats. He decided to take another look. He throttled up and made a tight turn, heading for the southeastern side of Fisher Island.

CHAPTER 42

The flight from Fort Lauderdale to Chicago was pleasant enough, except when Thomas made his mock vomit sounds, recalling their trip to Canada. They had a few drinks and talked. Thomas thought about asking what the next few days held for them but decided against it. He was going to hold his ground when it came to keeping him out of New York. The stakes were simply too high.

When they got off the plane Dergo looked at one of the screens for connecting flights, found what he was looking for and started down the concourse. Thomas knew something was wrong already.

"Dammit Dergo, where are you going?"

"I have a flight to catch." He stopped walking and dug around in his front pocket. He pulled out his keys and handed them to Thomas. "Take these and go to my house. Check in on my neighbor while you're there, he's getting old and I worry about him sometimes."

Thomas knew that Dergo lived in Morris Illinois, about sixty miles southwest of Chicago. Finding his house would be easy enough, but it certainly wasn't what he had planned.

"Fwock you and your keys." He said emphatically. "You're not prepared for this. You're going to get yourself killed."

Dergo had enough. "And what's the alternative at this point? Sit around and wait for them to come to us? I've already been shot, albeit by myself, but somebody tried to kill me. Vinny's son is dead and Tye's brother is dead. Who is to say they are not coming for you next?"

Thomas was completely confused. "What are you talking about? Nobody is trying to kill me. And you have no idea what the whole deal with Frank and the Indian was about. You're not even sure Frank had anything to do with it. His name and number was in the Indian's wallet. So what? So now we have to go to New York and poke a hornet's nest full of mafia bad guys? Seriously Dergo – what the Fwock?"

"I don't expect you to understand. I'm a cop…"

"You USED to be a cop. You aren't anymore…"

"Whether I'm a cop now or not doesn't matter. What matters is that for the last twenty-five years I've been a cop and I know when something is wrong. And dammit Switz, something is really wrong here. All of this stuff is linked, I'll bet my pension on it. And I'd bet everything else I have that a lot of the answers we're looking for can be found with this Maldonado guy. He can tell us everything, I'm sure of it."

"And I'm sure he'll be happy to sit down with us and have a little chat…won't he? What are you going to do when he puts a gun to your head and finishes what the Indian started? What then?"

Dergo thought about it for a second. He didn't have a plan and he knew that was a problem. "I know that I still have some time to figure it out. Besides, if these people are as bad as everyone seems to think they are, doesn't it mean they are much more likely to finish what they started?"

"You're paranoid Dergo. Plain and simple, you're paranoid. Give me your keys. I can't be a part of this anymore."

He reached back into his pocket and handed over the keys. "Doomer is eighty-two and he can't hear very well. Make sure he knows you're a friend of mine before you go on his property or he'll shoot you."

Thomas looked at the keys in disbelief. "Why did I even come to Chicago?" He asked Dergo. "If you knew you were going to do this why did you even have me get on that plane?"

"It was your choice amigo. I had nothing to do with it. Besides, consider it a vacation."

"To fwocking Morris Illinois? You're not paranoid, you've just gone stupid. You ate some retard pills this morning didn't you?" Thomas was visibly upset.

"Look, you have access to a bass boat with all the gear you would ever need. You can hunt birds on my property. Doomer has ducks on the north side of his property. My Harley is in the garage, go explore. Ride up to Sturgis if you want."

When he put it that way it didn't sound so bad. Thomas caught himself thinking about it and stopped himself. "Dammit, no. I'm not vacationing in Morris Illinois." He didn't know how Dergo had turned the conversation around on him so quickly but it happened, and he was upset with himself for allowing it.

"I've got to run. I'll see you in a few days and I promise I'll keep in touch. I want someone to know what's going on in New York."

Thomas didn't say a word. He didn't know what to say, or do. He couldn't physically grab Dergo and force him to stay in Chicago. So he stood and watched his friend walk away, silent and confused, all he could do was wonder how he got himself into this situation.

CHAPTER 43

Tye began to pay attention to the boats and yachts parked in front of the private residences. Most residents parked their vessels in the marina if they weren't on the island or knew they wouldn't need it for a while. It was just easier. The marina took care of basic maintenance issues like keeping batteries charged and making sure bilge pumps worked, bathrooms were kept spotless, etc. As a result there were fewer than ten boats parked in front of residences. He read the names, *Reely Mine, E-Fishin-C, She-Worthy, Liquid Asset, Jib–N-Tonic, For-Play*, and the *Halfmine*.

Finally, he cruised into the marina. There were three long rows of boats, but first he had to navigate the two break walls at the entrance. It was easy enough for the nimble jet ski, just two walls, jutting out from either side of the land, designed to keep large wakes from making it into the marina. It was effective. Tye carved a large 'S' shape in the water and found himself in front of the center row of boats. He veered to the left a little and slowly made his way down aisle one. He continued to read boat names, *On Pointe, Reel Estate, E-Sea-Livin*, and the *Winedown* were some that stuck out.

He made the right hand turn and continued to read. Some boats were backed in, rear toward the dock, so he was unable to read the boat names in those cases. He moved slowly down aisle two, and finished his recon. Nothing. Nothing at all jumped out at him.

As a last resort he tied up the jet ski to one of the empty slips and started to walk around the marina, hoping he might be able to see something from that vantage point that he was unable to see earlier. He was on the far left side of the marina and began to walk quickly, not sure how long he would be able to stay before being asked to leave. He could smell food being cooked on an outside grill and realized he was hungry. He had a cup of coffee and a fruit smoothie around four A.M. Nothing since. He couldn't help but become distracted by the scent of fresh hamburgers and hot dogs.

He walked briskly around the first corner and made his way toward the middle of the marina. He could see the smoke coming off the grill at this point and thought about grabbing a burger but realized he left his wallet and cell phone at the rental place in a locker. He gave a nod to the guy attending the grill and continued to move. He was pretty sure his time on Fisher Island was limited now that he had been spotted by one of the marina employees. Security and privacy are what separates places like Fisher Island from the public beaches and hangouts. Employees are trained to spot and report people who don't belong.

He was right. He looked back at the grill and saw the man cooking motion inside for something. He could have needed more BBQ sauce, but it was unlikely.

So he quickened his pace. The first two rows of boats were the sport-fishing and mini yacht variety, not many were longer than sixty feet, though all of them were beautiful. Every one of them cost more than Tye would make in ten years and that fact didn't escape him.

The third row provided much more room for the big yachts to maneuver. There were two football fields distance between row two and row three and Tye could see why that much room was needed. The vessels in row three were absolutely humongous. All of them seventy foot long and better. Most of them well over one hundred feet in length with multiple decks. Some had helipads, many had pools. They were floating cities with endless activities for the tenants.

Tye looked over his shoulder and could see two security guards with hand-held radios walking toward him. Once again his pace quickened. If his estimations were correct he could make it to the end of row three before they caught up to him, unless they started running. He was pretty sure that wasn't going to happen. Although when he thought about it, he was a middle-aged bald guy who probably had white drool slipping out of the side of his mouth who had just parked a jet ski in a place it didn't belong, in a place where he didn't belong.

He had gone to lengths to remain under the radar on this recon and now he was about to blow all of that if he wasn't careful. He decided cooperating with the security team was probably in his best interest, so he slowed down and eventually came to a stop. The security guys were in front of him within a few seconds asking questions. The tall black man asked him, "Do you own or rent on this island sir?"

Tye had to be quick on his feet. "No, but I have a friend who lives here, I thought I'd stop in and see if he was on his boat." Tye looked at them closely. They were buying it.

"And what's his name sir?" The shorter Caucasian security guard asked.

"His name is Jules, you don't happen to know him do you?"

"We are not at liberty to discuss any personal information relating to residents. And I'm sorry but we're going to have to ask you to leave unless you are an official guest of an island resident."

"That's O.K." Tye said. "Just thought I'd give it a shot. Didn't mean to upset anyone…and I'll be on my way. Thanks guys." Tye said with a genuine smile and started to walk away.

He had taken a few steps when he heard the taller security guard call to him. Tye turned to face him.

"Yeah."

The guard pointed at the yacht in front of him. "Looks like he's not on his boat today, but I can tell him you stopped by to see him if you want.

Tye took a look at the boat. "FAMILY JEWELS" was scripted on the back.

He looked again at the helpful security guard. "Yeah, if you don't mind, tell him that Darryl from the Texaco stopped in to say hello.

CHAPTER 44

The flight from Chicago to New York was approximately two hours long. This gave him enough time to come up with some sort of plan. Anything was better than what he had at the moment.

The plane approached cruising altitude and the pilot shut off the seatbelt signs. He got up and went to the restroom. While he was in the back of the plane he ordered another drink and asked that it be delivered to his seat whenever possible. The flight attendant smiled and said she'd be there in a minute.

He returned to his seat and pulled out a notebook from his carry-on bag. He started to thumb through the pages and found the one that contained the scribbling's from the conversation he'd had with his old friend from the Chicago police department. It was amazing the access law enforcement had in these big cities. Morris barely had computers and Chicago could link in to several FBI databases.

He'd made several notes. Wrote down names and addresses. Over the years he had developed a shorthand that he understood. Key phrases would incite him to remember other things. The resulting scribble was a conglomeration of one-word phrases and strings of letters. He looked at the page.

Tribeca. J Maldone, AKA Mal. Wrap sheet.

A&B (Assault and Battery), GBI (Great Bodily Injury), SOM (Suspicion of murder). AM (Attempted murder), R&R (Racketeering and Ricoh), Genovese family. FL cnxn (Florida connection). 1970 Benito.

What he hadn't written down, but remembered, was that according to reports, Mal owned a cigar shop and that he was known to spend long hours at the store. The fact that he was affiliated with the Genovese family threw up major flags for him. Whatever plan he would devise would involve a lot of avoiding anyone affiliated with the Genovese family. The only problem was that he didn't know who those particular people were. He was deep in thought when the stewardess arrived with his drink.

He thanked her and closed his notebook. Took a long drink and closed his eyes. He was tired. His plan was to take a quick nap and resume working on the plan in fifteen or twenty minutes. Instead, he slept through the entire flight and awoke only when the plane touched down at LaGuardia. The chirping of the wheels made him jump a little and he was afraid he'd spill his drink.

When he opened his eyes he realized his tray had been wiped clean and secured in the upright position.

"She didn't want to wake you so she just took your drink and put your notebook on the ground." Dergo never really acknowledged the man sitting beside him on the plane.

"Jeff Dunston. Nice to meet you." He extended his hand for Dergo to shake. He introduced himself and tried desperately not to make small talk with his new best friend. No luck.

"So what do you do for a living?" Jeff asked.

"I'm retired now. I do a lot of fishing. Just up here visiting some friends."

The plane had come to a complete stop and Dergo stood up.

"Where you from?" Jeff was relentless.

"He's from shitsville Illinois." Came a voice a few rows in front of him.

Dergo's eyes opened wide. He looked but couldn't believe what he saw. "What the hell are you doing on this plane you Swiss prick?"

Thomas turned to face him directly. "I figured New York City was a better vacation spot than shitsville Illinois." Dergo looked genuinely offended by Thomas's description of his hometown. "Besides, I figured you might need some company on this trip."

Dergo wasn't happy that Thomas got on the flight. "You know, sometimes less drama is better than more drama when it comes to vacation."

"I know. Believe me I know."

The door opened and people started to shuffle out. Thomas and Dergo made their way out of the plane and up the loading ramp into the concourse at LaGuardia. They didn't say much to each other during the brief walk. Once inside the cab Dergo instructed the driver to take them to a decent hotel in Tribeca.

Thirty minutes later they arrived at the Tribeca Grand Hotel on sixth avenue near little Italy in Manhattan. They checked into their room and settled in a little. Dergo took a shower and Thomas took a nap. By eight o'clock in the evening they decided to get something to eat. Thomas wanted to go out and Dergo wanted to order in.

"We need to develop some sort of plan. I think it's better if we stay here and get some work done."

Thomas agreed. They ordered room service and started to spread out across the desk. Dergo unfolded a map of lower Manhattan and began marking various places. After a while he began to explain himself.

"O.K. my source at Chicago P.D. tells me that the feds have been keeping close tabs on the Genovese family here in New York. There's this guy, his name is Johnny Maldone, but people just call him Mal. It turns out he has made a few trips to south Florida in the last month to see some guy in Miami." Dergo stopped to make sure he was keeping up with him. This gave Thomas a chance to ask questions.

"And of course you think he's linked to this whole thing somehow?"

"I do." Dergo reached back into his bag and pulled out a small folder. He opened it up and spread its contents across the table. Among the contents was a picture of Johnny Maldone. Thomas picked it up and looked at it..

"Holy Fwock.!" He said, the words drawn out slowly as if he had just discovered something.

"What?"

"I've seen this guy before. At the Lantana Airport. It was him and a few other guys that were in that Black SUV. I saw him!"

"Do you think he'd recognize you if he saw

you?"

"I'm not sure. There's no way to know."

"Well that changes things a little. We need to make sure he doesn't see you. Just in case."

Thomas looked at Dergo with genuine fear in his eyes. He could sense that his friend was concerned.

"I told you to take a few days off in Morris dumbass! You could be bass fishing right now." This didn't seem to be helping Thomas at all.

"Anyway." Dergo said, "Mal owns a cigar shop here." He pointed to the map indicating the shop was only a few blocks from where they were staying, on the outskirts of little Italy. "I also think he has ties to a warehouse here." Again pointing to another circle he drew on the map. "We can observe both of the buildings until we figure out some sort of pattern. There has to be some sort of structure involved in this guy's work habits. It won't take long to figure it out."

Thomas waited for Dergo to finish outlining the plan. Nothing else came. He raised his eyebrows as if to say, "O.K., keep going."

"That's it. Once we figure out where he goes every day we can tailor our plan to fit our needs."

Dergo sounded convincing, but the truth of the matter was that he still didn't have a logical plan. He'd just have to play this one by ear.

"So what do we do now?"

"Why don't you rent us a car so we can watch these two addresses. Get something comfortable. Maybe something big enough to sleep in if we have to." Dergo laughed under his breath. It was like having a rookie on the force again. He wanted desperately to toy with Thomas but figured he would need him as alert as possible in the next few days.

CHAPTER 45

Tye sat on his new information for a few days. He felt like he was caught between a rock and a hard place. That is, if he sat Vinny down and told him what he had found, he knew Vinny would want to drive down to Fisher Island and kill the guy. On the other hand, if he started asking a lot of questions about this Jules guy it might raise some unwanted flags in his direction.

So he sat on it for a day or two and just let it mull around in his head. Toward the end of that second day of mulling it was starting to get to him. He had information nobody else did and he wanted to share it with someone.

Officer Payne pulled in to the Texaco and chatted with the guys for a few minutes. Tye took the opportunity to ask a few questions.

"Hey Payne, the other day I saw some guy drive right over a dive flag out in the ocean. If I got the name of his boat is there any way you guys can look it up?"

Payne just looked at him funny. "Why the hell would you want to do that? I thought all you fishermen hated the divers?"

"Well we do, but still…I don't want anyone to get hurt out there. I was just wondering, that's all." Tye decided to drop it. Besides, what was he going to do? If he mentioned the name of the boat it linked him directly with Jules. That wasn't a good idea. He didn't know exactly why it was a bad idea at this point, but he was sure he didn't want it.

He decided that the only way to get more information was to go see Michelle about something unrelated, perhaps she knew more than she was telling.

Tye finished his diet coke and continued to chat with the handful of guys that were sitting in front of the candy shop. Today there were two regulars whom he had not seen in a while, Lloyd and the King. Lloyd was a retired corporate man from Proctor and Gamble who loved fishing almost as much as he liked to travel. He and his wife had just returned from a cruise that basically took them around the world. When Tye first met Lloyd he didn't pay much attention to his stories of travel. It wasn't something he was interested in. It was only when his brother had formed a bond with Lloyd, sharing stories of travel to Russia, Thailand, Prague, and various other places around the world that Tye really started to pay attention. Lloyd was a world traveler and highly educated man who had made it big in the corporate world. Tye guessed what intrigued him most about his relationship with Terry was that they seemed like equals. His dumbass brother was holding his own with this guy. To some extent it fascinated him how he could do that.

The King, on the other hand was a little closer in age to Tye. He rode a Harley-Davidson and seemed to live life on cruise control. Not much ever bothered him and he seemed to have found peace in his life. He was a Vietnam veteran who married a wonderfully nice woman. They settled down on the beach and raised a family. There wasn't much else to say about The King. Tye just liked to talk to him every once in a while.

He finished up his conversations with his old friends and when Vinny wasn't looking he told everyone he was going across the street to check his mail. He said his goodbyes and sauntered across the street. Just before he left, Lloyd told him to wipe the white stuff off of his face. Tye popped another lozenge in his mouth and wiped his face briskly with the bottom of his shirt.

He headed across the street and did in fact check his mail in the Briny Breezes office. He was still receiving junk mail for Terry. It reminded him of how important it was to get to the bottom of this. He tucked the mail in his back pocket and approached the little counter where Michelle's assistant worked.

"Hi there." Tye said with his genuine smile. Women seemed to like it. "Is Michelle around?"

"She is. Give me one second and I'll let her know you're here."

She ducked around a corner and within a few minutes she was back, Michelle was right behind her. They greeted each other and Michelle asked him to sit in her office.

"I only have a few minutes, I have to finish these reports and send them out before the end of the month."

"That's O.K." Tye said, "This will only take a minute..

CHAPTER 46

Dergo and Thomas woke up just as the sun started to peek through the windows of their hotel room. They got dressed and packed the necessary items they would need for the day in a backpack and headed toward the elevator. In the lobby they found the continental breakfast and both sat at a small table in a corner. Thomas had a muffin and Dergo went with a small bowl of oatmeal. They were both on their second cup of coffee.

"So what's the plan?" Thomas asked.

"I figured we'd stake out the cigar shop for a while. If that doesn't look promising we can head down to the warehouse for a while."

"Brilliant plan."

"You got a better one?"

"No, but I'm not a cop."

"Neither am I, remember?" Dergo gave him a shitty smile and finished his coffee. Thomas, though not impressed at the moment, had faith in Dergo's ability as a detective. He was sure the butterflies in his stomach would dissipate once they were actually doing something.

As they exited the lobby toward the parking garage Dergo stopped at the front counter and asked if a package had arrived for him. The young lady behind the counter went into a back room and returned with a UPS Early A.M. box. She handed it to him and he thanked her. Thomas didn't ask, he knew what it was. You can't take firearms on a plane but you can have them shipped to your destination. He assumed it was Dergo's firearm, and he was right.

Once inside the parking garage Thomas led the way to the rental car, Dergo wasn't paying attention. He was trying to open the UPS box tucked underneath his arm. When he finally did retrieve it he smiled and tucked it into his waistband just as he heard the rental car locks open up with a loud beeping noise. The flashing of the lights that accompanied the beep made him raise his head. He was staring at a Toyota Prius. His smile disappeared.

He looked at Thomas who replied, "It's all they had left." Dergo just shook his head and opened the passenger side door without saying anything. He had to turn sideways and put his butt in first, then swivel his body to gain full entrance to the vehicle. He tried to put the seat back further but realized it was already back as far as it could go. When he closed his door his knees were hitting the dash.

Thomas could see how uncomfortable the car was for Dergo and asked if he was going to be O.K. "Just drive Switz."

They arrived at their destination within a few minutes but it was another thirty before they found a place to park where they could keep eyes on the front entrance of Johnny Maldone's cigar shop. It was appropriately titled, "The Smoke Lounge." It was a nice enough looking place. Very professional and well kept. The front of the store was decorated in Italian colored fare, and an Italian flag flew above the front door. A canvas awning in tasteful colors shielded the front windows from the sun. On their first pass in front of the shop they could see through the windows into the store. It was small with floor to ceiling shelves of cigar boxes, and what appeared to be a half-dozen leather recliners and a couch. A small counter on the right side of the room had a cash register and more boxes of cigars on it. Toward the back of the room was a door.

Thomas decided to walk around the corner and grab some coffee for the wait. The cigar shop didn't open until nine A.M., which gave him a good thirty minutes to grab coffee for him and Dergo. On one of their trips around the block looking for a parking space they noticed a small newspaper vendor who also sold coffee and snacks.

"Be right back. What do you want in your coffee?"

"Cream, two sugars. Grab a newspaper while you're there."

"You got it." Thomas exited the small prison and shut the driver door behind him. It was a little warm already. He was thankful it wasn't Florida heat. He had to walk past the cigar shop on his way to the coffee stand. As he passed he took a good look inside. The lights were off but he could see everything plainly as the sun was shining deep into the store. He noticed the leather chairs were very high quality. The shelves that extended to the twelve foot ceiling were made of mahogany. From this vantage point he could see that the floors were an expensive Italian marble. The place was beautiful, it was a man cave and he suddenly wanted to smoke a cigar in one of the soft leather chairs while he drank his coffee and read the morning paper. He turned the corner and walked another block to the coffee stand.

He picked up a New York Times and ordered two coffees from the man on the other side of the small table that separated them.

"Just started a new pot. Gonna be a minute if that's O.K.?" The man said.

Thomas looked at his watch. He still had twenty minutes until the store opened, plenty of time to get the goods and find his way back to the Prius before the store opened. "Yeah no problem."

He started to thumb through the newspaper and landed in the crime section. There was a small write up on the Genovese family and their recent string of troubles. Thomas was no cop but it looked to him as though they were in for some trouble. Local, state, and national authorities all had a hand in these recent troubles. Everyone wanted to bring them down.

"Grab me one too while you're back there Jimmy." A voice with a thick Brooklyn accent said from directly behind Thomas. Someone had walked up behind him while he was reading the crime section.

"You got it Mal." Said the vendor.

Thomas almost pissed himself. He closed the paper and stared straight ahead, looking at the vendor, then at the coffee pot. It was less than half full. He would be here a few more minutes minimum. Thomas started to panic at the thought of

Johnny Maldone standing right behind him. It bothered him. No…it scared him. Which is why what he did next made even less sense. At some point in the future Thomas would see a psychiatrist and try to figure out what compelled him to ask his question. He made a mental note of that at some point, right after the words came out of his mouth.

"You sell cigars here?" He looked at the vendor and tried to keep a straight face.

"No sir I sure don't. Sorry." He said, as he handed the coffee cups to Thomas.

"No problem." He said, and paid the man. He never once turned around to see Johnny Maldone, and he wasn't going to now. He laid down a twenty dollar bill and picked up his coffee. "Keep it." He said, and started to walk away

Johnny Mal noticed the generous tip and looked at Thomas as he walked away. He was only five or six steps down the street when he heard. "Heya buddy."

Thomas turned around. He was sweating more than he should have been and was hoping nobody would notice. When he turned he confirmed that it was the man he had seen at the Lantana airport as well as the man in the picture that Dergo had in his manila folder. A few things hit Thomas all at once.

First, Johnny Mal was a handsome man. He had movie star looks and Thomas was sure he could have been an actor had he chosen another lifestyle. His hair was black and slicked straight back on his head. His eyes were dark and tilted a little upward, not enough to stand out, but enough to notice if you looked. He was tall and thin. Just a shade over six feet or so and broad shouldered. He looked tough, and that look came from the confidence he possessed that he WAS tough. He didn't need to act like a bad guy, he was a bad guy, which gave him a sort of endearing quality. He was a bad guy that would certainly hurt you if you crossed him, but only if you crossed him. He might even prevent someone else from bullying you if you didn't deserve it. So within a few seconds Thomas had developed a mancrush on an alleged mafia gangster.

"I'm talking to you buddy." Johnny said, his temper obviously shorter than most of Thomas's acquaintances.

"Yeah?" Thomas asked, trying to act normal.

Johnny paid for his coffee and started to walk toward Thomas. "You need a cigar, I know where you can get one. Just around the corner here."

"That's awfully nice of you. Thanks."

"Don't mention it." Johnny said, laughing a little. "I own the joint. Today must be your lucky day."

"Yeah, it must be." Thomas saw the irony in all of this. This may have been his unluckiest day ever.

"You a cigar aficionado?" Johnny Mal asked in his thick Brooklyn accent.

"I indulge every once in a while. I'm not really educated in the world of cigars though, if that's what you mean."

"Well then this truly is your lucky day. I can tell you everything you need to know about cigars." They suddenly stopped walking. Johnny pointed to the store front. "This is my place." He slid a key in the lock and opened the door. "Benvenuti!" He said as he gestured for Thomas to step inside.

CHAPTER 47

Tye sat across from Michelle. For the first time he noticed how attractive she was. Maybe it was the way she was dressed today, maybe it was the sweet smell of vanilla that he detected. Whatever it was, he hadn't noticed until today. He cleared his mind and stared her in the eye. He detected a small smile from her, not sure if she was just being friendly or maybe she knew her little thread had caused him to have more questions.

"You said the feds were interviewing this Jules guy. Did he have any information for them?"

"Not that I know of Tye. But I don't have any inside information. I just know that one of my old friends is married to a Fisher Island cop. He mentioned to her that they asked him questions about some of the events that took place up here. Some of the murders. I just thought I'd tell you since you were directly involved."

Tye thought for a minute. "Do you think you can find out anything else? I mean, maybe a last name or physical address. What does this guy do for a living and why would he have any motivation to involve himself in anything going on in the Boynton Beach area?"

"Tye that's all I know. But I will certainly ask

her if she finds out anything else."

"Thanks." He said. Then looked at her. "How often do you see her?"

Michelle could see that Tye had an interest in pursuing this lead. Maybe he had done some snooping up to this point. Maybe not. Either way, she decided to play along.

"I never see her. We just happened to run into each other by chance."

"Maybe you could call her? See if she has an update, or even put a request in to find out more information if possible." Tye was grasping a little at this point. He knew it but he couldn't help himself. He didn't know what else to do.

"Tell you what. I'll call her right now. Will that help?"

"Yes it would. And thank you very much." Tye seemed happier because of her gesture. She picked up the phone and dialed the number to her house. It rang once and she put her thumb on the "end call" button. She waited a few seconds then talked to nobody. She was making the conversation up as she went.

"Hi Lorrie it's me Michelle…"

"Yeah, it was great to see you too…"

"I agree, we should try to get together more often, But hey, I have a favor to ask if you have a minute?"

"Great. Remember you were telling me about the feds questioning the guy on Fisher Island? Did you happen to hear anything else?..."

"Oh… I see."

"Is that right?" She looked at Tye and winked,

signaling that she was getting some information. She paused for another twenty seconds.

"O.K. then, well thank you so much sweetie. And if you hear anything else be sure to call me, O.K?"

"Uh-huh, you too sweetie. Uh-huh…bye now."

She put the phone in front of her face and pretended to hit the "end call" button. She was very convincing. She looked at Tye and waited for him to ask her what she had found out.

Tye finally caved. "Well, what did she say?" He was leaning forward now, impressed with Michelle and her ability to help him.

She smiled, more than happy to help him. "Well, his last name is Friedman."

Tye asked her for a piece of paper and a pen. She had several on her desk and pushed them toward him. He took notes as she spoke.

"His last name is Friedman. Jules Friedman. He is a real estate developer worth a lot of money, he's in his mid-seventies."

Tye wrote everything down. Michelle paused and they looked at each other.

"Anything else?" Tye asked.

"Yeah. She mentioned something about New York. That's why they were interviewing him."

Tye cocked his head a little. He was confused. "What about New York?"

"I don't know for sure. She said that maybe he had some ties to some people up there." She didn't want to give him too much, just a crumb or two for him to follow. Besides, she really didn't know much more than what she had told him. She knew Jules' name and that he had contacted some people in New York to help him. That's it.

"What do you mean ..ties?"

"I don't know. That's what she said. I'm really sorry I couldn't be more helpful Tye, but if I hear from her again I'll certainly let you know."

"Well thanks for your help Michelle. I appreciate it." He stood and got ready to say goodbye. She remained sitting and extended her hand. He shook it and she went back to work. He showed himself out.

He folded the paper he had written on and put it in his back pocket with the few pieces of mail that were there from earlier. Then he crossed the little street that separated the Briny Breezes office from the Texaco station.

He took his seat in front of the candy shop and resumed talking to the King. Vinny came outside and joined them. He was done working in the garage for the day. Tye was done playing cop for the day.

CHAPTER 48

Johnny Mal held the door open for Thomas as he stepped inside. The place smelled wonderful and Thomas made a comment without thinking. "I thought a cigar shop would smell more like..." Then he caught himself.

"More like cigar smoke?"

"Yeah, I mean, if people sit around and smoke cigars here why doesn't' it smell like cigar smoke?"

"Because I don't want it to, that's why. And I pay a lot of money to keep it that way. Women and first timers tend not to shop in the store when it smells like an ashtray. Besides, I don't like to walk in to my shop and smell old, stale, cigar ashes. Know what I mean?"

Thomas nodded even though he wasn't exactly sure how he kept it smelling fresh and clean.

Johnny turned some lights on and started a computer. It wasn't a point of sale system because there was an antique cash register on the other end of the counter. It was a 'National' brand, made of bronze with an oak box to collect money. The register itself was a thing of beauty. It was over one hundred years old but looked brand new and Thomas was sure that it was completely functional. He commented on it.

"That's a beautiful antique cash register."

Johnny stopped what he was doing and looked

at Thomas. “Yes it is beautiful. You have a good eye.” Johnny kept eye contact with him and gave him a slightly confused look. He asked. “Have we met before? You look familiar to me.”

“I don’t believe so, no.” Thomas said. His ass was starting to pucker and he suddenly realized that Dergo must have seen him go into the store with Johnny Mal. If he didn’t see him, Thomas was afraid this might not end well. He was getting nervous.

“So what kind of cigar do you like?”

Thomas was clueless when it came to cigars.

Johnny asked again, “Blond, Colorado, Maduro?”

Thomas assumed these were color classifications, much like coffee. For some reason he associated cigars with coffee. Good guess.

“I don’t like them too strong, so I’m guessing I’m more of a Colorado man than a Maduro man.”

Johnny followed up. “I think I have what you are looking for.” He moved toward the back of the store, which was only twenty feet deep from the front door to the back door and grabbed a small ladder from the corner. He opened it up and climbed a few rungs until he could reach the top shelf. He opened a small glass case in front of the cigar box he wanted and pulled out two cigars.

“This is a Rocky Patel. It’s a maduro but it’s very light. I think you can handle it.” He stepped down from the ladder and handed one to Thomas.

Not knowing what to do he put it to his face and ran it the length of his nose, inhaling deeply. “I like it.”

Johnny turned and walked behind the counter. He opened a drawer and retrieved a cutter and a lighter. He handed them to Thomas. He then stuck his hand in his pocket and pulled out a silver cutter and a gold lighter for his own use.

"Cut the end of the cigar like this." Johnny said. The cutter was basically a pair of scissors that you slid a thumb into a hole on one end and a forefinger into the hole on the other end. Thomas placed the butt of the cigar into the opening between his two fingers and squeezed, sheering off the butt of the cigar, just as Johnny had done with his.

"Lighting the cigar is important. You don't want to burn the end so keep the flame off of the wrapper."

Thomas nodded.

"Twist it in a circle and heat the end of the cigar evenly, then stick it in your mouth and do the same thing while you suck the flame up to the end of the cigar."

Thomas never realized there were so many rules to smoking a cigar, and he hadn't even lit it yet. He did as Johnny instructed and within a few seconds they were both smoking cigars. Thomas made sure he didn't inhale, he didn't want to cough.

They both took a seat in leather chair and smoked in silence for a few minutes. Thomas really did enjoy the feeling. It wasn't just the cigar, it was the entire experience. There was something very fulfilling about smoking a good cigar and sitting in a soft leather chair. The mahogany shelving and the Italian marble tile seemed to add to the experience and suddenly Thomas noticed soft music in the background. He realized that's why Johnny turned a computer on when he'd first entered. It was Frank Sinatra playing something Thomas didn't quite recognize, but it was bluesy and jazzy and understated. For a few moments Thomas just enjoyed his cigar and the music and his surroundings. He'd just received a lesson in civility from a mobster and he was starting to think that today may in fact be his lucky day. Then everything changed.

"So who is your friend?" Johnny asked rather calmly, exhaling a long trail of smoke after his sentence was complete, never breaking eye contact with Thomas.

"What friend?" Thomas asked. He realized Johnny didn't ask him *where* is your friend. He asked *who* is your friend. This confused Thomas and made him hesitate for a few seconds. How did he know about a friend in the first place?

"You got two cups of coffee. I assume one is for a friend. Won't your friend be waiting on his cup of coffee?"

Thomas stumbled, "Um…yeah, actually now that you mention it. I should be getting back with his coffee. I guess I got caught up in my cigar lesson. Thanks for reminding me."

Johnny's expression changed and Thomas could see it. It made him even more nervous. He wasn't cut out for this kind of stuff. He stood up and offered a hand to Johnny. Johnny shook his hand. "Beautiful place you got here, thanks for your hospitality."

"Don't mention it, it's what I do."

He picked up the coffees, cigar still in his mouth and turned away.

"Hey amigo, you gonna pay for that cigar?" Johnny asked, his voice stern.

"Of course I am." He set the coffee cups on the counter and reached into his back pocket for his wallet.

Johnny walked over to the bronze and oak National cash register and hit a button. Thomas could hear the tiny mechanisms moving inside the register, the very things that gave a National it's unique sound.

"That's two hundred and fifteen dollars."

"Holy fwock." Thomas said. Johnny noticed the accent.

"Where you from?"

He almost said Florida. That would have been a mistake. "Switzerland." He squeezed the words out between the cigar and his lips that was now held in place by his teeth.

"No shit, always wanted to go there."

Thomas had a problem. He didn't have enough cash to pay for the cigar and his only credit card had in big bold letters – Florida Community Bank.

"I take credit cards." Johnny said, his patience starting to wear thin. Thomas was sure Johnny would give him a beat down if he thought he was going to skip out on the bill. Of course, if he recognized him from south Florida he might try to kill him.

He heard the door open.

"Jesus Christ Switz, where is my coffee?"

Dergo said in a loud voice. A wave of relief washed over Thomas. He tried to explain, hoping they could align their stories somehow.

"I was on my way back when I met this gentleman. He owns this cigar shop."

Dergo took a look at the cigar between his teeth and squinted a little. "Are you kidding me? You've got a Rocky Patel between your teeth? Don't you know anything about cigars?" Johnny laughed a little.

In fact he didn't. And he knew even less about what it was Dergo had in mind, but he was damn glad to see him. Dergo looked at Johnny without changing his expression.

"Let me have one of those too. Those are tough to get in Illinois."

Johnny decided to ring them both up before he climbed the ladder. "That'll be four-hundred and thirty dollars, for the both of them."

"No problem." Dergo said, and fished his Morris Credit Union card out of his wallet. He handed it to Johnny who inspected it closely before sliding it across something underneath the counter.

"You need a receipt for that?" Johnny asked

"Yeah, if you don't mind. I can put it on the expense account when I get back."

Johnny opened a drawer and pulled out a receipt book. He scribbled down the words – Rocky Patel Anniversary Maduros – 215.00 x 2 – 430.00 paid in full/credit card. He handed the receipt to Dergo.

"Illinois huh? I have some friends in Illinois, Chicago. What do you do for a living?"

Thomas started to turn pale. Dergo never missed a beat.

"I'm a land developer. Retired now, but I still dabble a little bit." He pointed to Thomas. "Simon here was thinking about buying an apartment in Manhattan. He was a big shot with Nestle Corporation and he has decided to spend some time in the big apple."

Johnny wasn't sure if Dergo was telling the truth. He didn't look like a wealthy land developer. He didn't look wealthy. He started to size the two of them up as he walked toward the ladder to retrieve the cigar.

"How do you two know each other?" He asked, as he began to climb the ladder. Dergo moved toward the base of the ladder to speak.

"Actually Johnny, we met in Boynton Beach Florida, at the Texaco station. You know where that is…right?"

Johnny didn't look at Dergo. He reached his right hand into his suit pocket.

"Don't do it Johnny." Dergo said. But it was too late, his hand was starting to come out when Dergo kicked the ladder over.

Johnny fell from twelve feet up in the air and hit the ground before he could fire. He hit hard and the sound of his head bouncing off the floor actually made Thomas cringe. Dergo grabbed him by the throat with one hand and secured his pistol with the other. He slid it on the floor over to Thomas and started patting him down. He found a knife in his sock and a wallet in his back pocket. His keys were in his front pocket. Other than that he was clean.

Johnny was unconscious and bleeding badly from the back of his head.

Thomas was speechless. Dergo pointed to the front door and threw Thomas the keys. "Lock it."

"Why?" Thomas asked. "Shouldn't we get the hell out of here?"

Dergo didn't respond. He grabbed one of Johnny's arms and started to drag him toward the back door. It was locked and he told Thomas to open it. He did. The three of them went into the back room and Thomas closed the door behind them while Dergo searched for something to tie Johnny up with.

CHAPTER 49

Tye and Vinny decided to go fishing. Dergo left for Illinois and Thomas wasn't answering his phone so they decided it would be just the two of them. Tye took a day off work and Vinny was able to adjust his schedule. The conditions were perfect. The ocean looked like a flat pond. There were no waves and no wind and the mahi-mahi were running, Of course, fishing always sounds better first thing in the morning as you are boarding the boat, sipping coffee, anticipating a beautiful day on the ocean.

The truth of the matter is that a day on the ocean is always better than a day doing something else, almost anything else. But it does have its drawbacks. In the middle of summer the weather was hot, even if you were two or three miles off the coast. As the day ticked past the halfway point of fishing, usually somewhere in the early afternoon, your thoughts started to drift toward cleaning up the fish and the boat. By this time your back hurt from all of the jostling, not to mention your stomach from all of the back and forth and up and down. Having to re-rig your pole after a Kingfish bites everything off. And, in Tye's case on this particular day, having to listen to Vinny sing. It was constant and for some reason he was stuck on Britney Spears. He had already gone through several renditions of "Hit me baby one more time" and was now on some bluesy version of "Oops I did it again."

"For the love of God Vinny… please quit singing."

Vinny laughed. "The fish like it you dumbass."

"I don't think that's quite right. Besides, I'm the only one that can hear it, not them."

"Fuck you."

"I would prefer you fuck me than continue to sing Britney Spears. Besides… how do you even know the words to any Britney Spears song, much less all of them?"

"She's a good singer dumbass. I know you listen to her in your car when nobody is around."

"I don't. I really … honestly don't."

"Well you should…"

Vinny quit talking midsentence and jerked his pole backward, which immediately bent in half toward the water. The drag on his pole started to whistle as the fish on the other end decided to dive to deeper waters.

"WHOOOAAA." Vinny said. "That's a big one. I told you they liked Britney Spears."

Tye just shook his head. He was about to comment but a fish hit his line before he could speak. His pole bent in a semicircle and his drag screeched as the fish took off.

"Nice one dumbass." Vinny said with a smile. "Maybe we're on a school." There was excitement in Vinny's voice. Every once in a great while they would stumble across a school of Mahi-Mahi. There was a trick to this type of fishing and both of them knew what to do.

As Vinny finished reeling in his fish Tye had his halfway in. "It's a Dolphin dumbass." Vinny's excitement was at a peak now and he started to sing again. Mahi-Mahi is a Dolphin fish. Not to be confused with the mammal dolphin, or porpoise. Mahi-Mahi simply means *very strong* in Hawaiian, and they are appropriately named.

Instead of landing the fish on the boat Vinny made sure he was played out and then put his rod in a rod holder, leaving the fish near the top of the water. Once you do this the others in the school will follow and see if there is any food on the top of the water. And of course there is food there, because Vinny was throwing a few pieces of cut up ballyhoo bait into the water.

When the frenzy was all said and done they had limited out, ten fish per person, per day. With more than one hundred pounds of Mahi-Mahi on the boat they decided to call it a day. The sun was brutal and both fishermen were a little sore so the decision was easy. The trip back to the marina is always more pleasant when there are fish on the boat, especially today's catch. Vinny raised his voice to talk to Tye, they were at full throttle making their way toward the inlet. Vinny had to roar above the noise of the engine.

"Did you hear anything from the police yet?"

Tye shook his head. "You?"

"No." He paused then took a hit off his cigarette that was cupped in his palm to protect it from the wind. They were travelling at forty miles an hour. His usual blue wisps of smoke exited his mouth like water being spit out that wrapped around his head and got caught in the airstream, disappearing immediately. He continued.

"No, no, but I did get a visit from a U.S. Marshall."

Tye looked at him funny. He was yelling also. "You have the bluest partial?"

"No dumbass. I said I got a visit from a U.S. Marshall. Marshall."

"Your formage is impartial?"

"Marshall. MARSHALL!" He screamed at the top of his lungs.

Tye throttled down to a stop. "Hold on a second dumbass." He reached up above his head and retrieved his nicotine lozenges. Vinny lit another cigarette.

They were floating now. The winds had picked up a little since the morning and the waves were a few feet high, making the boat rock gently as they sat and talked in the hot sun. Tye ducked underneath the roof of the console to shield himself from the blazing fireball in the sky. Vinny sat on the edge of the boat and they faced each other. The conversation was long overdue and both could sense they were about to divulge something to each other.

"I said, I got a visit from a U.S. Marshall."

"What did he say? And why didn't you tell me?"

"I didn't tell you anything because he didn't really say anything."

"He had to have mentioned something."

"Dumbass, if he had told me who killed my son and your brother don't you think I would have called you up right away?"

Tye nodded his agreement. They both knew that Vinny would have told him about the meeting if anything like that came out of it. Still, Tye wanted to know what was said. He sat silent and stared at Vinny. Finally Vinny told him.

"Basically… he said that Frank was in the witness protection program, but we already figured that out when Payne told us a U.S. Marshall was looking into the case."

"Did he tell you why he was in the Witness Protection Program?"

"Yeah… said that he was a caterer in New York. Catered some parties for a mob family. Genovese or something like that. A party was raided by the feds, everyone was arrested. They tried to get Frank to wear a wire or something."

"I can't believe he'd do that."

"He didn't. He told them to go fuck themselves."

"So why was he in the program?"

Vinny took a long drag off his cigarette. "I guess he killed a guy. Ran over him twice."

"No shit? I didn't think Frank had it in him."

"Neither did I, but I guess this guy tried to kill him or something. The feds offered him the Witness Protection Program in exchange for his testimony if the day every came. That's how he ended up in Florida."

Tye thought about it for a moment and took it all in. "Doesn't really help us much, does it?" He asked.

"No, but when I asked him why he was telling

me all of that he seemed to think that I could help him."

"How?"

"He said that he was confident that I would eventually find the guy who killed my son. He just wanted me to know that he was on my side, if I ever needed help from someone on that side of the law."

"Well that was damn nice of him." Tye said, half joking.

"Yeah, I thought so too. I'm still not sure exactly why he wanted to talk to me."

"Maybe he really does believe you'll catch the killer."

"Maybe. But I'm pretty sure if I do catch him I'll take care of things myself. Calling him might be the last thing I do."

Tye nodded. He understood what Vinny was talking about because he felt the same way. "I imagine the only person I'd call would be you… that is, if I found the guy."

Tye was being nice, setting up Vinny for what he was about to tell him. "I guess there are some things I should tell you as well."

Vinny took another long drag off his cigarette. The blue wisps dancing across his face and floating out to sea. Tye decided he needed another nicotine lozenge for this one.

"So I was talking to Michelle the other day."

Vinny interrupted. "Michelle… from Briny Breezes?"

"Yes. Follow along dumbass. Anyway, she told me that a friend of a friend is a cop on Fisher Island down in Miami."

"That's a private island, right?"

"Yes, it is. So the cop is on duty when he's contacted by the feds, asking about the address for a guy named Jules Friedman."

"Never heard of him."

Tye continued. "Me either, but I decided to go down there and look for myself, just see if I could find the guy."

"When did you go down there?"

"The other day. It was a half day at work so I used the other half to explore Fisher Island."

"I thought you weren't allowed on the island unless you lived there?" Vinny asked.

"You're not, but I rented a jet ski and drove around the outside of the island."

Vinny smiled. He wouldn't of thought of that, but it was a good idea. "Did you find him?"

"No, but I found his boat. It's called 'Family Jewels'. I thought you might be able to look it up, find his address or something."

"How am I going to look it up?"

"You used to be a cop dumbass. Don't you have connections?"

"I was a cop on the island of Trinidad. What makes you think I have connections here?"

Vinny thought about it for a second. "Maybe you're right. Maybe Payne or somebody can help us with that."

"I was thinking the same thing. But Vinny…" His voice trailed off a little and Vinny gave him a few seconds to respond.

"Yeah, what were you gonna say?"

"Maybe we don't want the cops to know that

we're on to this guy…because if we find out he's responsible for any of this…"

"I see where you're going with this." Vinny said. He thought about it too.

"I guess calling the Marshall is out of the question too?"

Tye nodded. "For now anyway. Maybe we can find him on our own. We'll use Payne and the Marshall as a last resort.

Vinny agreed and lit another cigarette. Tye started the boat and throttled forward, almost knocking Vinny on his ass.

CHAPTER 50

Johnny Maldone woke up tied to a wooden chair he kept in the corner of his modest office in the back of his upscale cigar shop. His head hurt and his back was wet. He knew the wet, sticky, feeling was blood. He'd felt it before. He'd smelled it before. There was no doubt it was his own blood. He didn't know how he got there or why. He couldn't see straight and everything was blurry. As he tried to focus on the movement in front of him he could hear a voice. He didn't know who it belonged to, but he did know that he'd heard it before.

"Wake up gangster. I have things to do today." Dergo said from behind Johnny's desk. His feet were propped up and he was smoking one of the finest cigars in the world – in his opinion.

Johnny was now able to focus enough to see Dergo at his desk, and Thomas off to his right.

"Who the fuck are you?" Johnny asked.

"I'm the guy who just kicked the ladder out from under you. Remember?"

It was slowly coming back to him. He started to remember Dergo telling him he was from the south Florida area.

"Do you know who the fuck I am Jabroni?"

"Yeah I know all about you Johnny Mal. See, I'm a cop, and I've got a file on you that's two inches thick."

"You think I give a shit about your file? I'm

going to kill you. And it's going to be a slow painful death. Then I'm going to kill your family, both of you's."

Thomas looked a little confused. He asked Mal. "What is a Jabroni?"

"YOU'RE A FUCKING JABRONI!" He screamed. He looked at Dergo. "What's with this fucking guy? He doesn't understand English?"

Dergo sighed. "He's foreign. He is from Switzerland. He's never heard the word before."

"Well… I don't care if I have to travel all the way to Switzerland to do it, but I'm gonna kill everyone in his family too. You fucking Jabroni." He spit toward Thomas. Everything that came out of his mouth was red.

"I'd try to relax if I were you Johnny. You're bleeding out from the back of your head, and you don't have a whole lot of time left."

"What's your connection to south Florida?" Thomas asked.

"Fuck you."

"Why were you at the Lantana airport a few weeks ago?" Thomas asked, his voice raised

Johnny smiled and looked at Thomas. "That's where I saw you. The airport."

"Why were you there?" Thomas asked again. Johnny Maldone smiled and didn't say a word.

"I'll tell you why he was there. He came down to Florida to kill a few people, didn't you Johnny?"

"I don't know what you're talking about?"

"Of course you don't." Dergo said, disappointed. He looked at Johnny Mal. "You know Johnny, we don't have time for this. So I'm just going to skip the niceties and get to the point. We can do this here, or we can do this somewhere else. I'm not going to stick around here and ask you questions while we have a pile of blood on the floor out there and employees and customers about to walk in at any second."

"Fuck you."

"That's what I thought." Dergo said as he stood up from behind the desk. He looked at Thomas and pointed toward the back door. "Open it up and see if you can pull the car around there."

Thomas opened the door and got his bearings. He nodded at Dergo, who pointed at the front door.

"Go out that way, I'll lock the door behind you." Dergo followed him out into the cigar shop and opened the door. Thomas made a quick left toward their rental car and disappeared from view.

Meanwhile Dergo moved quickly. He locked the door and grabbed the ladder making his way to the back room. He started to rifle through Johnny's desk looking for a pen or a sharpie and a piece of paper. When he found what he was looking for he scribbled a note. He took his phone out of his pocket and turned it on. They had kept their phones off so their location couldn't be traced in the future. As far as Dergo was concerned nobody needed to know they were in New York. Not now and not in the future. He scrolled through his contact list and found what he was looking for.

"You realize you're already dead, don't you? You'll never get away with this." Johnny said through his bloody mouth.

Dergo walked over to Johnny and punched him

as hard as he could in the jaw, knocking him and his chair over. He was unconscious.

He found some cleaning supplies and mopped up the puddle of blood in the cigar shop, then began wiping the place clean of prints. As he was finishing up the last of it he heard a knock at the back door of the back room. He drew his pistol from his waist and moved to the door.

"Yeah?" He asked.

"It's me." Thomas said.

Dergo opened the door and saw that Thomas had opened the hatchback and put the rear seats down.

"What happened to him?" Thomas asked as he looked at an unconscious Johnny Mal tipped over on the floor.

"Just grab him." Dergo said without explaining. Together they lifted him and put him in the back of the Prius. Thomas found some towels to lay underneath him and Dergo finished mopping up the last of the mess in the back room. When he turned to exit he could see Thomas wrapping one of the towels around Mal's head to stop the bleeding.

"It's pretty bad, split wide open."

"I don't care." Dergo said. "Let's get out of here while we still can."

They got in the car and Thomas drove. He pulled out of the alley and onto the main street. He looked confused.

"Which way?"

"South Switz. We're going to Florida."

Thomas closed his eyes and shook his head. "Another brilliant plan."

CHAPTER 51

Tye and Vinny were at the Texaco trying to develop a plan. It was early in the morning and Vinny had just opened the station. He had a Ford truck up on the lift and he was walking around underneath it. He was wearing an L.E.D. lamp on his forehead, held in place with a headband. Purchased from a camping supply warehouse it worked well. It enabled him to see tiny crevices he wouldn't normally be able to see. He unscrewed the oil filter and let the remaining oil drip into the pan he had placed on the floor. His attention returned to the bottom of the truck, and so did the beam of light emanating from his forehead.

"Call Dergo and see if he can help. He still knows people in Illinois."

"Every time I call him it goes to voice mail." Tye said.

"Try Thomas again."

Tye sat back in the plastic lawn chair situated in front of the truck Vinny was working on. He popped a nicotine lozenge and took another swig of his Diet Coke. "How is Thomas going to help?"

"I don't know, maybe he has heard from Dergo. Maybe he knows somebody who can help us?" Vinny sounded dejected and his patience seemed to be getting thin. He ducked from underneath the truck and walked past Tye to his shop bench where he retrieved a fresh pack of cigarettes. He lit one and took his required long drag. There were fans in the shop but none blowing directly on him at the moment, so when the smoke escaped his mouth it went straight for his eyes, making him squint.

"Maybe doing something is better than doing nothing dumbass." Vinny said emphatically.

Tye shook his head and picked up his phone. He dialed Dergo and it went straight to voice mail. He dialed Thomas and got the same thing.

"Where the hell are those two?" Tye asked.

"Well that's what I'd like to know." An unexpected voice came from the front of the garage.

A tall man with a sugary voice entered the shop and took off his cowboy hat, wiping the sweat from his brow.

"Austin Seebeck, U.S. Marshall." He said with an extended hand and a broad smile.

Tye stood and shook his hand. "Tyrone. Nice to meet you Marshall."

Vinny came from around the front of the truck to the back of the truck where Tye and the Marshall were talking, L.E.D . lamp still attached to his forehead.

"Hope I'm not interrupting your work Vinny."

"Not at all, just taking a break. How can I help you?" Vinny asked, not necessarily wanting the answer.

"Well, I wanted to talk to your friend Dergo but I can't seem to find him. He was supposed to be in Illinois doing some work for the Morris Police Department, but it turns out their Chief has absolutely no knowledge of him being scheduled to work. When I talked to him…it was as if I'd made the whole thing up."

Tye and Vinny looked at each other hoping that the other knew something. No such luck.

"Why do you need to talk to Dergo, Marshall?" Tye asked.

"Well, I have some follow up questions based on the last time I talked to him, just wanted to tie up some loose ends, if you know what I mean?"

Vinny nodded. Tye was thinking.

Seebeck looked at Vinny and cocked his head a little to the left. "You would call me and let me know if you hear from him…wouldn't you Vinny?" His tone was questioning, if not implicating.

"I'll pass it along that you're looking for him…if I hear from him." There was a slight emphasis on the word if.

"Well O.K. then." He said and put his cowboy hat back on. He smiled at them both and turned to walk away. At the edge of the garage he pivoted three hundred and sixty degrees in a graceful, fluid motion. His right arm up in the air with a finger pointing at them.

"Oh… and by the way. If you guys need anything from me just let me know." He tipped his hat and turned to leave.

"As a matter of fact." Tye yelled. The Marshall stopped in his tracks.

"Shut up dumbass." Vinny whispered.

Seebeck turned around, a big smile on his face. "Yes?"

"What can you tell us about Jules Friedman?"

Seebeck's smile got even bigger. He looked at Vinny. "See, I knew it wouldn't take long for you get on the trail. I just wish you had more faith in me."

CHAPTER 52

Thomas looked at Dergo, who was sleeping at this point. He heard Johnny Mal uttering something. They had been driving a few hours now and were on interstate ninety-five, southbound toward Florida. He wasn't sure if Mal was alive until he heard him muttering in the backseat.

"Where are you taking me?" He asked.

"Does it matter?"

"Well of course it does. When I kill you I'll need to be able to find my way back."

"You're not killing anybody. Not today anyway."

"Get me out of this chair. My whole body is cramping."

"Tell me why you were at the Lantana airport and I'll be happy to let you go."

"Fuck you."

Thomas turned the radio up. He had been listening to NPR for the last hour and wanted to hear some music. He turned the station until he found something catchy and then turned it up a little more. He could hear Jimi Hendrix playing his magical guitar in the background when Johnny Mal decided to talk.

"If I tell you why I was at the airport will you get me out of this chair?"

"I said I would."

"I was visiting some family down there. Got an uncle in Boca Raton."

"That's bullshit Mal and you know it. If you were visiting someone in Boca you would have flown into Boca Raton Airport, not Lantana."

"Just fucking untie me Jabroni and I'll tell you why I was there. I promise."

"Oh you promise do you? Guess I should just pull over here and let you go, because you promise to tell me the truth? Do you think I'm stupid Mal?"

"I do."

"Well, I'd rather listen to the radio than listen to any more of your bullshit." Thomas turned the radio back on, Dergo started to wake up.

Another twenty miles passed as Dergo slowly woke up and got his wits about him. "I want a beer, get off at the next exit. We'll get gas too."

Thomas looked at him funny. "A beer, really? We've got a certified gangster in the backseat half dead with probably half of New York's mob population looking for him… and you would like to have a beer?"

"Yeah Switz, I said I want a beer. I'm thirsty. We're going to have to stop at some point and get gas anyway. What's your problem?"

"You are my problem, dumbass." Thomas was

shouting now. "If you had just stuck to the plan and went back home, none of this would be happening. I wouldn't have a half-dead gangster in the back of my rental car."

Dergo was still a little groggy. "And if you had just went back to Morris for a vacation, like I told you to, then again – you would not be here with a half-dead gangster in the back seat of your rental car."

"So what do we do when we get to the gas station and he decides to scream? Then what?"

"He won't scream. We'll just pump the gas, get our food and drink, and be on our way." He yawned when he was finished.

"Trouble ladies?" Mal said from the backseat.

Dergo unfastened his seat belt and turned around to face Mal. He had his pistol in his hand now and made sure Mal saw it.

"Aren't you the tough guy." Mal said in disgust. "Untie me and we'll see how tough you are.

"Why would I do that? You're not very smart are you Mal?"

"I'm smarter than you…you pig." He spit toward Dergo.

Dergo pistol-whipped him. Hard. He was unconscious again. He turned back around in his seat and buckled up.

"Get off at the next exit. I promise he won't scream."

Thomas shook his head. "Yet another brilliant plan. Are you just going to pistol whip the guy into unconsciousness every time we have to stop? He's probably got brain damage already from the fall in the cigar shop."

"Thomas, you sound like you give a shit about this guy. Did you two become buddies while I was sleeping. Or was it when he was killing Terry and Darryl, and the Canadian… and Frank. You remember Frank?"

Thomas pulled the car off the interstate and down the exit ramp to a small gas station that had a fast food place connected to it.

The two men took turns watching the unconscious gangster while the other went inside. Fifteen minutes later they were back on ninety-five south.

Dergo opened a beer and drank it in two swallows, then opened another.

"Slow down or we'll have to stop for a bathroom break." Thomas said.

"Don't worry I'm not going to get drunk."

"That's not what I said."

"But it's what you meant. You're afraid of this guy aren't you?"

"What do you mean?"

"I mean you don't want to be alone with this guy if I pass out or something like that."

"That's not what I said."

"Well, don't be afraid to admit it Switz. Hell, he scares me too. He's a bad guy that does bad things. He wouldn't think twice about killing us."

Thomas thought for a long moment. They were south of Washington D.C. now. Richmond Virginia was only fifty miles away. It was raining lightly and the sun was nowhere to be seen.

"So what is the plan Dergo. I mean, what's the

end game here? What are we going to do with this guy? I don't have a good feeling about this."

"I have to be honest with you Switz, I haven't got it all figured out just yet. But it will come to me. For now, I just know that we need to get back to Florida. The more distance we put between New York and ourselves the better off we'll be. Once we're on our playground we can make the rules. I don't see him telling us anything until we get to Florida."

Thomas thought about that for a while. "Do you think he'll make it that far? I mean, he's bleeding out back there."

"He'll make it. These mob guys are tough. Besides, the bleeding stopped. Except where I pistol whipped him, but that's not too bad. Infection is what I'd worry about if I were him."

Johnny Mal was waking up again. He was moaning loudly and coughing.

"Good morning sleepyhead." Dergo said in a happy voice.

"Fuck you."

Dergo took his seat belt off and turned to face Johnny in the backseat. "Listen to me. You've got a gaping head wound that needs medical attention."

"So take me to a fucking hospital."

"I'd be happy to do that if you would just tell me what you were doing in Florida when Thomas saw you."

"I'm not telling you anything. It's not gonna happen."

"Then you'll just have to die in the backseat of this car my friend." Dergo turned around and put his seat belt back on.

"I need water." Johnny said.

"Fuck you." Replied Dergo. "Unless you have something to say to me I don't want to hear from you anymore. In fact, the next time you say something that isn't exactly what I want to hear I'm going to pistol whip you again."

Thomas kept driving, not sure how all of this was going to end. One thing was certain however, he had a new respect for Dergo's line of work.

CHAPTER 53

The three men moved from the front of the garage over to the chairs in front of the candy shop. Vinny wasn't sure why Tye had opened his mouth, but what was done was done at this point. Besides, they were about to find out if they could take the Marshall at his word.

"So tell me how you found out about Jules and I'll tell you what I know about him." Seebeck said, slightly amused.

Tye spoke up. "Just lucky really. A friend of a friend knows someone on the police force at Fisher Island. Someone there mentioned that Jules Friedman was questioned by federal authorities about the killings here in Boynton Beach. It got back to me."

Seebeck tilted his head a little in disbelief and smiled. "A friend of a friend, huh? You wouldn't happen to know the names of these 'friends of friends', would you?"

"No, sorry I don't." Tye decided to leave Michelle out of the loop on this one. If he gave up her name she wouldn't be so quick to help him in the future. At least that was his logic behind keeping his source confidential.

"So, is it safe to assume that you went down there and checked things out?" Seebeck asked. "Did you find anything? Did you find him?"

"No, we haven't been down there." Vinny said before Tye could speak. "You have to live on the island to get on it. What could we possibly find out if we can't get to him?"

Seebeck tilted his head again, not sure if Vinny was telling the truth. "O.K., fair enough. So you got a name. Is there anything else you guys have come up with so far?"

Vinny knew that the Marshall was on a fishing expedition and he wasn't going to play along. But he did play nice.

He laughed. "That's all Marshall. We were damn lucky to get that much. If the right person hadn't overheard someone talking about it we never would have heard about it. So what do you know about this guy?"

"Not much." Seebeck said. "I was the one that interviewed him. He's wealthy. He's a land developer. He was out of the country when most of the murders happened. He's got solid alibies for where he was at when every one of the murders happened. I don't think he was connected to this whole mess. But that's just my opinion."

"So why did you interview him?" Tye asked. "What made you go down there and talk to him in the first place?"

The Marshall smiled at Tye. "Maybe you're the detective out of this group? That's a very good question Tye. I interviewed Jules because he was linked to Frank. And as I'm sure Vinny has told you by now, Frank was under my watch."

"Yeah, he told me. But what you're not telling

me is how Frank was linked to Jules." Tye waited for an answer.

"Well, that I can't tell you. That's part of an ongoing investigation."

Vinny was visibly upset. He took a long drag off of a short cigarette and put it in the ashtray. "Marshall. How do you expect to gain our trust if you're not willing to tell us the truth? You know how this works. You give us something then we give you something. Give us something to work with and we'll make something happen."

Seebeck looked Vinny in the eye. He knew he was a straight shooter and he did in fact understand how all of this worked.

"O.K. then." Seebeck smiled a little and took his hat off. He leaned back in his chair and stretched his long legs out. They were so long he might have to move them if a car pulled into the "Full Serve" lane in front of them.

"According to Frank's phone records – the phone he thought we didn't know about – he placed several calls to someone on Fisher Island. We don't know for sure who owned the cell phone he called, but our best guess is that Jules Friedman was in possession of the cell at some point. We've never recovered it, and I'm sure we never will."

Tye didn't fully understand. "So you interviewed him and as far as you're concerned he's not involved in any of this? Is that right?"

"That's right. Perhaps those two were up to something bad…perhaps not. But whatever they were or were not up to seems unrelated to what's going on in Boynton Beach."

"So was Frank involved in any of this?" Vinny asked.

"Well, I'm not sure yet, but it doesn't look good. We've been able to connect Frank to the Indian, which means he may have played a larger role in this whole thing. That's why I'm hoping you guys will be able to help me out."

Tye and Vinny both thought for a while. Finally Tye spoke up.

"So, Frank and the Indian are dead, and Jules doesn't seem to be involved. So who is involved Marshall. Who are we looking for?"

Seebeck took a deep breath and didn't make eye contact with either of them, he just stared straight ahead, due east toward the ocean. There was a steady breeze blowing right into his face and it felt good. For a moment he felt envious. For a moment he wanted to live down here in paradise with these guys and drink iced-tea while sitting in front of the candy shop, having put in a hard day of fishing. "Well gentlemen, I don't know. What I do know is that someone out there has the information we are looking for, we just have to find him."

He looked at Vinny and Tye with a big smile. "And I believe you two will figure out something. Hell, most of the folks I work with couldn't have linked Jules Friedman to this investigation and you guys found him. I'm impressed."

Tye felt a little uneasy. "Don't be. Like I said it was dumb luck."

The Marshall continued to stare east and let the breeze wash over his face. He squinted a little bit and could smell Vinny's cigarette. He wanted one.

He let out another sigh. “Well, maybe it was…maybe it wasn’t…either way I don’t care.”

Now he faced both of them and his tone became more rigid. “I honestly don’t care how you came up with his name. What I do care about is that you come up with another name, because I’ve hit a wall.”

None of what he said was true. He hadn’t hit a wall and he wanted desperately to know who gave them Jules’ name. The information on Jules in particular was inside information. Nobody should have known about that except for the people that tapped Frank’s phone. Seebeck knew that whoever told Tye about Jules – had to have been close to Jules. He was deep in thought when he heard Tye’s phone ring.

Tye looked at his phone, it said that Dergo was calling. He quickly shut it off and put it back down on the small table next to the ash tray. He looked a little nervous and the Marshall noticed.

“I was about to leave. If that call was important you should have taken it.” He paused, waiting for Tye to respond.

“Not important. Just work, and I really don’t feel like going in to work on the weekend. Whatever it is, it can wait.”

The Marshall stood up and stretched. Tye and Vinny both noticed how tall he was. A few of the female patrons pumping gas noticed how handsome he was. “Well, I guess I’ll talk to you two later. And when you hear from Dergo, please tell him we need to chat.” The Marshall smiled and tipped his hat before he walked to his truck. Tye and Vinny watched him pull onto A1A and head north toward the Woolbright bridge.

Vinny thought about giving Tye a hard time for mentioning that thcy knew about Jules, but he felt better knowing that it was likely a dead end. They wouldn't have known that had Tye not initiated the conversation with the Marshall. Vinny lit another cigarette.

"That was Dergo on the phone." Tye said.

"Well… call him back dumbass."

Tye turned his phone on and hit the redial button.

CHAPTER 54

Thomas had been driving for more than twelve hours with only a few brief stops to refuel. It was dark now and the sky was clear as they approached Savannah Georgia. The moon was bright and he had his window down, the temperature a cool sixty degrees. Dergo was sleeping and Thomas was starting to fall asleep when he heard Johnny Mal.

"Keep your fucking eyes on the road."

"I'm awake." Thomas said quickly, as though he had been caught doing something wrong by his mother. He had in fact started to nod off and drifted into the lane beside him. Interstate ninety-five southbound had been congested all day, but now it was empty. There were a few tail lights in front of them and some white lights in his rear view mirror, but they were far off.

He had forgotten that Johnny Mal was in the backseat behind him. It was dark inside the Prius, and had Johnny somehow worked himself free in the last two hundred miles, he could have easily choked Thomas to death or clubbed him with something. He suddenly felt sick and decided to wake up Dergo. He pulled the car into a designated rest stop thirty miles north of Savannah. There were a few cars scattered amongst the available parking spots, most of them close to the bathroom facilities. The rest stop was dark except for a few lights illuminating the restrooms. Thomas pulled all the way to the end, far away from the other cars.

When he exited the vehicle he slammed the door behind him, waking up his friend. He stretched a little bit and heard the passenger door close.

"Where are we?" Dergo stretched and yawned. "When did it get dark?" He looked at his watch and was surprised to learn that he had been sleeping for several hours.

"We're just outside of Savannah. I'm getting tired. Why don't you drive?"

"No problem. Gotta piss. Be right back." Dergo walked in front of the car to a tree that he felt would be just right for relieving himself. When he was finished Thomas used the same tree. Neither of them wanted to get back into the car.

"I'm sure the gangster has to go to the bathroom." Thomas said.

"So."

"So I don't want the car stinking for the next four hundred miles."

Dergo yawned and stretched some more. "You got a point there Switz. Let's see if he's still alive first."

They opened up the hatch and could see that Johnny was O.K, or at least still alive. They each grabbed one side and slowly yanked him out, sitting him directly behind the bumper.

Thomas took a knife out of his pocket and made quick work with ropes and duct tape that fastened the gangster to the chair while Dergo pointed his pistol in Johnny Maldone's face.

"Listen up you piece of shit. I'm going to say

this once. I will not repeat myself. Do you understand me?"

Johnny nodded his head.

"We're going to walk over to that tree and you are going to go to the bathroom. I will be right beside you with this gun pointed at the back of your head. If you try anything… and I mean anything, I will not hesitate to kill you. Again…do you understand me?"

Johnny nodded again and they started to walk to the tree. From behind, Dergo could see that the gash in his head might not have been as bad as they thought. It was big and it needed stitches, but he was definitely going to live. He could also see that the pistol whipping had left some big marks on his head, along with a big lump on his temple.

Johnny finished his business and they returned to the back of the car. Dergo told him to sit down in the chair and Thomas picked up the roll of duct tape. Dergo reached into his back pocket and produced a pair of handcuffs, which he quickly put on Johnny, with his hands behind his back.

"Listen guys, don't put me back in that chair." Johnny said. His voice was a little different this time. He wasn't as angry or threatening.

Dergo raised his gun to pistol whip him again but Thomas intervened. "Wait a minute."

"What? I told him not to talk unless he had something for us. He knows what is coming." Dergo raised his gun again and this time Thomas physically stepped in between them.

"That means he's going to tell us something." He pleaded with Dergo who temporarily halted his assault on the gangster. Thomas then turned to Johnny. "You are going to tell us something, aren't you? Because if you do, we won't put you back in the chair."

Johnny looked a little defeated. "O.K, alright. I can tell you that the day you saw me in Florida I was there to see an old friend of mine."

Dergo raised his gun and swung it at Johnny, who moved out of the way at the last second, potentially saving himself from brain damage. Once again Thomas got between them.

"O.K. Johnny. What was your friend's name?" Thomas asked.

"Anthony."

"Anthony what?"

Johnny looked at them a little uneasy. "Anthony Aiello."

"Never heard of him." Dergo said, and raised his weapon again.

"O.K, alright." Johnny was almost pleading now. " He had a different name in Florida. People called him Frank. You guys called him Frank. I've known him for twenty years."

Thomas looked at Dergo and nodded his approval. "Now we're getting somewhere."

"I'm, thirsty. I need something to drink."

"Fuck you." Dergo raised his gun again and started to push Thomas out of the way. When Thomas pushed back Dergo explained, "He knew we knew Frank. He hasn't given us anything. He's playing us. He's trying to play you against me." Dergo was getting upset. He'd seen this sort of thing before and he knew the gangster was dangerous. At no point was Dergo ever going to put them in a position to be attacked by Johnny. He figured the longer he was unconscious the better.

"O.K., I'll tell you who he was working for." Johnny said, almost pissed off.

Dergo settled down a little. "Who."

"Me. He was working for me."

Dergo and Thomas looked at each other, not sure whether or not to believe him. Dergo did believe him however. "Did you kill him?"

"I ain't saying nothing else till I get something to drink. You want to kill me with that fucking pistol go right ahead. You wanted me to tell you something and I told you. It's the truth. Now get me something to drink and don't put me back in that fucking chair." Johnny made his point with conviction. If he was lying, he was the best liar Dergo had ever come across.

Thomas reached into the front seat and pulled out a bottle of water and a bag of chips. He looked at Dergo for approval, who nodded and uncuffed the gangster.

Dergo pointed the gun at him. "I'll give you a few minutes to eat those chips and drink that water, then we're getting back on the road."

Fifteen minutes later they were on 95 south. The gangster was cuffed behind his back and seat belted securely behind the passenger seat. There was also a surplus of duct tape and rope securing him and his feet directly to the seat, along with a blanket that covered him, hiding the restraints from other drivers.

Dergo was driving now and Thomas was

almost asleep. The adrenalin rush of trying to keep Dergo from killing the gangster was subsiding and he was nodding off. It wasn't until he started to snore that Dergo started on Johnny again.

"So tell me gangster. Why was Frank working for you? That means you were working for somebody. I guess that's the real question, who were you working for?"

Johnny didn't say a word.

"So you killed your friend. Who does that?"

Nothing from Johnny.

They were past Brunswick Georgia, headed toward the Florida line. They still had more than six hours until they would arrive at the Texaco station.

Dergo looked in the rearview mirror, straight into Johnny Mal's eyes. "So tell me why you had to make a trip to Florida just to kill a good friend of yours. It doesn't make sense."

Nothing from Johnny, but this time when Dergo looked up, he was smiling. It took him a few seconds to figure out what was going on. By then it was too late.

Johnny Mal had worked his way out of his restraints and slid his handcuffed hands underneath his butt and legs. His hands were now in front of him and wrapped around Dergo's throat. He was yanking as hard as he could and Dergo's head was pointed at the sky. He could no longer see the road. Dergo took one hand off of the wheel and haphazardly punched Thomas who didn't wake up. He then grabbed him by the hair and yanked backward. He was only seconds away from passing out.

Thomas woke up and panicked. He turned around and punched Johnny in the face but it had little effect. He grabbed him by the throat but he could tell that Dergo was going to pass out before Johnny did.

Dergo slammed on the brakes. Everyone in the car moved forward, including Johnny's cuffed hands that were wrapped around his throat. In that instant he turned his head toward Thomas and said.

"Gun."

Johnny regained his stranglehold on Dergo and within seconds he went limp. The car started to drift a little to the right. Hitting the brakes had slowed them down to nearly thirty five miles per hour and their speed seemed to be slowly decelerating.

Thomas reached for the pistol Dergo kept in his waistband and retrieved it. He pointed it at Johnny Mal and screamed, "Let him go or I'll kill you."

Dergo was unconscious and limp.

Johnny screamed at Thomas. "Fuck you, you won't do it. And you're next. I told you I'd kill both of you."

Thomas fired the gun at Johnny's shoulder. His ears immediately started to ring. He couldn't hear anything else. He turned to Dergo. The cuffs were still wrapped around his throat. Johnny intended to kill him even if it meant his own death.

Thomas looked at Johnny. He was wounded, shot in the shoulder. Thomas put the gun to his head. Johnny didn't stop. He started to squeeze the trigger and closed his eyes. He really didn't want to kill a man in cold blood but he had no choice.

He opened his eyes and pistol whipped Johnny

who immediately passed out. Thomas wasn't sure if he was dead or not, but at least he didn't shoot him in the head.

The car camc to a stop. Thomas turned around in his seat and could see that they had run into a guard rail. There was little damage to the car and less to the guard rail. They couldn't have been going very fast when they finally hit it.

Thomas jumped out and ran over to the driver's side. The window was down and Dergo was slumped over, his head resting on the door jam. He wasn't breathing. In his panicked state Thomas undid Dergo's seat belt and pushed him into the passenger seat. It took him a minute to get his entire body out of the driver seat. It felt like twenty minutes and he was afraid that a state trooper might be passing by, or even another car that might call nine-one-one.

Once Dergo was in the passenger seat Thomas got in the car and started it. He backed away from the guardrail and resumed south, not sure what to do.

CHAPTER 55

Vinny looked at Tye as he held his phone to his cheek. He noticed the white streak that trailed out of his mouth and met the phone, almost like it was a string attaching the phone to his lips. Dergo's phone rang twice before Tye heard him answer on the other end.

"Dergo, where have you been?" Tye asked.

Dead silence from the other end of the line.

"Dergo, are you there?"

Silence.

Tye looked at Vinny. "Nothing." He said with a puzzled look.

Vinny grabbed the phone from Tye. He spoke loudly. "Dergo quit playing games, we need to talk to you."

Silence.

Tye grabbed the phone from Vinny and hung it up. "I wonder if something is wrong?"

"Why did you hang up on him dumbass? Maybe he was trying to tell us something."

Tye frowned at Vinny. "Have you ever known Dergo to be short on words? If he was on the other end of the line…"

Tye's phone rang. It was Dergo. He let it ring twice before he answered and put it on speaker phone. He placed it in front of himself and Vinny so they could both hear it.

"Hello, Dergo? Is everything O.K.?" Tye asked.

"Where's Johnny?" Came a voice from the other end of the line.

Tye and Vinny looked at each other, wondering if the other recognized the voice. Neither of them did.

"I said where is Johnny?"

This time Tye listened more carefully to the voice. He could hear an accent. It was definitely New York, and most probably Brooklyn or Long Island. He'd heard enough New Yorkers in south Florida to know that accent.

"Who is Johnny? And who are you?" Tye asked.

"You don't worry about who I am. Just know that I'm going to find you. You have no idea what you've done or how bad the price is that you will pay."

Tye looked a little confused. He had no idea he was talking to a gangster. He asked. "Umm… what is it that I've done?"

The voice on the other end screamed so loudly Tye almost dropped the phone. "You took Johnny you son of a bitch."

Tye was getting a little upset. "Look, I don't know who you are or what you think I've done, but I sincerely hope that you find your…Johnny." Tye hung up the phone and looked at Vinny.

"What do you think he was talking about? And who do you think he was?"

Vinny was as confused as Tye. "Well." He said. "The one thing that we do know is that whoever he is, he has Dergo's phone."

Tye laughed. "And apparently he's missing a Johnny."

Vinny got a little more serious. "So why did he call you?"

"I have no idea. Maybe it's Dergo's idea of a joke?"

Vinny's phone started ringing. His eyes got big as he looked at Tye and fished his cell out of his pocket.

It was Dergo. Or at least someone calling from Dergo's phone. He clicked the green button to answer then hit the speakerphone button.

"Hello?" Vinny asked

Silence.

Vinny spoke. "Somebody wants to say hi." He placed the phone in front of Tye's mouth.

"Uhh…this is Johnny. How the hell are you?"

Screaming came from the other end of the line. "You think that's funny? You have no idea what you got yourselves into. You think you can kidnap a made man? All of you's are gonna die." He hung up.

Vinny hung up his phone and put it back in his pocket. He lit a cigarette and started to think. Tye did the same. If it weren't for the difference in skin color they would have looked like twin brothers. One reaching for a smoke the other for a nicotine lozenge.

"I think Dergo may have found himself some trouble while in Illinois." Tye said.

Vinny continued to stare straight ahead. “I don’t think Dergo’s in Illinois. You heard the Marshall. He tried to contact him there and couldn’t. Police Chief in Morris said hc had no idea that Dergo was coming home to work.”

“Where do you think he went?”

Vinny took another hit off his cigarette. “I don’t know, but you heard angry guys’ accent. He’s from up north somewhere.”

“Yeah. New York.” Tye looked at Vinny. “Why would he be in New York?”

“Don’t know.”

Tye leaned forward a little in his chair outside the candy shop. “I suppose this is something the Marshall would want to be aware of?”

“Probably.”

Tye leaned back and stretched. “Guess we’re not going to tell him though…are we?”

“Not yet.”

“When?”

Vinny shook his head. “I don’t know dumbass, but I do know it’s nice out. Let’s go fishing.”

CHAPTER 56

Thomas was in a panic. Dergo looked to be dead and the the gangster wasn't far behind. He took a few deep breaths and assessed his situation. First, get out of here. Get some distance from the scene of the accident. If anyone called in the accident the police would be here in minutes. Thomas was careful not to speed. He didn't want to draw any unnecessary attention to himself. Second, he had to get Dergo to a hospital.

As he continued to head south he looked at his friend in the passenger seat. He didn't look so good, slumped over and limp. He didn't seem to be breathing.

"Dergo!" He yelled. "Dergo wake up." He grabbed the back of his head and pulled him by the hair. "Wake up!" His body was lifeless. There was no time to find a hospital.

Thomas pulled off at the next exit into a large truck stop. He drove toward the far end, away from people and big rigs. He purposely parked the car so that the passenger side of the car faced away from the truck stop and a curb was a few feet from the door. He pulled Dergo out of the car and laid him on his back. He could feel a faint pulse and began CPR.

He started to count with each chest compression. Of all the things for him to remember at this particular moment – was an episode of 'The Office', one of his favorite television programs. In this episode the gang has to take CPR training and the instructor tells them that they should sing the song, 'Staying Alive' by the Bee Gee's in order to get the correct rhythm. So Thomas started singing and pushing down on Dergo's chest at the same time, "Uh – Uh – Uh – Uh – Staying Alive – Staying Alive – Uh – Uh – Uh –Uh - Staying Alive – Staying Alive. Fuck – You – Der – Go – Stay – Alive – Stay - Alive. Fuck – You – Der – Go – Stay –Alive – Stay –Alive.

Dergo's head turned and he gasped for air. "Get off me you Swiss prick." Dergo yelled. He took a few deep breaths and kept his eyes closed. Thomas rolled over and laid on his back. Tears were coming out of his eyes.

"Oh God…I thought you were dead."

"Yeah, well I'm not."

"No thanks to me."

Dergo thought for a second. "The CPR may have helped but your singing had me running toward the light. I was hoping I'd die before you got to the next verse."

Thomas laughed. It wasn't a happy laugh. It was an exhausted, I'm at the end of my rope laugh.

"Did you kill the gangster?"

"I think so… not sure though."

"Why don't you sing to him and get it over with?"

"Fwock you."

"I need a beer."

"No you don't. You need to drive and I need to get some sleep."

"That arrangement didn't work out so well for us last time Switz. Why don't you drive and I'll make sure the gangster doesn't kill us."

"I think he's dead."

Dergo got up off the ground and coughed. He put his hands on his throat and tried to massage his neck muscles. His neck hurt and he was having trouble talking. He opened the back door of the Prius and checked on Johnny.

"He's got a pulse. Not much, but it's there."

Thomas hopped up off the ground. "I'll drive. You make sure he doesn't kill us."

They loaded up and went back to the truck stop to get fuel for the last time. Dergo went into the bathroom to clean up and Thomas decided it was time to call Vinny and Tye and let them know they'd be there soon. They were going to need some help with the gangster as both of them were exhausted. Thomas had little sleep in the last two days and Dergo had almost been choked to death, though Thomas thought he looked pretty good for almost dying.

When they were back on the road Thomas asked Dergo to retrieve his phone out of the glove compartment. He did so and handed it to him. The sun was up now and they were in Florida, so turning on his phone didn't seem to be an issue – until he turned it on. His phone made several beeping sounds as it retrieved messages and missed calls.

"Popular guy." Dergo said with half a smile.

Thomas looked at his phone while he was driving, which made him drift a little into the other lane.

"Watch where you're going Switz, you wanna get pulled over?"

Thomas handed him the phone and stared at him for a few seconds longer than he should have. They could hear the rumble strips from the side of the road.

"Christ Thomas, watch the road."

Dergo looked at Thomas's phone. He had seventeen missed calls. "You are popular."

"Look at who they are from." Thomas said, without taking his eyes off the road this time.

Dergo scrolled through the list which started with ten calls from Vinny and Tye combined, mostly Tye. Then there were seven missed calls from Dergo.

His brow scrunched a little and he looked genuinely confused. "When did…"

"Exactly." Thomas said. "When did you make those calls? Because one of them came just about the time Johnny Mal was choking you to death, and I don't remember any phone breaks during your little episode."

Dergo turned white. His eyes were big and his mouth was open. Suddenly he started going through his pockets and then the glove compartment. He looked on the floor of the car and in the center console.

"Aww man!" He said and then put his head in his hands, looking at his own knees. This was bad and he knew it.

"So tell me how you called me seven times without me ever seeing you do it." Thomas's tone was firm. He knew the answer because it was obvious, but he wanted Dergo to say it.

"I think I left my phone in the cigar shop."

Thomas was yelling now. "And WHY would you have left your phone in the cigar shop Dergo? I thought we agreed to turn them off so nobody could trace our movement. Nobody was supposed to know we were in New York."

"Aww man." He said again, head still in his hands. "This is bad Thomas."

"No shit it's bad Dergo. How could you have possibly left your phone at the cigar shop? Tell me. Why wasn't it in the car with mine…where we agreed to leave them until we got back to Florida?"

Dergo lifted his head up and explained. "I took the phone into the cigar shop with me when I saw you and the gangster standing at the front door. I didn't know if he recognized you, I didn't know if he had a gun to your head – all I could see was that your hands were full with coffee and he let you in. I never thought you would have gone in there by yourself. I thought I was going to have to call nine-one-one. That's why the phone was with me when I went into the cigar shop"

Thomas looked at him for a second. "I didn't think I would go in either. It just sort of happened."

Dergo continued. "Anyway…when you went

to go get the car I cleaned the place up, hoping it would buy us a few hours before anyone got suspicious. Then I left a note."

"What did you just say?" Thomas thought he heard him wrong.

"I said I left a note."

"I thought that's what you said. You left a note? Really? A note? Was it a thank-you note? Birthday wishes? Congratulations on being a FUCKING MOBSTER?" Thomas was screaming now and had accelerated to ninety miles per hour without noticing.

"Slow down. Keep your head on straight."

Thomas slowed down and took a few deep breaths, then a few more. The reality of the situation was sinking in. He checked the speedometer – sixty five miles per hour. He took a few more deep breaths.

"Dergo, what did the note say?"

"It said – I have Johnny. If you want him back call the police. Or you can call me at 561-788-4710."

"Dergo…why did you leave them a note?"

"Honestly, I had a pretty good plan, but now that they have my phone that plan isn't the one we're going with anymore."

"Of course not." Thomas said in a condescending tone.

"Leaving a note doesn't explain why you left your phone at the cigar shop. Why did you need your phone for the note?"

Thomas thought about it and then laughed. "Really? You don't know your own phone number?"

"It's the cell I use when I'm in Florida. It's not my main phone. No, I don't have the number committed to memory because I don't use the phone that often."

Thomas looked ahead at the road and tried to ignore Dergo. They were almost in Daytona Beach, which meant they were only a few hours from the Texaco in Boynton Beach. He took another deep breath and put the cruise-control on seventy miles per hour.

"Why don't you call Tye and let him know we're only a few hours out."

"Do you want me to check these voice-messages for you?" Dergo asked politely.

"No." Thomas said. "I'm pretty sure we know who they are from."

CHAPTER 57

As soon as Tye and Vinny loaded the boat with supplies the wind picked up. Since Vinny sometimes got seasick when the seas were rough they decided to fish the river. Fishing the river simply meant that they would stay in the intracoastal waterway instead of heading out into the ocean. Wind didn't affect the intracoastal and it would be as calm as a river on a day like this. It was the right time of the year to fish for pompano in the river and they were a great sport fish.

It took a while to get to their favorite spot, maybe thirty minutes or so, which gave them some time to talk. Along the way they had to pass underneath the Woolbright bridge, the place where Tye's brother had been murdered. He felt a pang in his chest and he simply wanted to get past the bridge and get it out of his mind. It made him realize that Vinny went to work every single day and was reminded of his son's death each time he walked into the candy shop.

"How do you do it Vin?"

"I'm just a better fisherman than you. You know that." Vinny said with a smile.

"No…I mean…every time I see this bridge it reminds me of Terry. I get a sick feeling in my stomach."

Vinny took the last drag off his cigarette and threw it in the water. He looked away and Tye decided maybe he shouldn't have asked the question. A few minutes went by with nothing said. The boat continued to head north in the intracoastal and Tye turned the radio on.

There are a lot of ancillary victims involved in any death, especially a murder. They aren't always people, sometimes they are things, events, objects, and memories. Sometimes those things are killed right along with the person. For Tye, one of the innocent victims of Terry's death was slowly becoming – fishing. Every time he took his boat out he had to pass underneath the Woolbright bridge, and each time he did, it became harder and harder to do. Tye was beginning to think that if it got much worse he might just avoid that bridge forever, which would put a damper on his fishing. He decided he wasn't going to let that happen.

Vinny wasn't looking at him, nor was he talking. He was alone in thought with his cigarette and the salty breeze that chased the smoke away from his face. Tye realized that the briny breeze was half the reason they came out here. It was soothing. More so than the waves or the sun. That salty breeze was as therapeutic as it was subtle. Today however, they felt like bloody breezes. Each one that hit him in the face reminded him that death happened here. He couldn't get it out of his mind. He stopped the boat.

Vinny didn't even turn and ask why they had stopped. His mind was somewhere else. Tye spoke to him.

"I know I've said it before but I'm sorry about your boy."

Vinny continued to stare off into the distance, not saying a word.

"Shouldn't we talk about this? I mean…I'm not a psychologist or anything, but…aren't we supposed to talk? Isn't it supposed to help? I could use some fucking help about now." Tears started to come to Tye's eyes and he got embarrassed. He turned away from Vinny and wiped his eyes even though Vinny wasn't looking at him. It was instinct. Grown men didn't cry in their world. He hadn't cried yet and he wasn't going to do it now.

"Talk to me Vinny." Tye was angry now. Not at his friend but at life in general. "Tell me how you do it, because I can't. I'm trying, but nothing seems to be working."

He noticed Vinny's shoulders moving up and down gently. At first he ignored it, not knowing what was going on. Then he realized that Vinny was crying. Suddenly he felt a little better. He didn't feel alone. Vinny was hurting as bad as he was. The façade they had put on was cracking and neither of them could control it. Tye turned up the radio and faced the other side of the boat, away from his friend, and they both cried.

CHAPTER 58

Dergo tried to call Tye but he didn't answer his phone. He and Thomas both started to wonder if some of Johnny's friends had made it back to the Texaco before them. It was possible. Not likely, but possible.

They were an hour away and decided to just keep going. They would fill them in when they arrived. Dergo checked on Johnny Mal, who was curled up in the backseat. He was barely alive. His pulse was faint and Dergo had trouble finding it at first.

"I think the gangster is just about dead." He told Thomas.

"Well, we'll be there soon. Try to keep him alive."

He had already put a pressure bandage on the gunshot wound, but that didn't seem to be his main problem. Thomas's shot went straight through the meaty part of his upper shoulder without hitting any bones or arteries. His head, however, was a different story. Between the initial fall and the pistol whippings he had a concussion that seemed to keep him in an unconscious state. He was dehydrated and that didn't help either.

"I think he'll make it." Dergo said and turned back around.

An hour later Thomas exited interstate ninety-five at the Woolbright exit and headed east toward the ocean. As they crossed the Woolbright bridge they both remembered Terry. Thirty seconds later they pulled into the gas station and thoughts of Darryl and Frank raced through their heads.

"I hope this was worth it." Thomas said to Dergo as he turned off the car and got out.

They left Johnny in the backseat and looked for Vinny and Tye, who were sitting in front of the candy shop. Thomas could see they had been fishing based on the clothes they were wearing. Since the Prius was a rental neither had noticed that Thomas and Dergo were the occupants. They surprised them.

"Catch anything?" Thomas asked loudly.

"Hey.. where have you been dumbasses?" Vinny asked them.

Dergo spoke. "We had to take a little trip, but we're back now."

Tye asked. "Did you happen to run into Johnny on your little excursion?" Vinny laughed a little. Thomas's eyes got big.

"Oh Fwock. They called you too?"

"Yeah." Tye said. "They weren't happy. By the way… who are they? And who is Johnny?"

Thomas looked at Vinny. “Open the garage up. I need to pull in. We’ll introduce you to Johnny in there.”

A few minutes later Thomas pulled the Prius into the open garage bay and Tye closed the door behind him.

Dergo pulled Johnny Mal out of the backseat and sat him on one of the lawn chairs near the workbench. He was still unconscious.

“He looks dead.” Vinny said with a bit of surprise. “What the hell did you guys do to him?” He didn’t wait for an answer. He walked over to one of the cabinets on the wall and retrieved a first-aid kit.

“It’s a long story.” Thomas said.

Tye walked around him and sat in one of the other lawn chairs. “We have time.”

“I should probably explain.” Dergo said. “Anybody want anything?” He asked as he made his way across the back of the garage to the door that led to the candy shop.

“I think I need a beer.” Tye said, and reached for his lozenges. A minute later Dergo returned with a handful of Corona’s and passed them around. He sat Vinny’s on the workbench while he tended to Johnny. He dressed his wounds and cleaned those that needed it.

Dergo sat in a chair and started his story. “I’ll just cover the bullet points or else this will take all day, and I don’t think our friend here has all day.”

Everyone nodded.

“My contact in Illinois came up with this guy’s name. Johnny Maldone, AKA Johnny Mal. Turns out he and Frank grew up together. So my guy makes a phone call to his Fed buddies and he finds out that just before Frank was killed he made a few phone calls to this Johnny Mal guy. Right after I finish thanking him for the information he apparently called Thomas and told him not to let me go to New York, it was too dangerous."

Tye laughed and held his beer up to Thomas. "So not only did you let him go, you went with him. Nice job Thomas."

"That's not exactly how it happened dumbass." Thomas said.

"Anyway." Dergo interrupted. "It turns out Thomas saw him at the Lantana airport the day Frank was murdered.

"This guy?" Vinny pointed to Johnny.

"Yeah." Thomas replied.

"So why is he sitting in my garage. And why is he almost dead?" Vinny looked serious.

"Well, he doesn't like to answer questions and it turns out he has a propensity for violence." Dergo showed his neck to Vinny and Tye. "And the reason he is sitting in your garage is that I'm sure he knows what happened to the others."

"That's it. That's the whole story?" Vinny asked.

Dergo looked shocked. "Yeah that's it. What more do you want me to say?"

"No, I mean, do you have any other information that might help us or do we focus completely on this Johnny guy?" Vinny asked.

Dergo thought for a minute. Well, the only other thing that I know isn't very helpful. My guy in

Illinois told me that the day Johnny Mal flew to south Florida, this wasn't his destination. Miami was. He actually spent some time in Miami somewhere before he returned to New York. But I don't know where or what he did. So yeah…let's start with the gangster in front of us."

"Gangster?" Tye asked and almost choked on his beer. "You forgot to mention that part."

"You know what else he forgot to mention?" Vinny asked angrily. "Why this guy's friends are calling us. And how they even got our numbers in the first place."

"Dumbass left his phone at the place we picked up the gangster." Thomas said, and raised his beer to Dergo.

Tye sat up in his chair. "So let me get this straight. This guy is a gangster. All of his friends know where we are and who we are, and we're sitting around in the garage as if everything is O.K.? Does anyone else see anything wrong with this picture?"

Vinny nodded. "Yeah, we have to get out of here." He looked at Tye. "Let's take him down to the trailer."

"The trailer is only a block and a half away from here. Don't you think we should go somewhere far away?" Tye said.

"They don't know the trailer."

"How do you know that?"

Vinny was losing his patience. "O.K. dumbass, I don't know that for sure, but I'm positive they know where the Texaco is. Let's just get out of here, then we can think of a better plan."

Everyone agreed. Vinny closed the gas station early and locked up. He put a sign on the door that read "CLOSED FOR REPAIRS UNTIL FURTHER NOTICE." Ten minutes later the four fishermen and the gangster were sitting in the tiny white trailer by the sea. Tye noticed a strong breeze coming in from the east as he shut the door behind him.

CHAPTER 59

Michelle's phone rang in the Briny Breezes office, it was Jules. "Meet me for lunch. We need to talk."

"Sorry but today isn't a good day. I'm busy with…"

"I'm not asking you sweetie. I'll be at the Old Key Lime House in thirty minutes." He hung up the phone.

Michelle was weary of this meeting. If Jules found out that she had given Tye his name there would be a heavy price to pay. On the other hand she knew she had been careful. She couldn't imagine a scenario where he would be able to link her with any sort of information leak. Besides, she really had no other choice. She wasn't in a position to just walk away from everything and go on the run. Instead, she went to the bathroom and freshened up. She looked good, and she felt confident. She told her assistant she had a lunch meeting and that she'd be back in an hour.

Jules was walking across the parking lot toward her when she pulled in. They arrived at the same time. Old Key Lime House was one of her favorite restaurants. It sat on the intracoastal overlooking the water. It was a place to party and let your hair down. Many of the tables were waterside and the music was always live. The food was fantastic and she was looking forward to eating.

"You look gorgeous." Jules said and smiled at her, extending an arm. She grabbed it and they walked hand in hand through the colorful blue doors in the front of the lime green building. She could smell the ocean and see the water of the intracoastal.

"Thank you sir. And of course you are as handsome as ever." A genuine smile came across her face. She had known Jules long enough to understand that his greeting always set the tone for the conversation. Whatever the issue was, or was not, it had nothing to do with Michelle. She felt safe.

There was a line to be seated but Jules was greeted inside the door by the manager. "Right this way Mr. Friedman."

"They are busy for a weekday." Michelle said.

"They're always busy."

The manager took them to the best seat in the restaurant, which was the last table down a long walk that resembled a thin pier and was fifty feet out over the water. It was wide enough for a small table on one side, which allowed enough room for a waitress to walk on the other side. A blue and lime colored shade umbrella jutted out from the center of the table and provided ample protection from the sun for both of them. As they sat, a cool breeze washed over them, taking with it all of the humidity in the air. It was nearly ninety-degrees in the middle of the day but they were comfortable with the umbrella and the ocean breeze. The manager said that a waitress would be with them shortly and a young lady who must have been right behind them sat a pitcher of sweet-tea on the table along with two glasses. She poured them and left.

Jules took a long sip of iced-tea and sat his glass down. By the smile on his face he obviously enjoyed it.

"Good stuff huh?" Michelle asked.

"The best in south Florida." Jules looked around at the packed house. "People come here for the view, the food, and the ambience. I come here for the sweet-tea."

Michelle got to the point. "So why am I here sir?" Her tone was all business.

"I missed you. Just wanted to see you."

She wasn't buying it. "Uh huh. You're a very busy man Jules. Time is money with you. If you are taking time out of your day to sit face-to-face with me, then you're ignoring somebody else. What gives?"

"I like that about you Michelle. Always did." He said, and took another swig of tea. "You are my eyes and ears at Briny. Tell me what's going on there."

Michelle looked confused. "I'm not sure I understand. Things are running smoothly. Other than some maintenance issues the place runs itself."

"When was your last meeting with the board of directors."

"A couple of weeks ago. Why?"

Jules took another sip of his tea. "I'm just asking Michelle. Is there anything I should be aware of?"

She sat back in her chair, crossed her arms, and squinted her eyes. "What the hell are you talking about Jules? Am I missing something here? You know that if anything out of the ordinary happened I would call you. I haven't called you. So apparently something is going to happen, or maybe should have happened, or maybe I just plain missed it. Would you like to fill me in?"

"It's nothing dear. Truly it's nothing. Let's eat and celebrate the joy that is this wonderful day." He refilled both of their glasses and toasted her.

She smiled and toasted her glass with his. He was lying and she knew it, but it wouldn't be prudent for her to pursue the issue, so she left it alone.

What Jules wasn't telling her is that he received a nasty phone call from some ex-associates in New York. Someone kidnapped Johnny Maldone and they were sure it was someone from Florida. Specifically, they were sure it was someone from the Texaco station next to Michelle's office.

What he also wasn't telling her was that things were going to get ugly, and fast. He was amazed the New Yorkers had waited this long. In the back of his mind he'd hoped they would burn it to the ground and force Vinny out, making it easy for him to buy it from the insurance company.

Michelle thought long and hard about the conversation with Jules on her drive back to work.

She couldn't figure out what he was getting at. Obviously something was about to blow up but she couldn't put her finger on it. He'd asked if she met with the board of directors but couldn't figure out why. This was simply a bunch of retired people enjoying some time at the beach.

As she passed the Texaco and turned into Briny she couldn't help but notice the station was lifeless. No people and no cars. There was a handwritten sign in the door which she couldn't quite read from the road, but she thought it said that they were closed.

CHAPTER 60

Tye turned on the air conditioner after closing the door. Within minutes it was cold inside the trailer and he thought about turning it off.

Vinny was rifling through his first aid kit for smelling salts. Dergo opened the refrigerator and grabbed a few beers, handing one to each of the guys.

"Before you wake him up Vinny, let's fill in these two about Jules."

Everyone was seated. Johnny was slumped over the edge of the couch.

"Who is Jules?" Thomas asked.

Tye took the lead. "A friend of a friend gave me some information a while back. I didn't think much of it at the time, but now…with all of this going on…I think it fits in somewhere."

Tye pulled his lozenges out of his pocket and opened the cylindrical container.

"Spit it out dumbass." Dergo said

"Alright, relax." He popped a white lozenge in

his mouth and rolled it under his tongue so he could talk.

"So, a couple of weeks ago I heard that the Feds interviewed someone on Fisher Island about all of the things happening here in Boynton Beach."

"Oh?" Dergo said and leaned back in the couch, eyes widened with anticipation.

"Yeah, they said the guy that was interviewed was named Jules Friedman. So one day I went down to Fisher Island but all I found was what I think was his boat. A yacht called Family Jewels."

Dergo had a smile on his face. "That has to be where Johnny went, after he killed Frank."

Tye continued. "Well, it makes sense I guess. Miami's a big city though, could just be a coincidence."

"Only one way to find out." Vinny said. "Let's ask him." Vinny walked over to Johnny Mal and snapped the smelling salt in half, releasing its chemicals into the air. He waved the tiny cotton cylinder underneath Mal's nose and nothing happened.

"I believe he's dead." Thomas said.

"No he's got a pulse. Not much of one but it's there." Vinny said. He waived the cotton cylinder under Mal's nose again and got the same result.

"Maybe he is in a coma?" Thomas aksed. "I mean, Dergo pistol whipped the shit out of him a few times. He may have some serious damage."

Vinny sighed. "Well, one thing is for sure. We need to keep him alive at least long enough to interrogate him. His blood pressure needs to increase. He's lost a lot of blood and the only way to replace it is for him to rest. He should be able to talk in a day or two."

"I am not keeping a gangster in my trailer." Tye said.

"Where would you like him to go?" Thomas asked.

Tye snapped back quickly. "How about your house Thomas?"

"I don't think so."

"I don't want him here either"

Vinny interrupted. "Shut up, both of you dumbasses." He looked Tye in the eyes. "You remember earlier this morning when you asked me how do I do it? How do I keep going in to work every day. Well it's for this. It's because somewhere in the back of my mind I think that I might have a chance to catch the son of a bitch that did this to my boy. That's the only thing that keeps me going to work. It's the only reason I have to wake up in the morning. We're close. We're going to find out who did this to Darryl, and to Terry, and Frank."

"Fuck Frank. I think he tried to kill me." Dergo said. The beer was starting to get to him.

Vinny concentrated on Tye. "It's only for a day or two, I promise, then we'll get him out of here. But we need to talk to him."

Tye looked at Vinny. He'd never asked anything of him before, so when he pleaded with him about Johnny Maldone he knew it was important. Besides, maybe he was right. Maybe catching the people who killed their family members might somehow take the bloody smell out of the breeze.

"O.K." Tye said. "But just a day or two. I mean it."

Tye looked at Vinny. "Maybe you should tell them about the Marshall?"

Vinny nodded. He'd forgotten about the Marshall. He looked at Thomas and Dergo who were sitting on the same couch as Johnny. "I got a visit from a U.S. Marshall the other day. He worked Frank's Witness Protection case."

Dergo looked a little worried. In the previous few days he had committed several felonies. The idea that a U.S. Marshall was sniffing around didn't set well with him.

Vinny continued. "He seems pretty sure that I will find the guy that killed Darryl, and he wanted me to know that he would help me if I ever needed it. I think he meant it. I think he's on our side."

Thomas asked. "Do you think we should call him now, let him know about Johnny?"

"No." Dergo said confidently. "That would be a bad idea."

The others weren't sure but were content to trust his instinct in the matter. His skill set as a detective had served them well to this point…except for the half-dead gangster in the living room. That was going to be a problem.

CHAPTER 61

The next twenty-four hours consisted of the four men taking shifts keeping Johnny alive, resting, and sharing information. Thomas decided to take notes on a makeshift bulletin board to see if they could make more sense of the information they were aggregating, and it seemed to help.

On his notepad he had listed all of the players and everything they knew about them. He started with Frank and his background in the Witness Protection Program. He drew a line to Johnny Mal's name and wrote that they were childhood friends. Johnny Mal's name had a line drawn to Jules Friedman, who they assumed knew each other and had met in Miami the day of Frank's death. Dergo made sure that Thomas included the Indian, who didn't seem to fit.

Nothing really seemed to fit. Thomas started over again, rearranging the names to fit on a timeline according to death. First Terry, then the Canadian, then Darryl, and Finally Frank. In between Darryl and Frank he drew a vertical line with Dergo and the Indian jutting out of the bottom of the timeline. There still didn't appear to be any rhyme or reason to the list.

"Well let's put it in context." Tye said. "We do know that Jules is rich and he got rich developing land. We think Briny Breezes might be for sale but we can't confirm."

Dergo added. "But we do know that the Canadian was going to make an offer on the trailer park, and maybe on the Texaco. But he died before he could make the offer."

Thomas joined in. "And then we went to Canada and next thing you know someone tries to kill Dergo, and we think Frank had something to do with that."

Tye spoke next. "Then we think that Johnny Mal flew down to Florida to talk to Jules, but decided to kill Frank along the way."

Vinny summed it up. "So…it looks like Jules…the land developer…wants to buy Briny and the Texaco, and has his old friend Frank kill the Canadian before he makes an offer. But why kill Frank, and what about the others? Doesn't explain any of that."

Tye helped. "What if Frank screwed something up and pissed off the gangster? Maybe that's why he's dead."

"Maybe Terry and Darryl were accidents. Maybe Vinny was the target all along." Thomas thought out loud.

"That doesn't make any sense." Dergo said. "What Frank messed up was killing me. That's pretty obvious isn't it?"

"It does fit." Tye said. "But Terry and Darryl still don't fit."

Vinny interrupted. "Forget about Terry and

Darryl for a minute. We know that Frank was involved in all of this. We know that Jules probably wants to buy the trailer park and the gas station. We know that the gangster is linked to both Frank and Jules. What we need to do is ask the gangster some questions and see what he knows about Jules. Between the two of them we can figure this thing out. Everything else will fall into place after that. We need to wake up Johnny. I'm tired of waiting."

They all agreed and focused their attention on Johnny Maldone. He was looking a little better than he had the day before. His bleeding had stopped and his breathing was heavier now, consistent at least.

Vinny grabbed the last smelling salt capsule from the first aid kit and snapped it in front of Johnny Mal's nose. He didn't move. Vinny waived it a few more times under his nose. Still nothing. He threw it in the garbage and sat down at the kitchen table.

Tye got up from the couch and filled a cup with water. He walked over to Johnny and threw it in his face. His head snapped back and they could all see him move his mouth muscles. He was alive for sure and regaining consciousness.

Tye's phone rang.

"Great Johnny. No doubt your friends are trying to find you." He walked back to the table and looked at the number. It was Dergo's phone calling him.

Tye looked at Dergo. "It's from you - dumbass." He said as he put the phone to his ear.

"Yeah." Tye said in a very nonchalant voice, as though he wasn't sitting in the trailer with a kidnapped gangster hanging on to life.

"I want Johnny." Came a relatively calm voice from the other end. "Just tell me where he is and we can end all of this. We just want him back safe."

Tye smiled a little as if he was about to laugh. "Oh sure, you just pick him up and go back home…and forget all of this happened, right?"

"That's right."

"I'm pretty sure that's not how you operate. I'm gonna have to get back with you. Keep the line open and I'll call you back." Tye hung up the phone.

He looked at the others in the room and he could see they were all worried. Who wouldn't be given the situation? For some reason Tye wasn't. He was upset. He was trying to figure out why he wasn't afraid when Thomas spoke to him.

"Well dumbass, what did they say?"

Tye answered. "They want their friend back. Said if we tell them where to pick him up they will just leave and go back to New York."

"And you believe them?" Vinny asked.

"Of course not."

Dergo let out a deep sigh. He had a pained look on his face as though he was constipated. "I think we have to bring the Marshall into the fold at this point. We're in over our heads with this one. We need help."

"I don't think so." Vinny said. "We're close. All we have to do is wake up the gangster, find out what he knows about Jules, then take care of business."

"Then what Vinny? We all go to jail for killing

a mobster and a land developer? Think about what you are saying. If we get the Marshall involved now, maybe we can all walk away from this."

Vinny ripped back at Dergo. "I don't care about walking away from this. I don't care if I end up in jail. The only thing I care about is bringing justice to whoever killed my son."

Tye added. "I'm with Vinny. I don't really care what happens…I can do time. I'd rather get justice and do time than watch these two slither away unpunished."

"You guys aren't thinking clearly." Thomas said. "You don't want to end up in jail."

Vinny shook his head. "You don't get it dumbass. And you won't. You'll never understand what it means to lose a son."

Thomas decided not to argue anymore. He knew he didn't understand what Vinny or Tye were going through.

Dergo had seen this sort of thing before and he knew not to argue either. He did know that there was a way out of this however.

Johnny Mal started to groan and the men turned their attention to him. They almost didn't notice when Tye said that he was going for a walk to clear his head.

Vinny noticed. "Stay away from the Texaco. The gangster's friends will have eyes on it." Tye nodded and put his sunglasses on as he walked out the door.

CHAPTER 62

Tye kept a golf cart outside the trailer door for shuttling surfboards to the beach and fishing poles and beer to the boat at the marina. He unplugged it from its charging station and made a left, headed east toward the beach. It was only a hundred feet away but he didn't want his friends to know his true destination. He needed to talk to Michelle. He felt guilty about not telling the others that she was the informant who gave up Jules name but it just didn't seem that important.

At the top of the row of trailers he made a left and headed north along the beach for a minute then made another left and was heading due west toward A1A and the gas station. Part of him wanted to see if Vinny was right, if Johnny's friends had eyes on the station. He would blend in with the others riding around in golf carts. Everyone had them and since the gangsters didn't know who he was he figured he could drive right past them without being identified.

Vinny was indeed correct. A very noticeable black suburban was sitting in front of the Coastal Star newspaper pointed directly at the gas station. The windows were tinted and though Tye wanted to stare and see if he could see if anyone was in the vehicle he knew better. He simply looked straight ahead and waited for the light to turn green so he could drive his golf cart across the road to the Briny Breezes office.

The light turned green and instead of pulling into the office Tye decided to circle around behind the office building to the marina. He wanted to see if anyone was watching his boat in case he needed it. He drove slowly past the marina and his boat staring straight ahead as though he had a destination. His friends Tom and Jeannie lived a few trailers past his boat and he decided to stop in and say hello. Tom's boat was not in its slip so he knew they were out on the water somewhere.

But for good measure he walked up the three little steps in front of his big trailer that faced the marina and knocked. He forced himself to wait a few seconds, feeling exposed, then jumped back on the golf cart and made his way back to the office in search of Michelle.

He was careful not to look around. No reason for him to be suspicious of anything. He parked in front of the office and walked in the front door to check his mail, just as everyone else had been doing all day. The front door was in plain sight of the black suburban. The less he was in their view the better, he thought to himself. Once inside he asked for Michelle at the front desk

"Sure thing Tyrone." The pretty little assistant said in a sugary voice. He wasn't happy that she'd used his name, then realized how paranoid that sounded, even to himself at this point. A few minutes later Michelle came out from behind her door and invited Tye to join her for a walk.

"No thanks, is it O.K. if we just sit in your office?" He asked, trying to stay calm.

"It's so nice outside though, sure you don't want to take a little walk around the marina?"

"I'm sure." He said with a smile.

They walked the few steps down the hallway and into Michelle's office.

"So what can I do for you sir?" Michelle asked with a genuine smile on her face. She knew something was going to blow up around here and she knew there was a good chance Tye was going to be a part of it. She found herself chomping at the bit to get it all started, that is, if she could help in any way.

"I need you to tell me everything you know about Jules Friedman."

Michelle had a confused look on her face. "I'm not sure what you mean. I told you that a friend of mine heard something about him. That's all I know."

Tye eyed her up. "So you've never heard of him before?"

"No. Should I know him?"

Tye was in full bluff mode at this point. "Actually yes, you should know all about him. He's a land developer, the biggest in south Florida. He owns more real estate than anyone else from Jacksonville to the Keys. And guess what Michelle, you're in property management, It's what you do. Seems like you ought to have at least heard of this guy before."

"Well, I can assure you I have not."

"Something else doesn't sit right with me. Why did you tell me about him. I mean…why even mention his name in the first place. It's almost as though you wanted me to look into him. What good could have come from that?"

Michelle pushed herself away from her desk slightly. The plastic wheels on the bottom of her chair made a squeaky sound as she did so. Her arms fully extended she stood up and glared down at Tye, who remained seated.

"I don't like the tone you are taking with me sir. I did what I thought would help you…not hurt you…and here you are in my office accusing me of…" She paused. Tye waited for her response.

"Of what Michelle?"

"I don't know. I don't know what you think, but you are wrong. And I'd appreciate it if you left." She stood and moved toward the door.

Tye remained seated. He could hear the phones ringing out in the office now that the door was open. Michelle stood firmly by the door and repeated once more for Tye to leave.

He sat, hoping she would calm down.

Michelle started to yell. "I've asked you twice to leave. I'm not asking again."

Tye could see some of the office workers peeking their heads down the hall from behind their desks.

Michelle became louder. "If you do not leave I'm going to call…"

Just then the pretty little girl with the sugary voice decided to intervene. Things were getting out of control. She raised her voice and shouted, "Michelle, line one is for you…it's Mr. Friedman."

They locked eyes and both appeared to be afraid. Tye spoke to her on the way out.

"Or you'll call who…the police? I think that might be a good idea." He walked out the door and hopped on his golf cart. On his way out he noticed that the black suburban was gone.

Michelle closed her door behind her and picked up the phone. "Yes Jules."

"Any news?" He asked.

"As a matter of fact yes, but I'm not sure it's what you're looking for."

"Tell me."

"I just had one of the residents ask if I knew who you were. Of course I told him no."

"What trailer does he live in?

"A-10"

Jules hung up.

CHAPTER 63

Tye circled around the back of the office to check the marina again. The black suburban was nowhere in sight so he was confident they didn't know he had a boat docked there. If wouldn't take long for them to find out though. He pulled his golf cart behind Tom and Jeannie's trailer and walked back to the boat. On the way he dialed Thomas's number.

"Hello?" Thomas said, not sure who was actually on the other line.

"It's me dumbass." Tye said. "And we've got problems."

"What kind of problems?"

Vinny and Dergo turned their attention away from Johnny Mal and looked at Thomas.

"There was a black suburban parked at the Coastal Star, pointed at the Texaco. Jules Friedman called Michelle while I was talking to her. He knows we're here, which means the gangster's friends will know we are here in a couple of minutes."

"How does Michelle know Jules Friedman?" Thomas asked.

"Don't worry about that right now." Tye said. "Right now I need you to get everyone out of the trailer."

"Where are we going to go with a half-dead gangster? We're going to look awfully suspicious walking down the street with him."

Vinny and Dergo could infer from the conversation that they needed to get out of the trailer and they started to gather their belongings.

"We could just leave the gangster here, that might solve a few of our problems." Thomas said to Tye.

"No. No that's not going to work. We need him. He's the only leverage we have right now."

"We're not leaving this piece of shit here." Vinny said. He was thinking like Tye.

"I've got it." Tye said. "Listen to me. There are a spare set of keys for the neighbors golf cart hanging on the key rack by the door. Take his golf cart and load up the gangster. Head over to Ferber's alley and I'll pick you guys up there."

"Ferber's alley?" Thomas asked in disbelief. "You're picking us up at the beach?"

"Yeah. I'll be in my boat. Just meet me there as soon as you can." Tye hung up his phone.

Ferber's alley was a small walkway just wide enough that a golf-cart could fit through. It provided beach access for Tye and Thomas to bring jet-ski's and other equipment onto the beach without having to haul them up and down steps. It was nestled in between two multi-million dollar ocean-front homes and was only a stone's throw away from the trailer. It would provide good cover and concealment and since it was all private beach there wouldn't be many sunbathers out either.

Tye fired up the engine on his boat and started to back out of the slip. He kept a vigilant eye out for anything unusual but saw nothing. Nobody knew he was leaving. Within minutes he was under the Woolbright bridge, past the restaurants by Ocean avenue and headed out the mouth of the Boynton inlet. Once out in the ocean it would take him a little bit longer to make the two mile trip south because the wind, current, and waves were all working against him.

Ten minutes later he passed Briny Breezes private beach and was sitting in front of Dog Beach, where Ferber's alley emptied onto the sand. He had binoculars on the boat and pulled them out. He was anchored about three hundred yards offshore. From where he sat the trailer was five hundred yards away and he could see the neighbor's golf cart had not moved yet.

"Something is wrong." Tye said to himself. "Why haven't you left yet?" His phone rang. The caller ID said it was Dergo.

It rang again and Tye looked at it, not sure what to do. He put the binoculars back up to his eyes and this time he could see movement. Vinny and Dergo were helping the gangster onto the golf cart, which Thomas had retrieved and pulled in front of the trailer. From his vantage point he could see clearly down ocean avenue, which ran parallel to the beach. At the far end of the trailer park, to Tye's right, he could see the black suburban heading due south at a slow pace toward A-row.

His phone rang again.

He needed to call Thomas and tell him not to drive up to the beach. He needed to warn them.

His phone rang again. This time he answered it, keeping the binoculars up to his face.

"What the hell do you want?" Tye said, unsure what to do. His friends were five seconds away from being blindsided by the bad guys and he was helpless to provide any support from where he sat.

A deep voice came from the other end of the line. "My name is Tony, and we're going to get to know each other very well."

Tye thought for a second. He wanted a nicotine lozenge but realized his hands were full at the moment. "I can see you." He said to Tony.

The suburban pulled over to the side of the road and stopped moving. Inside, Tye let out a big sigh of relief.

"Is that so?" Tony asked. "Why don't you tell me where you are?"

Tye played along. He moved the binoculars to his left and could see the golf cart now moving toward the beach. In a few seconds they would be within view of Tony and what Tye assumed to be a suburban full of bad guys with guns.

"I'm behind you. You just passed me up. If you turn around and come back a few blocks I'll give you Johnny."

Tye moved the binoculars back to the right, he could see the suburban backing up. He spoke.

"Turn around dipshit. The cops will pull you

over for backing up this far. Just turn around and I'll make sure you get Johnny back safe and sound."

Tye watched as the suburban cut the wheel and turned around. Just as the suburban pointed north the golf cart turned onto ocean avenue and headed south toward Ferber's alley. He looked at the suburban knowing he only had to stall for about ten more seconds.

"O.K." Tye said in a calm voice. "You see that white house in front of you?"

"Yeah I'm at the white house." Tony said, losing patience.

"Well keep going past that until you get to a stop sign. Make a left and you will see Johnny."

Tony was angry. "If you're fucking with me kid, I'm gonna kill you. Do you understand me?"

Tye was careful not to laugh. "Yeah tough guy, I got you." He kept the binoculars focused on the suburban until he saw it make the left turn at the stop sign. Then he panned left until he saw Ferber's alley. The golf cart was empty. He panned further down the beach and saw his friends scurrying toward the water.

"I gotta go dipshit." Tye said and hung up the phone. He started the engines and throttled forward, lifting the front of the long boat into the air. Once it planed out he was within a hundred yards of his friends. He eased the boat gently past the breaking surf, careful not to go too far and beach the craft. This was the only place along the coast he could bring his boat in past the surf without hitting a reef or a sandbar. Had he not spent so many years in this water he might not have known exactly where to go.

He was happy that he did.

Dergo and Thomas threw a garbage bag onboard, then boarded the boat from the back and climbed over the transom. Vinny stayed in the water with the gangster until the others could help him lift. A few minutes later and everyone was in the boat.

Safe. For now.

CHAPTER 64

"O.K. genius, what now?" Thomas asked. Tye throttled forward and was heading south along the coast. He reached into his pocket and retrieved his nicotine lozenges.

"Now we head south and wait for the next move."

"And what's the next move?" Dergo asked

Tye realized everyone was soaking wet. It didn't really matter, it was warm out and if he went fast enough everyone's clothes would dry within an hour.

Vinny reached inside the gangster's shirt and pulled out a large gallon Ziploc baggie full of cigarettes, cell phones, and wallets. He distributed them to their rightful owners and then lit a cigarette.

Dergo exclaimed. "We would have been here a lot sooner but Vinny wanted to make sure everyone had dry clothes and some essentials on the boat."

Vinny opened the garbage bag full of dry clothes and everyone changed. Dergo emptied the other garbage bag of its contents. There were snacks and bottles of water which he stowed away. Once everyone was settled Tye throttled down so everyone could hear him.

"Johnny's friends are in town. They're driving a black suburban and they just about ran into you back in Briny."

"Yeah I think we saw them." Thomas said.

"I think we should go to Fisher Island. From there we can call Tony back."

"Who is Tony?" Dergo asked.

"He was driving the suburban. He's not real happy with us, but he'll do anything to get Johnny back." Tye said.

He looked at Johnny who was slumped over in a chair near the front of the boat. He could see that he was awake and that his eyes were open. There wasn't much more life to him than that, but at least he wasn't dead.

Tye pointed to him. "Keep the sun off him, we're going to be out here for a while."

Vinny was waiting for answers and they weren't coming, at least not fast enough for him. "Why are we going to Fisher Island dumbass?"

"Because we are going to arrange a meeting between us and Jules Friedman, and I want to have eyes on his boat when they load it up to meet us. I want to be able to see who gets on it."

Vinny looked off to the side as he pondered what Tye had just told him. He drew in a long puff of smoke then exhaled. "So you think we should arrange a meeting with Jules. Make sure he gets on his boat alone, then we will board his boat before he gets to the meeting place. Is that right?"

"Yeah that's about it, except that you left out the part where we can get the hell off of his boat whenever we want without anyone stopping us. Namely Tony. He doesn't sound very friendly, and frankly, I don't want to meet him."

Dergo took a swig of beer and smiled. "I like that plan. It actually sounds pretty good."

"Where did you get a beer Dergo?" Tye asked in disbelief.

"Your refrigerator. I threw them in the garbage bag. You want one?"

Tye looked at Dergo. "Yeah…I do."

Dergo handed Tye a beer and they both drank. Tye was about to say something when his phone rang. He looked down at it, then looked at Dergo. "It's you again."

"Hello." Tye said.

"I guess you want to play things the hard way, don't you?" Tony said.

"I don't see why I have to make it easy on you, so yeah, I think we'll do things my way from now on."

Tony paused on the other end. Tye was sure that if he were standing in front of him he would not hesitate to kill him in a second. But he wasn't standing in front of him. On top of that he had something Tony wanted really bad.

"Let me tell you how to get your buddy back Tony. You get a hold of Jules Friedman and you have him call me. He's the guy I want to talk to. I'm pretty sure he's the guy I need, not Johnny, and definitely not you." Tye hung up the phone and announced to all on the boat. "The next time this phone rings it should be Jules Friedman on the other end." He put his phone back in his pocket and throttled down. Everyone sat back in their seats and enjoyed the ride south to Fisher Island.

Along the way they stopped to get gas and more refreshments. The sun was hot and Johnny Mal wasn't looking great. Tony had called twice during the jaunt south but Tye sent it to voicemail both times.

The sun was no longer above them in the hot Florida sky. It was starting to drop behind the scenery in the west, behind the luxurious waterfront homes of South Beach and the beautiful people that dotted the sandy landscape.

They were anchored in the ocean just outside of Fisher Island's marina where they could see the "Family Jewels." It was quiet. The breeze was warm but efficient. The water was calm and the sky was beginning to change color. Blues and whites gave way to oranges and reds, outlined in grey and white.

The four fishermen and even the gangster took a few minutes to stare at the sky. It was impossible not to be in awe. They finished their beer and ate snacks, enjoying a day on the water. Then Tye's phone rang.

CHAPTER 65

Everyone watched Tye as he looked at the caller ID and then put the phone to his face. "Hello." He said in a relaxed voice. It was a private number, unidentified. It could have been Tony calling from another phone, but he was thinking this was Jules on the other end. He was right.

"I hear that you would like to speak with me?"

Tye was a little surprised at the voice. It was meek and a bit…tender. He had expected something more sinister, but Jewels sounded more like his grandfather than a cold blooded killer.

Tye gathered himself. "Yeah, I have some questions I'd like to ask you. I think we should meet."

"Why don't we just talk on the phone? I'll answer your questions right now."

"No, I'd like to meet face-to-face. I'm not going to do this over the phone."

There was a pause from the other end. "Well, I'm a little busy right now. How does tomorrow.."

Tye interrupted. "I don't really care what you are doing. We meet now or we kill Johnny Maldone."

There was another pause on the other end. "Well…O.K. then. Where would you like to meet?"

"The Ocean Reef Club.. Do you know where it's at?"

Jules replied. "Of course I do. It's on Key Largo, but it's only accessible by boat."

"Well, you do have a boat don't you?"

Jules snipped a little. "Of course I have a boat."

"So here are the rules." Tye continued. "You get on your boat – alone - and you head to the Ocean Reef Club. We will have dinner and I'll ask questions. If I like the answers then I'll give you your friend back. Sounds simple, right?"

"Well, it's not that simple." Jules said. Tye could hear the trepidation in his voice. He could tell there really was a problem. "My boat is rather large, and I have a crew that…"

"No crew. You come alone or I kill the gangster."

"I don't think you understand how big my boat is. In fact it's not a boat, it's a yacht."

Tye was upset now. "Well I'm sure you can figure it out, because if you don't, Johnny Maldone dies. You got it?"

Another long pause. "Yes, of course. I'll come alone. When would you like to meet?"

"Now. I'm here. And I'm waiting for you." Tye hung up the phone. He looked at the others.

"It's thirty-five miles by boat to the Ocean Reef Club. That should give us enough time to be pirates."

Dergo took a drink of beer and looked at Tye. "You think he's going to make the trip?"

Thomas spoke up. "Either he will or he won't. Pretty cut and dry."

Vinny chimed in. "If he does make the trip, and Johnny's friends get on the boat with him it could get ugly. We only have two guns."

"Three." Tye said, and pulled out the flare gun from the cabinet above his head. He stuffed it into his pocket.

"What if he doesn't make the trip? Then what do we do?" Thomas asked.

Tye responded without looking at him. "Then we'll come up with another plan. Until then we need to figure out the rest of this plan."

"We don't have a plan." Dergo said.

"Exactly why need to think this through a little bit."

"Good point." Dergo agreed and finished his beer. He reached for another.

Over the next hour the four men talked about what they would do and how they would do it. Who would remain on the boat and who would board Jules's yacht. Where each of the weapons would be at all times, and what their exit strategy was. What they didn't talk about was the fates of the people likely involved in the killing of Terry and Darryl. They didn't speak of who might be alive and who might be dead in a few hours. They also didn't talk about the longer term implications of their soon to be pirate-like behavior. How they would deal with Johnny Maldone's friends or how they would bring the Marshall into the mix. The entire time they kept eyes on the yacht owned by Jules Friedman. They had seen no movement on or near the vessel.

As they sat and watched the last of the sun tuck behind the Miami Beach skyline, Dergo asked Tye, "So how Did you find out about Jules? Who was the friend of the friend?"

Everyone on board focused their attention toward Tye and his forthcoming answer. It had been a mystery long enough he thought to himself. He spoke.

"Well…I guess it doesn't matter at this point anymore. It was Michelle. Michelle from Briny Breezes gave me his name."

Everyone looked surprised. "How did she know?" Thomas asked.

Tye frowned at Thomas. "I told you she has a friend who is married to one of the cops on Fisher Island. That's where it came from."

"Or maybe it came from the Marshall. That's more likely." Dergo said and laughed as though he knew something the rest of them didn't.

"What do you mean?" Vinny asked.

Dergo looked at the others in a bit of disbelief. "I've seen him go over to the Briny office a few times. They went out to lunch…I don't know…I thought they liked each other. Besides, the Marshall would have had access to the Witness Protection files. He would have been involved in any interrogation of Jules. Doesn't it make sense that she might have heard his name from him?"

They all looked at each other not really knowing what this meant. Maybe it didn't mean anything.

Vinny was the first to try to make sense of it. "Well…if Michelle is fucking the Marshall and he mentioned the name, then it makes sense that she would make up a story about how she heard it in order to protect the Marshall."

"Yeah." Thomas interjected. "It makes sense. I mean, they're both attractive people, why wouldn't they hook up?"

Everyone looked at Thomas.

"You dumbass." Tye said as he laughed.

"What the fwock?" He asked.

"You think the Marshall's attractive? Is everyone in Switzerland gay?" Dergo asked him.

Thomas just shook his head and reached for another beer. As he did he noticed someone walking along the dock toward the "Family Jewels." Thomas pointed toward him. "I think our man is ready to start moving."

CHAPTER 66

Jules had just finished packing an overnight bag for the trip to Key Largo. He wouldn't need one but it was habit. He had made a phone call to his boat Captain and was now confident that he could safely navigate to and from his destination.

"Just call me once you're in the wheelhouse and I'll walk you through the navigation settings. The boat will steer itself, just like a plane does on autopilot. Once you get to the Ocean Reef Club contact the harbormaster and I'll make sure he has a slip available that you can pull up to…nothing tricky. There are cameras that show you views of everything in all directions. There is even a night-vision function that allows you to see in the dark if you have to…but you won't need any of that boss, that place is lit up like the fourth of July. It's just like any other boat…just a little bigger."

Jules wasn't so sure, but he had to sound confident. He didn't want to raise any red flags.

"Well I may just get down there and turn around and come back. If I do that I may call you again if you don't mind."

The Captain didn't hesitate. "You know Mr. Friedman, I'd be happy to go with you if you want. I don't mind the short notice. I don't mind at all."

"Well that's very nice of you, but this is something I've wanted to do for a long time and I've decided to do it now."

"It might be a better idea to wait until morning when you have more light. Can you do that?"

"No, no I think I'll do it now. Besides, why have all of these toys if I can't play with them?"

The Captain laughed. "You got that right sir. Good luck and don't hesitate to call me if you need anything."

The truth was that Jules was terrified of piloting the mammoth yacht by himself but he had no choice. Tony "E" was very convincing.

Once Tye had told Tony he wanted to talk to Jules the black Suburban made its way south to Fisher Island. Jules was hesitant to let security allow them access to the island but he knew they would find a way to speak with him one way or another. He had made the choice to work with Johnny Maldone and now he was realizing some of the unwanted consequences of getting into bed with some unsavory characters.

Tony "E" was from Connecticut, formerly of New Jersey, and formerly a soldier for the Genovese family. He had served fifteen years for second degree murder and while in prison had a terrible accident that left him nearly blind. For a brief time after his release from prison the Feds watched him but he gave them nothing to worry about. He was an aging gangster who could barely see during the day and not at all at night. He travelled with a companion, his best friend and former Genovese associate – Salvatore (Torre) Merola. Torre served not only as best friend to Tony E, he also drove him everywhere and helped with day-to-day activities. Tony still held power within the Genovese family, albeit from a distance. They called on him whenever they needed someone "outside" the family to take care of business. Travelling to Florida and recovering Johnny Mal was his latest task delegated from New York.

Tony was on another line listening to the conversation between Jules and Tye. The first time that Jules said he was too busy to meet Tye, Tony pulled out a gun and pointed it at his head. The conversation took on a different tone at that point, eventually leading Jules to pilot the Yacht himself.

After he hung up with Tye he looked at Tony. "What am I supposed to say to this guy once we meet?"

"Whatever it takes to get Johnny back. I don't care what you tell him." Tony put his gun back in his shoulder holster. Torre kept his gun in his hand.

"What if he's wearing a wire?"

Tony laughed. "A wire? This kid is small time. I don't think we have to worry about him. Besides, I'm going to take care of him and his friends. Don't you worry about that."

"He may be small time, but he's got Johnny doesn't he? Seems to me like he's more of a threat than you give him credit for."

"I told you not to worry about it didn't I?" Tony said in a decidedly pissed off tone. "You just do as you're told and this thing will take care of itself."

Jules was starting to get antsy. "You guys gonna be there with me…in case it gets nasty?"

"Trust me." Tony said with conviction. "We'll be watching you the entire time. Until we get Johnny back nothing is gonna happen to you."

"And once you get Johnny back?"

Tony laughed again. "I told you not to worry about it." He was losing patience quickly. His mind turned to other matters. "One more word from you and I'm gonna kill you right here and right now."

Jules got up and walked away from the table. "I have some things to do before I leave. Are you going to be on the boat with me?" He asked, hoping this wouldn't upset Tony any more than he was already.

"No, we're not gonna be on the boat. You heard him. You go alone."

"Great." Jules said and turned to pack.

Torre waited until Jules left the room before he spoke to Tony. "Whaddaya mean we're not gonna be on the boat? He asked. "How the hell are we gonna get there. You heard him yourself…only accessible by boat."

"I got orders from higher on this one Torre." Tony said as he made his way to the front door. "We need to get out of here."

Torre looked confused. "Where are we going?"

"The airport."

CHAPTER 67

Jules boarded the boat using the long flight of stairs that stretched from the dock to the first floor entrance. He punched in the combination on the electronic keypad and could hear the magnetic lock release itself. The door opened slightly. He stepped inside and shut the alarm off.

A few minutes later he was in the wheel house. He turned the lights on and called the Captain. Together, they powered up the boat and warmed up the massive diesel engines. Twenty minutes later they had completed all of the necessary checks and Jules was on his way to Key Largo. Once outside the marina and break walls he handed over the steering to the GPS computer and sat back in his chair, still a little nervous about the whole thing. He did feel better though. He was on his way. There was an empty feeling in the pit of his stomach. He wasn't hungry, although he did decide to make himself a drink while the yacht was steering itself. Upon returning to the wheelhouse with a bottle of Jack Daniels, a bucket of ice, and some root beer, he mixed a drink and put his feet up on the dash. It was the most comfortable he had been in a few days and decided to enjoy the moment.

Outside, the fishermen kept a close eye on the vessel, making sure it was headed south and more importantly, making sure nobody was following it.

Dergo had jumped in the water to cool off. The breeze wasn't knocking down enough of the humidity for his liking. He had two life jackets stuffed between his legs that provided enough flotation for him to be mostly submerged in the warm water, but just enough above the waterline to keep his beer safe.

"Get back in the boat dumbass, we're gonna be leaving in a few minutes." Vinny said as he threw the stub of his cigarette in Dergo's direction. It hit the water with a sizzle and Dergo started to paddle gently toward the back of the boat.

"How's he doing?" Tye asked of their guest.

"He's doing pretty good." Thomas offered. "He's conscious. He drank two Gatorade's. Still a little thirsty I think."

"Can he talk yet?"

Thomas shook his head. "He can definitely hear what we are saying. He makes eye contact now and then, but I don't think he's fully coherent."

"Well maybe the salty air will do him some good." Tye said sarcastically. "Keep him away from the guns."

Dergo climbed into the back of the boat. "And keep the fucker away from the beer. You know how those gangsters are always drinking someone else's beer, dammit!" He opened the cooler and grabbed one.

Tye and Vinny were focused on the boat ahead of them. It had left the marina and pointed south. It was picking up speed now and was becoming smaller on the horizon.

They panned their field of view searching for movement from another boat. Tye put his hand on the key.

"Not yet." Vinny motioned for him to stand down. "We can catch up with him easily. We know where he's going. Let's wait a few more minutes."

While they waited everyone seemed to focus on Johnny, as if they were suddenly concerned about his well-being.

"Should we tie him down in case we hit choppy waters?" Thomas asked.

"I think we should tie him down because he's a bad guy who wants to kill all of us....especially me." Said Dergo.

"Dergo's got a point." Tye said. "Why don't we make sure he's tied up before we get going. Who knows when he will wake up out of his fog."

Thomas grabbed some rope from one of the storage cabinets on the side of the boat and started to tie him up. "I'll do it." He said. "Last time Dergo tied him up he got himself free and almost killed him."

"Good idea Switz." Dergo raised his beer and took a drink.

Tye dropped another nicotine lozenge in his mouth.

Vinny lit a fresh cigarette.

"Here we go boys." Tye said as he started the

engines. “No turning back now.” He made sure everyone was seated and then throttled up. The front of the long boat tried to stand up but the back of the boat wouldn’t allow it. Eventually the vessel planed out and was horizontal on top of the water, scooting along at an increasing speed. Within a few minutes the Family Jewels was in sight ahead on the horizon. Vinny motioned to Tye to back off the speed a little, which he did. They were still going fast enough to close the distance between them, but it would take a little while.

The sun had disappeared somewhere in the west and the only light left was a faint glow on the horizon. It reminded Tye of when he and Terry used to play baseball when they were kids. Sometimes they would play until it got dark, when there was just enough light to see each other clearly but not enough light to see a baseball coming at your head.

“Running out of daylight Vin. Think we should get up there?” Tye asked in a soft voice, not wanting to alert the others. He was getting nervous now. They all were.

“Just keep this pace. We’ll be there in a few minutes. Besides, better if its dark.”

CHAPTER 68

The Family Jewels was a few hundred yards away when the sky finally went pitch black. Johnny Mal had regained consciousness and was trying to speak, but his words were muffled and he wasn't making any sense.

They approached slowly from the rear of the yacht, trying to be as stealthy as possible. Tye had shut down the running lights and their boat was nearly invisible in the inky blackness of night. The Family Jewels was not invisible, quite the contrary. It was large and lit up for all to see, and one could not miss the travelling city on water. It almost looked like a cruise ship.

Everyone knew what to do when Thomas inched the boat closer to the yacht. They were only a few feet away when Tye, positioned at the front of the boat, threw a rope around one of mooring bollards on the rear of the yacht. The rope fell over the top of the mushroom shaped metal post and fell to the ground, linking the two boats together. Thomas put the boat in neutral and cut the engines while Tye secured a buoy to the front of the boat to minimize chances of them running into each other.

Vinny climbed onto the Family Jewels and

drew his handgun, loading a round into the chamber. He waived to Tye, signaling that he was on his way up the ladder. Up he went. A minute later he was out of sight, pulling security for the others to board the boat.

Dergo and Tye grabbed the gangster. He was able to move by himself, which was helpful. They hadn't developed a plan to get him up the ladder while he was unconscious. That would have slowed everything down, maybe even brought the mission to a halt.

Dergo climbed the ladder next. He had a rope tied around his waist that was tied to the gangster on the other end. Once on top he saw Vinny, who gave him the thumbs up. This deck was secure, nobody home.

Dergo looked down and gave Tye the thumbs up and then yanked on the rope, almost pulling the gangster face-first into the ladder. Tye kept him standing up straight and quietly instructed him to climb the ladder. He had the flare gun at the ready in case Johnny Mal decided to try anything funny. Ten feet above the gangster, Dergo had his weapon at the ready as well.

A few minutes later the four men, Vinny, Tye, Dergo, and Johnny Maldone began walking toward the front of the yacht to find Jules.

Their destination was easy enough to recognize from the rear of the boat. It was brightly lit, even brighter than the rest of the boat, one deck above their current location. Music could be heard coming from the wheelhouse as well. As they got closer they could actually see someone moving around behind the large panes of glass.

Vinny pointed out the moving figure to Dergo, who then made sure Tye was aware of the movement. Johnny Mal also noticed Jules and thought about yelling, but Dergo's pistol was in his face as though he was able to forecast the move. Johnny decided to remain silent. He couldn't take another pistol whipping.

At the base of the wheelhouse was an elevator door and a set of stairs, both leading to Jules. Tye and Vinny told Dergo to babysit the gangster while they secured the wheelhouse, just like they had discussed earlier. Dergo nodded his head in agreement, though his face couldn't disguise the fact that he wanted to ascend the stairs and meet Jules himself. Babysitting the gangster seemed like a job for someone without police training. But he obliged.

Tye and Vinny looked at each other and nodded, as if to say, "This may be the last hurrah." After a brief pause Tye nodded toward the steps. "You first dumbass." Vinny turned and started to climb, Tye was close behind.

The staircase was spiral and steep. It was the second preferred method of entering the wheelhouse behind the elevator, but it worked. Dergo could still see Tye's feet above him as Vinny opened the door. He kicked it so hard that it bounced off the wall behind it and nearly closed again. Vinny pushed against the door and entered the room quickly. He turned to his left, then right.

"Hands!" He yelled at the top of his lungs. "Show me your hands!" Vinny continued to yell as

Tye stepped into the room behind him, unsure what to expect.

What he saw was a man in his seventies leaning back in a Captain's chair drinking a Jack and root beer. He didn't seem disturbed by Vinny's outburst, and he certainly didn't seem surprised to see them.

He looked at Tye and spoke. "I'm guessing that's Johnny Maldone…the one everyone is looking for?" He pointed over Tye's shoulder.

Tye turned around to see a bank of five closed circuit television screens, each about eight inches in width. The center screen showed Dergo and Johnny patiently waiting downstairs. Tye stuck his head out the door and yelled down. "It's clear. Use the elevator dumbass."

He turned back to the screen and watched Dergo push the button for the elevator. It opened and he pushed the gangster inside.

When Tye turned around he could see that Vinny had holstered his weapon and was pouring a drink. Jules was finishing his off and asked Vinny to mix him one.

"Sure Jules, I'll make you a drink. You just need to answer some of our questions." Vinny said as he filled two glasses with ice. He was unscrewing the lid on the bottle of Jack when the elevator door opened. It startled him a little and he reached for his weapon.

"A little nervous sir?" Jules asked in a slightly condescending tone. "An appropriate feeling given the people that you are dealing with."

Vinny stopped what he was doing. "Let's start there Jules. Who exactly are we dealing with… and why is it that we are dealing with them?"

Jules laughed a little in disbelief. Vinny stared him down. Jules' tone became more serious and his head cocked a little to the side. "You really don't know, do you?" He sat up in his chair and took his feet off the console in front of him. "I'm sure you're aware of the mafia, the New York mafia? Well Mr. Maldone there is a Captain for the Genovese family." He nodded in Johnny's direction.

Dergo had positioned Johnny in one of the chairs next to Jules, his hands still tied. He also tethered the gangster to the chair itself so he couldn't move.

Vinny continued. "I know who he is Jules. And I know who you are. What I don't know is how he is involved in all of this. Why are you involved in this?"

"Define.. "This", will you please?" Jules asked for clarification.

"This," Vinny seemed to be struggling a bit.

Tye entered the conversation. "By.."This," he means "Who killed my brother and who killed his son?"

"And who killed Frank…and the Canadian?" Dergo asked.

Jules looked at Dergo in disbelief. "You are referring to the young man from the Wellington Group?"

"I am."

"Well that I can explain. The others you speak of… I have no idea why they met their demise."

"So start explaining." Dergo said and raised his weapon."

Jules started to speak. “Be careful…” when shots rang out and everyone in the wheelhouse ducked.

“Don’t shoot” Jules yelled from the floor. Everyone was on the floor except for Johnny Maldone, who was much more alert. He was smiling and looking at the bank of television monitors.

“Time for you to die now.” A trickle of blood was running out of Mal’s mouth as everyone turned their attention to the eight inch security monitors on the wall. In the top right monitor was a picture of the rear of the yacht, with about half of the boat Thomas, Tye, Vinny, Dergo, and Mal had used to board the Family Jewels. In the monitor next to it was a helicopter sweeping from left to right above the small vessel firing machine gun rounds into it.

Johnny Mal started to laugh. “I told you motherfuckers I was gonna kill you.” It was a scary vision. Mal was tied to a seat and couldn’t duck for cover, nor would he have if he were not tied to the chair. “I’m gonna kill every one of you motherfuckers…especially you.” He looked at Dergo and winked.

“We’ll see about that.” Dergo said, and pistol-whipped Johnny, knocking him unconscious.

“What the fuck dumbass?” Tye objected to the unnecessary violence.

“Were you listening to him? He wants us dead. Maybe it’s best if he’s not awake for a little while.”

“Thomas!” Vinny yelled at the top of his lungs.

Everyone focused on the screen again and watched the small fire turn into a large fire and explode after the helicopter made a final pass, nearly sawing the boat in half.

"Did anyone see Thomas get off the boat?" Vinny asked.

Silence filled the room. Johnny was quiet. Jules was afraid for his life and huddled in a corner not making any noise.

Tye looked at Dergo. "Check on Thomas, we'll meet you at the back of the boat when we're done here."

Dergo hesitated for a second trying to figure out the strategy. The back of the boat no longer provided an escape route, especially with an armed helicopter circling in the skies.

Tye could see the hesitation. "Just go!" And with that Dergo exited the door and climbed down the spiral staircase.

Vinny put a gun to Jules' head. "Tell us what you know now or you will die."

Jules stood up, one eye on the security monitors. "Terry's death was an accident. The sniper on the bridge was supposed to shoot somebody else."

"Who?"

Jules didn't speak. He was visibly scared and he knew that once he told them everything he knew either they would kill him or Johnny Maldone would kill him.

"If I tell you…" he looked at Johnny Mal, "he is going to kill me."

"That's not my problem." Tye said, more interested in the conversation now. He grabbed him by the collar and pinned him against the wall with the security monitors. “Tell me why you killed my brother.”

“It was supposed to be him!” Jules nodded at Vinny.

They didn’t believe him. “Bullshit.” Tye said. “It doesn’t make sense.” Tye was deep in thought and released Jules’ collar.

“Dumbass, we’ve got trouble on top.” Vinny was pointing at one of the monitors. Tye turned and could see the helicopter landing on top of the boat.

Tye turned to Jules. “Listen to me very carefully. You fucked up old man, and you should die for your sins. But I’m not your judge or your jury. Your judgment will come one day. Do as I say and you will live. Do you understand me? Do you understand what I am telling you?”

“We’ve got to go Tye.” Vinny was almost begging.

“No. No we don’t have to go anywhere Vin. They want Johnny Mal and we have him. Our best play is to let them come to us.

CHAPTER 69

Through the security monitor they watched the helicopter land and then watched Tony E. and Torre walk confidently across the open deck toward the elevator. Just short of the elevator Tony E. pulled out a cell phone and put it to his ear.

Jules' phone rang. He pulled it out of his pocket and held it in front of him for all to see, waiting for instruction.

Tye looked at Jules. "Tell them we're in the wheelhouse and we have what they want. Tell them to put their weapons down…Fuck it – just give me the phone." He grabbed the phone and hit the green button.

"Tony my old friend. We're in the wheelhouse and we have Johnny. We are willing to do this peacefully, we just need you to answer some questions."

"Oh yeah?" Tony asked, clearly not shaken. "And who is to say that we don't just come down there kill all of you and take Johnny."

"Because we'll kill you and Johnny if you try something that stupid."

Tye looked into the security monitor. Tony didn't know he was on camera. He could see Tony hold the phone away from his face and ask Torre a question. A moment later he spoke into the phone. "Look, there's an easier way to do this. You ask your questions and I'll answer them. Then you send Johnny up and we leave."

Tye thought for a minute then looked to Vin for advice. Vinny pointed at Johnny Mal and shook his head.

"Ok…Ok." Tye said. "I don't want to see you anymore than you want to see me."

"So shoot." Tony E. said.

"Shoot?" Tye was confused. "Shoot who?"

"Ask your fucking questions already. I aint got all day to play with you fucking hillbillies. Ask your fucking questions or I'm gonna come down there and kill all of you."

"Ok. Relax man." Tye was preparing his first question when Jules grabbed him by the shoulder. In one movement Tye dropped the phone and buried a right hook into Jules' stomach.

A gasp of air exited Jules' mouth, as did all the color in his face, and he went down on one knee. He was waiving his hands in front of him signaling that he didn't want trouble. He remained quiet and started pointing vehemently toward one of the security monitors on the bottom row. Tye and Vinny were so fixated on Tony E. that they missed it. Another boat was approaching the Family Jewels. It was a U.S. Border Patrol vessel.

Tye picked up the phone. "Who killed Darryl?"

"Who the fuck is Darryl?"

Tye looked into the monitor, Tony was asking Torre if he knew who Darryl was. He didn't.

"Darryl was the guy that was shot at the Texaco. Who killed him?"

"I don't know. I don't't' know who he was or who killed him. Honestly."

Tye was stalling. He scanned the monitors to find the Border Patrol agents.

"I said I don't fucking know. Next question."

Tye and Vinny continued to monitor the screens. "That's good. I believe you. You didn't know. So tell me. Who killed Frank?" Tye asked in a remarkably calm voice given the situation.

"Who the fuck is Frank?" Tony E. was visibly upset at this point. Tye could see his face steaming on the screen, unbeknownst to Tony E.

"You know… Frank, the guy that lived across the street from the Texaco. The caterer from New Jersey. The guy who ended up drowning in his own toilet. That guy."

On one of the middle screens Tye and Vinny could see two people making their way up a ladder toward the helipad. He had to distract the gangsters.

Vinny stepped up to the wall and put his face six inches from the screen trying to get a better look. He thought one of the Border Patrol agents looked familiar but he couldn't tell. Tye didn't understand what Vinny was doing. His hands were full at the moment.

"Like I said, I don't know who you are talking about." Tony E. pulled the phone away from his face and whispered something to Torre. Torre laughed a little.

"Now see, I don't like it when you lie to me." Tye said with a disappointed tone in his voice. "And I know when you are lying to me you WOP fucker."

Tony E. started to scream at the top of his lungs, just as Tye thought he might. "You calling me a WOP you motherfucker! I'm gonna kill you. Enough of your games." Tony E. hit the button for the elevator to go down and then proceeded to punch the elevator doors until his fists bled. Though he could no longer hear him he could see the temper tantrum taking place on screen. Tye didn't necessarily want to come to blows with this guy after watching him go psycho on a metal door.

Suddenly Tony E. stopped punching the door and Torre made a half turn. They both put their hands in the air. Seconds later the Border Patrol agents were behind them, guns at the ready. Tony E. and Torre put their hands behind their backs and were cuffed using large black zip strips.

The lighting was better by the elevator door and once again Vinny approached the screen, his nose almost touching it.

"You need glasses dumbass." Tye said.

"Do you know who that is?" Vinny asked.

"Now I know you need glasses. Did you see the gigantic "U.S. BORDER PATROL painted on the side of the fucking boat?"

"It's the Marshall. It's Seebeck. He's with a Border Patrol agent." They continued to stare at the screen. The capture of the two gangsters went off without a hitch. The bad guys and the good guys seemed to be talking to each other when the Marshall hit the elevator button and the door opened up.

CHAPTER 70

Tye and Vinny prepared themselves. Tye stood behind Johnny Mal, flare gun at the ready. Vinny stood next to the elevator doors in case he needed to flank the bad guys as they exited.

Tye wondered why Vinny would take up such a posture when the bad guys were obviously in custody, but there was no time to talk about it. The elevator door beeped, the light came on and the door opened.

Tony E. and Torre exited first, hands behind their backs, with Seebeck and the Border Patrol agent behind them.

"Well hello there gentlemen. How is everyone doing today?" Seebeck said in a jovial tone. Tye nodded. Vinny was speechless, his eyes never leaving the bad guys. He recognized that something was wrong but he couldn't put his finger on it.

"This is quite a boat you have Mr. Friedman." Seebeck said to Jules. "You boys alright?" He asked, making eye contact with Vinny.

"Yeah, we're Ok. One of our guys went down with the boat. We're not sure if he's Ok." Vinny seemed to loosen up a little bit.

Seebeck looked at Tye. "So everyone is accounted for then?" Tye began to answer when Vinny interrupted. "Unless there are more bad guys out there."

Tye played along. "Glad you showed up Marshall. Things were getting a little dicey around here." He then moved from behind Johnny Mal to behind Jules. He slowly placed the flare gun in Jules waistband. This was the time of reckoning for Jules. He would either alert the bad guys of Tye's actions or let the scenario play out and not give up Tye.

The Marshall paused and looked around. He took a deep breath and considered his next move. "Yeah, sometimes that happens in this line of work. The trick is that you have to stay one step ahead of everyone. And it seems to me that you guys were close."

His comment was confusing. The Border Patrol agent shook his head and looked at Seebeck for clarification. When he did, Seebeck put a hole in his forehead and he dropped to the ground. Vinny reached for his weapon and Seebeck aimed his gun at Vinny before he could draw. "Easy there partner. You wouldn't want to do anything that could get yourself hurt now, would you?"

Tony E. started to laugh and Seebeck cut his wrists free with a pocket knife, then cut Torre loose. Tony E. made his way to Johnny Mal and started to untie him. Torre made his way over to Tye and searched him. He found nothing, looked at Seebeck and announced that he was clean.

Seebeck kept his eyes on Vinny. The red dot from his laser sight shining on Vinny's forehead.

"Drop it and kick to me."

Vinny did as instructed. Seebeck picked the gun up off the floor and handed it to Tony E. who immediately pointed the gun at Johnny Mal and put a bullet in his head.

"Ok I'm just confused." Tye said in a smart ass voice.

"What's so confusing?" Seebeck asked. "You guys kidnapped a made man. Not a smart move. Then you hijacked a yacht belonging to Mr. Friedman here, who was at one time thought to have been involved in the murders of your brother and Vinny's son. You killed Friedman and Johnny Mal. When we got here there was a shootout and you killed the Border Patrol agent, and dammit, you tried to kill me too. It makes perfect sense." The Marshall's syrupy southern slang was providing a little extra drama for the story.

"Not really." Tye said. "Why would we kill a Border Patrol agent?"

Seebeck shook his head. "Why wouldn't you? You already killed Friedman and Johnny Mal in revenge. You didn't want to go to jail so you tried to escape."

"So why are you going to kill Jules? I mean....why did we kill Jules?" Tye asked.

"Now that is the first good question you've asked. You see, Jules was never involved in any of the murders. Sure, he hired Johnny Mal to put the fear of God in Vinny in the hopes that he would sell the gas station, but when he found out that your brother was killed he tried to call off the whole thing. Which of course I couldn't let happen."

"You couldn't let happen?" Jules asked, genuinely surprised.

"That's right old man. Once you put this plan in motion there was too much money at stake to back out."

"And what about Darryl?" Vinny asked, more than a little upset.

"Darryl was collateral damage, and I am truly sorry about that. But you see, with Jules calling the operation off I had to get rid of Frank. I knew I was going to kill Johnny in the end, he knew about everything. I wasn't sure if Frank was going to keep his mouth shut so I had to make something happen. I had an associate at the FBI call Frank and tell him that he wasn't happy with the progress that had been made and that I was going to have to come down from New York to fix it myself. We used a voice modulator that made the call sound like it was coming from Johnny Mal. Basic stuff so far. So I killed two birds with one stone, actually three if you count Darryl. Johnny was so pissed at Frank he actually did come down from New York and kill him. In the end his death helped me pit you and Tye against Jules."

Jules was upset. "That still doesn't explain why you have to kill me?"

At that moment Seebeck reached into his pocket and pulled out a handful of papers. "Well compadre, it's gonna make a whole lot of sense here in a minute." The Marshall unfolded the documents and placed them on the table in front of Jules.

"What is this?" Jules asked.

"Power of attorney documents that you are

about to sign."

"Why would I give you power of attorney. Who would believe that?"

"Not me!" Seebeck was disgusted and the look on his face showed as much. "Christ, are all of you guys retarded? Don't you ever watch Law and Order or anything like that?"

Jules continued to read. He turned the page and saw what he was looking for. He looked like someone had just punched him in the stomach. "Wow, I didn't see this coming." He said. His eyes drifted off into space as though he were trying to put it all together. "How long?" He asked and looked at Seebeck. His voice raised, demanding an answer. "How long!"

"Easy old man… easy. Long enough I suppose."

Jules was heartbroken.

Tye decided to talk. "I'm still confused."

"It's Michelle." Jules answered. "He wants me to assign power of attorney over to Michelle."

"Michelle from Briny Breezes – Michelle?" Tyrone asked.

Seebeck smiled. "That's right, Michelle from Briny Breezes. You didn't know that she has worked for Jules for more than twenty years did you?"

"No…no I didn't." Tye said.

"Well, his plan was to get Michelle the position of manager so he would have eyes and ears on the place, someone working from the inside when he decided to make his move to buy the place."

"So Jules was never really responsible for any

of the murders, and when Michelle told me that he was questioned…it was all a lie to throw suspicion onto him?"

Seebeck smiled. "That's right. It was my idea in fact. I wasn't sure you guys were going to take the bait, you waited so long to investigate on your own." Seebeck took a deep breath. "Well, I just thought you would want to know before this was all wrapped up. He turned to Vinny and put his hands on his hips. "See amigo. I told you a long time ago you were going to help me solve this case, and you didn't disappoint. It played out exactly like it was supposed to." The Marshall pulled a pen out of his jacket pocket and handed it to Jules. "Sign it."

CHAPTER 71

It was cool in the air-conditioned wheelhouse, maybe seventy degrees. When Tye looked at Vinny and saw the sweat running off his forehead he knew something didn't fit. Vinny looked nervous. Tye assumed that Vin was going to make a move. They had to, the Marshall had made it clear he was going to kill everyone once the power of attorney was signed. Tye was hoping for a little more time to figure things out but the reality was that they had less than a minute to live. He looked again at Vinny for a clue.

Seebeck and the others were looking intently at Jules, making sure he was signing as instructed. Several billion dollars were about to exchange hands with Michelle in charge of it all. For a brief moment Tye wondered how long she would remain alive. The Marshall was a mad man with a badge and a high I.Q, a truly formidable opponent.

As they stared at Jules, Tye looked at Vinny

again. This time Vinny moved his eyes toward the elevator. “Does he want to make a break for the elevator?” Tye thought to himself. “That can’t be right.” It wasn’t right… but it was enough.

The elevator beeped and the door started to open. For a split second everyone in the room froze in fear, including the Marshall. Tony E. was the first to respond by moving his weapon in the direction of the door and away from Vinny, a natural instinct for the gangster, and one that cost him his life.

Tye had never seen Vinny split a coconut in half with his bare hands, he had only heard about it. But it must have looked a lot like Tony E.’s skull. It took less than a second.

The elevator door opened and Dergo yelled, “I found the Switz, damned near drowned …” He fell silent when he saw what was happening. Thomas was in the elevator sitting down, eyes barely open.

The Marshall took one step back and had everyone in his view. “Freeze!” He yelled. Torre started to yell something in Italian and rushed to Tony E’s lifeless body. The blood was thick on the floor already and the smell had become noticeable.

Tye was still standing behind Jules and reached into the back of his pants where he had hid the flare gun earlier.

“Sal!” Seebeck yelled at Torre. “Salvatore!” Still no response. “Torre!” He yelled again, this time the gangster turned to him. “Search him!” He pointed to Dergo. Torre got up and thought about punching Vinny for what he had done. But he thought twice about it after realizing what the man was capable of. He’d never seen anything like it before in his life.

"I'm going to kill you for this." He calmly said to Vinny as he took a few steps toward the elevator.

An explosion came next, along with a blinding light and heat, all of which was followed by the smell of something burning. Tye had fired the flare gun at the Marshall. The flare hit him in the chest with such force that he fired his weapon before dropping it on the floor. Vinny took care of Torre before he ever reached Dergo and Tye jumped on the Marshall, who was on fire.

They wrestled for a few moments before Vinny and Dergo secured the Marshall's gun and shot him in the leg, essentially disabling him. Dergo found a fire extinguisher and put out the fires that were burning in the wheelhouse, including the one on the Marshall's chest.

From the time the elevator door opened to the moment the fire was extinguished a brief forty seconds had passed.

Tye looked at Vinny. "Let's get out of here dumbass. You think you can drive this thing?"

"Of course I can, but I think we should take the helicopter."

They all looked back toward the elevator. Thomas was standing up now.

"Can you fly the helicopter dumbass?" Dergo asked.

"I don't know, what is it?"

Jules stood up, holding his leg. He was bleeding. The last shot the Marshall fired grazed his leg but he was bleeding pretty badly. Tye tore off a piece of his shirt and wrapped it tightly around the bullet wound. Jules winced but was happy for the help.

"It's an MD-500." Jules said to Thomas.

"Yeah I can fly it. I'm not rated for it but it's not a problem."

Dergo let out a small laugh. "I'm not rated for it.. but I can fly it." He said mocking Thomas. He followed up with, "Is everyone in Switzerland as gay as you?"

Vinny cuffed the Marshall with a set of zip strips he found on the Border Patrol agent. He and Dergo muscled him into the elevator, along with Jules and headed toward the helipad. Tye and Thomas took the stairs. There was not enough room in the elevator for everyone.

Thomas started everything up and within minutes they were airborne. He called in a "Mayday" for the Family Jewels and reported that he had two injured on board the helicopter and several dead on board the Family Jewels. The U.S. Coast Guard instructed him to land at Jackson Medical Center, University of Miami. Thirty minutes later Thomas sat the bird down on top of the hospital. They were met by several doctors, gurneys, police, and Federal agents.

CHAPTER 72

SEVERAL MONTHS LATER…

The men sat in front of the candy shop drinking a few beers and laughing. Life had changed for all of them. The Marshall was in jail awaiting sentencing, likely to receive the death penalty. The same held true for Michelle.

Vinny narrowly missed being brought up on murder charges himself, but Jules helped him get out of that mess by making a few phone calls to the DA's office.

Dergo decided to move to south Florida full time and open a bait shop next to Vinny's gas station. It still stands there today, and every once in a while you can find him working there – if he's not fishing.

Tye and Thomas are both retired since Jules decided to give each of the four men a million dollars for saving his life.

The sun started to set on the tiny trailer park of Briny Breezes. Dergo opened his last Beck's for the day. Vinny lit a cigarette and Tye popped another nicotine lozenge in his mouth. Thomas was about to comment on the white streak that was still on his mouth from the last lozenge when a limousine pulled into the full serve lane. The rear window rolled down and the four men could see Jules. It was the first time they had seen him since he was released from the hospital.

Tye pulled his brothers' lighter out of his pocket and used it to open a Corona. He lifted it in the air toward Jules and said, "come have a beer with us dumbass."

Made in United States
Orlando, FL
03 August 2022